SHUT UP, THIS IS SERIOUS

Carolina Ixta

SHU
THI
SER

Quill Tree Books
An Imprint of HarperCollinsPublishers

Quill Tree Books is an imprint of HarperCollins Publishers.

Library of Congress Control Number: 2023936916
ISBN 978-0-06-328786-0

Typography by Joel Tippie
23 24 25 26 27 LBC 5 4 3 2 1
First Edition

For Fruitvale, forever

AUTUMN

ONE

IF YOU REALLY KNEW ABOUT IT, YOU'D KNOW LETI'S MOM NEVER
even taught her about birth control. That woman holds the cross so
tight in the house, it's what she used to pry open Leti's legs. That's
what I tell Leti, anyway. And if you really knew about it, you'd know
that despite this, Leti was pushing to do it with Quentin. But if you
really knew her like I know her, you'd know she only slept with him
twice before she got pregnant. And the first time didn't even count
because he finished before he was inside her. She called me to tell me
about it and was all like—oh, you know, he got nervous, you know
how it gets. I don't know about any of that, but I popped my gum and
said uh-huh anyway.

If you grew up with Leti's family like I did, you'd know that her
ma is always pinching Leti's cheeks and calling her prieta or India.

That's to say, she's calling Leti ugly in a racist-Mexican way. She'll be standing there giving Leti a bendición and then turn Leti's palms over, praying she'd lighten to their color.

So, you'd know why Leti still refuses to tell her ma who the father is. Cuz if you knew about the situation, you'd know that the father, Quentin, is, God forbid by her family's standards, Black.

You'd know that Leti chose not to tell her ma because if her ma found out she was gonna have a grandchild darker than her own daughter, a *Black* grandchild, hail Jesús, María, and José, her ma would shoot herself in the head right then and there.

And if you knew Leti's pa, you'd know where the scar on Leti's eyebrow came from. You'd know his hands and his mouth and his temper bigger than the sky. When Leti's pa drinks, he goes on and on about what he cannot stand. At the top of that list is Black people, and right below that is loose women.

But you don't know any of that.

And really nobody else does either. If there's anything I've learned since my pa left, it's that people think they know somebody, but it turns out nobody knows anybody at all.

Which is why when Leti is pulling her sweatshirt tight over her stomach, I tell her to cut that shit out. Leti is the smartest person I know—like, she's a fat nerd. But she's tugging at that fabric so tight it might rip open at the seams. She's not even showing yet, but she's always been hella dramatic this way.

She gets it from her ma, but Leti is a whole other ballpark. At least her ma has that immigrant shit to put her stress on—Leti's just stressed to be stressed. If the bus is late, if that A isn't plus, if a paper is wrinkled—big Virgo behavior.

When she stops tugging at her sweatshirt, her backpack slips off her shoulder and slides onto the concrete. It thuds with weight.

"How many books do you have today?" I ask her, while swiping lip gloss over my mouth. It smells like cherries.

She smacks her lips. "Two."

"You got that calculus one?"

She shakes her head. "No. Just chemistry and history."

"All that homework is gonna make your brain thicker before your stomach can catch up."

She sighs. "Stop, Belén, that's not funny."

I look over at her and raise my eyebrows.

Then we both laugh.

Every morning we wait for the bus together. We've done this since middle school. Rain or shine, we wait for the bus across from the Wendy's on International and 31st Avenue. We sit right by the shop where my sister cuts hair. At this time of the morning, six thirty, not even Ava's awake. The sun isn't even out yet. But here we are, cuz it's the first day of our senior year and Leti already has zero period AP Chemistry. And if she goes early, I go early. There's no way I'm riding the bus by myself.

The routine has been the same since I met Leti in the sixth grade—back when she'd get up early to dig her nose in a library book at school. I wake up, scrunch some mousse into my hair, then make my way to the bus stop where Leti is already waiting.

She's early—always.

Wakes up at five just to get up and study. For someone real smart, she can be hella stupid sometimes. I keep telling her that with that time she could play with some makeup or put a wave in her hair, but she's always like *no, Belén, I have to pass my AP tests.* I don't even know what those are.

Leti is straight as a board. No hips, no ass, no chest. No mascara on her lashes or gloss on her lips. Pin-straight hair she always stays braiding. Flat all around— not like me. When we first became friends, her ma looked me up and down and crossed herself. She told me I was pretty to my face, and I am, but behind my back she told Leti she had to be careful because I had a Jezebel body. My family doesn't go to church like her family does, but I knew enough to know what that meant. Not my fault everything about me has a curve. Curly hair, wide hips, big thighs, full chest.

But I never fooled around with anybody.

I mean, I fool around, but I never went *that* far. Not that I don't want to—I do. People just don't offer it up to me like that. Not anybody good anyway. I get the honks when I walk down the street, but I'd rather die than mess around with men like that. Sometimes I don't think there's anybody for me to even mess around with at all.

That's why when Leti met Quentin, I couldn't even be mad. That boy is smart, kind, and tall. Studying after school and doing homework on the weekends. That's how they met, dug deep in some studying at the library. Typical nerd shit, she'd read him flashcards while he made eyes at her. Homework dates where they took breaks to go to the liquor store and share a bag of Takis. I mean, Leti said they were only little breaks. But now she's pregnant—how little could they be, you know?

I look over at Leti, her stomach covered by her AP Chemistry binder spread open on her lap. A group of men in a pickup truck zoom past us, whistling at us as they go. The rush of air sends her summer reading notes flying, ripping along the metal binder rings. Leti sighs, and I help her reorganize before the bus comes.

I swear, if I ever date somebody, they better have a car. No way am I taking this bus if I don't have to. I'm dead tired of sitting here every morning getting sexually harassed by somebody's tío while reading the same graffiti over the same real estate ads. Always Liam and Lauren selling some Oakland property to some white people, always the same 510 area code spray painted over their pantsuits, always the same FOREVER dripping over that white person's face. If I had somebody, he'd pick me and Leti up, no question, from the cleaner curb down the street.

But I don't.

Leti's the one with somebody, and that's still hard to wrap my head around. It just doesn't make sense. If I'm the one out here with this Jezebel body, why can't anybody put that shit to use? And if Leti is out here with not a curve on her face, how is she pulling more than me?

Not that I'm jealous—Quentin is good for her. When she told me she was pregnant, I couldn't even stop crying. Like, can you imagine *me* as a madrina? Madrina Belén? That's the flyest shit I've ever heard.

But everybody thought it'd be me.

Even Leti's ma was upset she couldn't pin this one on my shoulders.

Señora Barragón would've had the time of her life. All this: *I always told you about Belén, you know she's always up to no good, can't trust a body that looks like that one, can't trust a family that doesn't know God, can't trust a girl sin papá.*

But here I am at the bus stop with Leti, with her stomach growing rounder with a baby and mine growing flatter since my ma turned into a ghost. Leti's ma can't say anything anymore.

TWO

I CUT SIXTH PERIOD. IT'S A HABIT AT THIS POINT. I HAVE NO BEEF WITH English class or reading or any of that—I'm smart, I like reading. But, the moment I saw Ms. Foley's name on my schedule, I knew I had to cut. I spent some of junior year watching Ms. Foley slowly die right in front of me while she read books written by other dead, white people. It made me want to die more than normal. So today, I crawl through the hole in the wire fence by the dumpsters, holding my breath the whole way.

I've never gotten caught. With a school as big as mine, we can't keep track of anybody. It'll be a miracle if people even notice Leti is pregnant.

But even though we go to this big-ass school, the office is always buzzing at my house: letters, voice mails, emails, texts. Always the same script in the voice of a robot mildly trained to roll its r's: *Belén Dolores Itzel del Toro was marked absent in one or more classes—please call the attendance office to excuse Belén Dolores Itzel del Toro's absence.* I have to give it to that robot, though. When you don't speak Spanish, getting through my name is like combing through tangled hair.

When I cut class, I take my pick of places to read. Today it's gray out. The pavement smells damp, like it's about to rain, so I duck under the awnings on International and go to Ava's salon. She hates when I cut class, but when she's in a good mood, she'll throw me some cash for sweeping the hair off the floor.

When you walk around Oakland, you have to look like you know better. I put on a pair of headphones and stick my nose up like it's guiding me around corners. Like nobody can talk to me.

But everybody tries.

People say things without saying anything at all.

I walk down these streets every day, alone or with Leti, and it's always the same shit. The same old men, wrinkles sagging off their faces, eyeing me like I'm something to eat.

And if it's not them, it's the tías and abuelas and mamás pushing strollers and sweeping sidewalks and selling tamales who look me up and down like I am a sin. You'd think they'd know better, since somebody probably did that to them when they were younger and looked like me. But I've learned that if there's anyone who has been trained to hate women the most, it's usually other women.

I see Ava's salon in the distance. It's called Güera's and sits on top of an auto body shop on International and 31st Avenue, right across from Wendy's. I told her not to work here off the name alone, but ends gotta meet one way or the other. Despite the corny name, it's grown on me. It feels mismatched and comfortable, like somebody's living room. It's on the second story of a strip of gray, painted gold with a bay window tight against the telephone wires. When I approach it, I pass the bus stop Leti and I were waiting at this morning.

I hike up the staircase, holding on to the new railing as I go. Ava's been doing hair here for a minute, but the repairs have only recently come. And you can't even call them that. Matías, Ava's useless boyfriend, painted the stairs one winter when he was out of work. He thinks he's an artist because he tags up BART stations after hours, but he's really just an asshole. The stairs were supposed to be black, but you can still see bits of the original hot pink beneath the smears of paint. Matías isn't a good boyfriend to Ava, and I'm beginning to believe he isn't good at anything.

When I walk into the salon, the welcome chime above the door rings. It's supposed to prevent robberies, but the three synth notes that play sound like a death announcement. Ava looks up at the mirror ahead of her and glares at me in its reflection. A woman is seated in the salon chair, half of her hair clipped up as Ava blow-dries it big and round.

"Belén, what're you doing here?" Ava asks.

I shrug, then dump my backpack onto the seat of a hooded hair dryer. "Sweeping, if you need me to be."

She smacks her lips. "How about school, huh?"

I don't say anything. Ava is always ending her sentences with *huh*, like some question you can never answer.

She calls to me as I walk away. "Belén, it's the first day. Don't repeat that shit you pulled last year. You don't wanna end up like Pa."

And there it went.

Ava's favorite thing to do was use my pa as leverage. She did it often and did it well. Small, backhanded things to remind me what she really thinks of me.

I used to think it was annoying, even kind of harmless. But since he left, it's been a power move she likes to exercise. I know I look a lot like my pa, but I wonder all the time if she knew how I felt—being compared to someone so awful. She had no idea how difficult it was for me to look in the mirror. I sometimes wondered if she ever reminded herself of him—like, he makes up half her DNA too. But she takes after our ma too much, down to the appearance.

She could never understand what it was like.

I ignore her, walking toward the waxing room where she keeps her cleaning supplies. I pull the beaded curtain to the side, the scent of melting wax singeing my nostrils. I feel like I lose a brain cell every time I inhale this shit, which leaves me to wonder how many Ava's got left.

I walk past the waiting area, a bunch of leather chairs aligned side by side and saggy fashion magazines arranged on a glass coffee table. Nobody's touched them in years. I keep telling Ava she has to get real subscriptions to current magazines and not let the clients thumb through haircuts from 2006, but she always smacks her lips and is like, *Belén you know I only rent a chair, why don't you tell my manager that, then who's gonna help feed you, huh?* Like, Jesus Christ.

The room has a box-TV with a VHS player that wheezes every time you try to turn it on. Next to the mirror on the wall, there's an inexplicable poster of white motorcyclists and fashion models collaged onto a beach.

I go back into the salon and start sweeping around Ava's shoes. Old, vieja shoes that she described as "sensible" when she put them on her Christmas list. Her client stands up and checks out behind a glass counter full of jeweled hair clips and cheap, Quinceañera tiaras. As she leaves, she drops a few dollars into the flower vase Ava uses as a tip jar. Ava fishes her hand in and pulls out a bill, folding it sharply and handing it to me between two manicured fingers.

"Just in case Ma doesn't make it home in time for dinner."

Most days that I come home from school, I see my ma has left me a box of Rice-A-Roni next to the stove. Not like she cooks anything better—she'd make the Rice-A-Roni herself if she was home. Since my pa left, all we eat are pobrecita meals: Rice-A-Roni, Maruchan, and frozen TV dinners. So, when Ava knows she'll be closing the shop, she'll sometimes throw me a five to spend at Wendy's. If she wasn't around, I don't know what I'd do. When she was still working to get her cosmetology license, I'd have to microwave frozen vegetables and eat them with Tajín.

You'd think we were broke or something, but that's not really it. I mean, my ma doesn't make a bunch of money. She's a teacher, she's underpaid, she's busy. And I know we don't have it like that, but we have *something*. We used to eat the way most families do, and it wasn't excessive, but it didn't rely on a seasoning packet for flavor. But since my pa left, this is how my ma operates. She'll eat instant oatmeal for dinner if we don't tell her to stop.

Ava's no chef either, but she keeps an eye out for me. I take the bill from her hand and shove it into my back pocket, sweeping the last strands of the woman's hair as I go.

I set aside the broom and slump onto one of the seats of the hooded dryers. Ava counts her tips and taps her long, acrylic nails on the glass of the counter. I reach for my backpack and pull out some poems I'm reading, excerpts from a collection by this nun named Sor Juana Inés de la Cruz.

This is what I wish I was reading in my English class, but I'm in the "College Prep" track. International High sorts us into three tracks: Advanced Placement, Honors, and "College Prep." Fat quotation marks around the last one. The school sells it to families as a way to prepare kids for college, because no principal is telling a parent to their face that their kid is in a low-level class for students with poor test scores or truancy issues or bad attitudes. But we look at our books and look at our assignments and we know the truth.

In Leti's AP English class, they read all kinds of good shit. The school is always announcing the grants they receive for the AP track, so their books are usually brand-new, without any creases in the spines. Most of the books in my classes usually have penises drawn on the pages, missing covers, or entire chapters that are illegible from being warped by spilled coffee.

Leti gives me her assigned reading when she's done with it. It's like a hand-me-down book system, and each time she gives me one, I am amazed by what they get to read out there. She gave me this collection of poems earlier, during passing period, and I shoved it into my backpack.

"You're all done with it?" I asked.

14

Leti nodded. "I finished in class."

I rolled my eyes at her. I never understood how she had so much homework after school if she was constantly doing it in class.

"Ms. Barrera says that Sor Juana is the first Mexican feminist ever recorded in history," Leti continued, eyes wide with excitement.

"Inglés Sin Barreras told you what?" I moved my hair from my ear. It's so big that it sometimes blocks out people's voices, which I've grown to be grateful for.

Leti nudged me. "Stop calling her that."

I shrugged. "It's not my fault she chose to teach English with that name."

"She's not a commercial, Belén." She rolled her eyes. "She said there weren't any other feminists at that time period. She began a whole movement."

"It doesn't have to be *all that*," I told her. "I don't ever do what people tell me to do and I am not starting shit."

She tugged at her braid, which fell over her shoulder. Not even a fishtail braid, a regular three-stranded braid that began at the curve of her neck and ended right below her paper-flat chest. It made me sad to look at. "You *could* start something. You have to start doing your work, college applications are due soon."

I rolled my eyes again. "I'm not going to college. I'm not even going to sixth period. You think I'm gonna go and be around Ms. Foleys and people who want to become Ms. Foleys? I'd rather die."

Leti smacked her lips and looked ahead, something she does when she's frustrated with me. "You're a good reader, Belén. You just have to do the work."

But I hate "doing the work." It's not that I can't do it, I just don't want to. Applying to college seems like the largest waste of my time—if I can't even go to class, how do people expect me to go to college? Leti lectures me about it sometimes, but *nobody* lectures me more than Ava.

All of spring semester last year, she'd go on and on about my potential that was being wasted. She'd be in the middle of giving someone a blowout, holding the round brush in one hand and her hair dryer against her hip while saying, "Do you wanna end up like Pa, huh? That shit is not as good as it seems, Belén."

But I don't know who I want to end up like.

I don't really know what I want to be.

It isn't my fault. After my pa left, I'd cut class, collect my Wendy's money, and go home to lie in bed. I lay there because I felt like I couldn't move, like my body was tethered to the mattress. Some days, I'd find things to help distract me from the feeling. I was seeing this guy Jeveón, but when that fell apart, I'd just look out the window at the sagging telephone wires with sneakers tied on them. I'd think about how my chest felt so full, so heavy, but how my house was so empty.

Ava let that slide for a few weeks.

But after a while, the nagging started.

Since my ma began to disappear after work, Ava began to multiply. I knew she meant well, but after a while, it all became background noise. The feeling on my chest demanded so much of my attention. It only lightened when I was distracted by something that brought me joy—sleeping, reading, kissing. But Ava would die before she heard about that.

I peek up at her now. She's looking at my backpack with her eyes squinted and tight. That means she's about to ask me what's for homework today. I don't really feel like making up a lie, so I quickly dump the book into my backpack and zip it up fast.

"I'm hungry, I gotta go home," I tell her.

Her face scrunches up. "It's not even three yet."

"Bye," I call from over my shoulder, brushing past her next client in the entryway.

She calls out after me, but I'm already taking the stairs two at a time to get back on International. There, I breathe in that Oakland-smell of damp air and exhaust from whistle-tipped cars. I walk across the street and into Wendy's, passing the iron bars against the windows.

I get what I can afford—a 4 for 4 combo with fries, chicken nuggets, a junior cheeseburger, and a Coke. When the money is right, I treat myself to a spicy chicken sandwich and a Frosty.

Since my pa left, the money is almost never right.

Even now, when I know I have enough to pay, my palms start itching when I hand the cashier the money through the bulletproof, plexiglass barrier.

But she rings me up fine.

I carry the greasy bag in my hand, preparing myself to walk down the street again, digging my heels into the pavement. I sit in front of Liam and Lauren on the bus bench opposite my morning stop. While I wait, I shove handfuls of fries into my mouth, listening as an old man honks at me, rolling his window down to blow me a kiss. I don't react. I've learned these men are like pigeons—if you feed them, they come back expectantly. So, I sit and watch cars pass, people walk by, graffiti fade beige.

Once I'm inside the bus, I sit near the middle exit and press my head on the thick, plastic windows. I begin eating my burger while peering out onto the street. I think of the time Leti and I walked to her house, and how the honking was so bad and the cars kept circling like vultures. When we got to Leti's house, Leti's ma told us to never speak to those men. But she looked at me and at my hips as she spoke. Like I was speaking to them to begin with. Like I invited them to talk to us.

At the bus stop in my neighborhood there's less staring, less honking, less worrying. I walk down the block to our house—boring, plain, white walls with a miserable excuse for a lawn. I see my ma's car with its mismatched door parked in the driveway. Milagro.

But then I see my tía Myrna's car parked beside it, and everything makes sense. I groan. I think I hate my tía Myrna. I know you're supposed to love your family or whatever, but since my pa left, I no longer think that rule applies.

She is the definition of a metiche. She's always in people's business, always proudly bearing bad news and peacocking in her Ross outfits and clearance-rack Michael Kors purses.

I don't know why my ma is always so happy to see her—after my tía delivers her gossip and leaves, my ma usually goes to cry in her room.

I stand on the front stoop, stuffing the Wendy's evidence into the bottom of my backpack before my tía can think of commenting on my lonjas. I sigh, preparing myself to go inside, and grab the mail along the porch steps. I see an envelope from our electricity company.

18

Bold, red letters are printed at the top, unmistakable as they read: PAST DUE.

This is our third one since my pa left.

I slide my backpack down into my hand, preparing myself for the shift I experience when I enter the house. I feel so noticeable around the city, a choice I've never made myself, but one my hips made for me. But once I'm home with my ma, it's the opposite. No matter my hip size or the truancy notices or my big mouth, I'm invisible. On the rare times she's home, she just sits at the kitchen table, sipping tea and gazing off into the distance with emptiness in her eyes. I wonder what she thinks about, what she looks at more than she looks at me, but sometimes I think it's better this way.

Sometimes it's better not to know at all.

THREE

WHEN I WALK INSIDE, THE SMELL OF HOMEMADE FOOD HITS ME across the face. The only semidecent thing about my tía Myrna is that she'll usually bring us something to eat. Her husband, my tío Berto, works in construction in the East Bay, so she's a real Mexican housewife. Making flan on a Tuesday and needle-pointing every pillowcase in their house. On good days, she criticizes my ma for having gone to college instead of learning how to be more domestic. On bad days, she claims this is the reason my pa left.

I peer into the kitchen, where I see Tía Myrna, my ma, and Tía's twin daughters, Veronica and Valeria, sitting around the kitchen table. My cousins are probably the only thing worse than my tía herself. When we were younger, they'd cut off my doll's hair and laugh while pointing at the fat on my stomach.

Their whole family is crazy, just like Leti's. Parents who are too strict to know their kids. My tía Myrna is so Catholic that she makes her daughters kneel on rice and recite Bible verses. The girls host Bible study on Thursday evenings. They wear Virgencita chains around their necks like dog collars.

But whatever, at least I'll get to eat a real meal today. I walk into the kitchen, where I see the pot of caldo de res my tía brought simmering on the stovetop. I set down my backpack and my ma stands to greet me.

"Hi, mija. How was the first day?" my ma asks, hugging me gently. It's ridiculous what Mexican parents do in front of company. I can't remember the last time I hugged my ma. I didn't even know she knew that today was my first day of school, and she's a *teacher*. But when she embraces me, the smell of her perfume triggers something in my brain, phantom limbs of past comfort wrapping their arms around my body.

"Uh, fine," I tell her, then bend down to hug my tía Myrna, who never stands up for anything. "Hi, Tía."

"Ay, Belén. Every time I see you, you're more and more grown-up. Dolores, have you seen those minimizing bras? They might do her good, I got some for the girls last year."

Like I said, it's ridiculous what Mexican parents do in front of company. Veronica and Valeria are fraternal, but their mosquito-bite bra size is identical. I want to tell my tía that sometimes I don't even wear a bra. She'd faint.

But I bite my tongue and sit down in an empty seat, desperately wishing for Ava to finish with her clients and come home. Ava is like family glue—she's older and nicer, so she usually cleans up my messes when I say too much.

"Hey, guys," I tell Veronica and Valeria, who are texting expertly, fingernails clicking against phone screens. They look up for a moment and both say "hi" in unison. Then they give me a fake smile and an up-down.

I look across the table at my ma, who looks tired. She has her hair up in a bun, a pencil woven through it. She's out of her teacher-clothes and into her house-clothes—a pair of leggings and one of my pa's old T-shirts he left behind when he discovered they wouldn't fit into his bags.

My tía Myrna looks at me. "Mira, Dolores. I always forget how much Belén looks like her pa."

I immediately regret sitting down at the table, kicking myself for not expecting my tía to be such a chismosa. I blink at her, feeling a heaviness travel from my stomach and into my chest. She reaches to grab a piece of pan from the pink panadería box at the center of the table. Then she slurps her mug of coffee loudly, her brown eyes peeking up from the rim, expectant. "¿Y Rodolfo? How is he?"

I hate talking about my pa—it's always the same story and the same updates wrapped up neatly. My ma has become this ex-wife politician at answering these questions, always surface-level responses and little smiles and a tone that suggests that she's totally fine. A bunch of garbage. Right after people ask her, she goes into her bedroom and lets her mattress soak up her tears.

My ma shrugs and sips her coffee.

Veronica and Valeria look up at me, their eyes narrowed and slim like they're peering through my body. I can already hear them on their car ride home, gossiping about how it's just so sad about my pa, how it's gonna ruin my life and make me hate men and how I'll never get married or be a good wife, their tones thick with fake sympathy and ego-soaked pity.

If I could sit between them in their SUV, I'd tell them that everything is going fine. I don't know where my pa is, but I'm still flunking math just like I was before, and so what if I never get married? Even while my parents were together, they were unhappy. Maybe I'll just skip a step.

"Pues, I hear he's in México." Tía Myrna takes a bite of her pan, a cochinito that looks plump like her. "I hear he moved back to Michoacán."

Everybody's always hearing things about my pa, but nobody really knows any truth.

Not even me, and probably not even my ma.

When he left in the spring, he took all my ma's emergency savings she kept in the freezer. He didn't even say bye to me or to Ava. It was so abrupt that I didn't even know that day would be the last day I'd see him. I went to school like normal, but my ma came to pick me up early.

She told the front office I had a dentist appointment, and when that pink office pass floated my way in sixth period, I began feeling sick to my stomach. My ma never leaves her school for anything, so I knew something was wrong. She was parked crookedly in the student lot, Al Green audible even with the windows rolled all the way up.

I got into the passenger seat, expecting her to say something. But she just looked ahead, at the sunlight beating down against the hoods of cars, and told me that her savings that she kept in the freezer had gone missing.

I popped my gum. "*I* didn't take it, if that's what you're asking."

"No, mija. I know you didn't take it."

Then she didn't say anything. The radio was set to 102.9 KBLX, my ma's favorite station. DeBarge sounded through the speakers, static crackling between us when the high notes hit. And then Chaka Khan came on, and still, she said nothing.

I sat there with her, her knuckles bone-white from gripping the steering wheel, expecting her to cry and tell me somebody robbed our house or died or something, waiting for tears to stream down her cheeks.

But she was expressionless, her smile lines had gone flack.

Chaka Khan turned to Luther Vandross, and we sat stiffly.

And then she just told me that he left. My pa left. He took her money and just left. About four thousand dollars in cash.

She said it just like that, with her sentences all broken and pausing to catch her breath.

The number stuck in my head the most—what could somebody do with so much money? But the next thing we know, we hear from his coworkers that he's got an apartment twenty minutes away. Apparently, he'd go to sleazy bars after work and pick up girls as young as Ava. Isn't that fucked up? How can you fuck somebody as young as your own daughter?

My ma cried about it for weeks. Every time we hugged her, her face was damp with tears, even her hair began to smell like salt water. She

24

loved him, I guess. But how can you love somebody like that? When I'd ask her, she'd pin my hair behind my ears and say, "Mija, you don't understand. You shouldn't understand. We both came from different places and met here. And then, he gave me the two of you. I will always love him."

I hope I never love anybody like that, enough to water me down and make me so pathetic.

"I haven't heard from him," my ma says, "but everything is going great. Ava's at her salon and Belén keeps reading."

My one redeeming academic quality is always shared. My tía Myrna perks up in her seat, the posture she has each time she's about to gloat about something ridiculous. "That's great. Valeria is varsity captain of her volleyball team this year, and Veronica is first chair in violin."

How disgusting. I'd rather chew on cement than be in the band, and even worse in a sport. My tía continues. "They're both thinking of applying to UC Berkeley and UCLA. Belén, where do you think you'll be going to school?"

I look at my ma, who hasn't bothered to ask me about college in years, but she's looking at the floor.

"I'm keeping my options open," I deadpan, practicing my ma's politician-style.

My tía Myrna clicks her tongue. "Well, you'd better hurry. Those applications are due soon."

I feel like banging my head on the wall. I get this shit all the time from everybody at school. I almost like coming home to be ignored just so I don't have to keep hearing about it.

Thank God my ma gets up to begin serving dinner, pouring caldo into the brown-rimmed bowl set every Mexican family seems to own. I have to eat cautiously, eyeing my tía every now and then. If I eat too quickly, she'll ask my ma if she even feeds me. If I eat too slowly, I must be depressed because of my pa.

I get so overwhelmed that I don't want to eat at all, but I do.

I shovel homemade food into my mouth for the first time in weeks. I'm full from Wendy's, but I don't know when I'll get another home-cooked meal. So, I dig in, tasting fat off a bone and lime juice that sours and splinters.

I don't remember the last time my ma prepared a big, traditional meal like this. A few months ago, she tried to make frijoles and ended up scorching the bottom of the pot. She stood over it, smoke wafting over her face, asking why she couldn't do anything right anymore. Ava, desperate to get her out of that slump, went to KFC and bought us a family meal. She put the bucket of chicken in the center of the table, surrounded it with its greasy sides, and we all picked at it without a word. That was the last meal at this table that I can remember.

When I look up at my ma, I see she is looking down at her bowl, the brown of her eyes melting into the oil swirls in the broth. When we were younger, she'd make this caldo for us during the winter.

While my pa was out at work, she'd cramp up her fingers chopping vegetables and ask Ava and me to watch the garbanzo beans boiling on the stove. Most times, because he came home late, we ate without him. Just the three of us around a table that was too wide, reaching over each other for tortillas. Hands too small and stomachs too big, but enough food for the three of us, and the fourth one always missing.

As I scrape rice into my bowl and slice chayote into smaller bits, my tía Myrna begins to speak. Something about my ma's job, something about the union, something about how teachers should be on strike. I look at my ma's hands, calloused with work, and my ma looks over at me. Her eyes melt into my own. She does not smile, but her mouth twitches as if to say that she is remembering too.

After my tía Myrna is gone, I go to the bathroom to take a shower. Our shower is always full of Ava's half-baked experiments, the shelves stacked with mixes of conditioners and surplus shampoo bottles from Güera's. The bathroom has only one small window to let out steam, and between the plastic bottles and the tiny glass window, I'm constantly struggling to breathe.

What's worse is that whenever I shower, I squint at the grout between the tiles that is smeared sloppy. Between them there's dirt and soap scum, but there are also tiny black hairs. Each of them belongs to my pa. After he'd get his hair cut, he'd come home to shower, the evidence sticking onto the walls.

One afternoon, I caught my ma weeping in the bathtub, trying to scrub the hairs out with steel wool. No matter how much she scrubbed or how much bleach she added, they remained stuck to the grout. Sometimes, I still find the bits of hair on the soles of my feet after a shower and spend minutes picking them off my skin with the tip of my nail. I begin to check once I'm out, balancing one foot on the bathmat and lifting the other with my hand, making sure I am not carrying my pa anywhere he no longer wanted to be.

But Ava pounds at the door, her acrylic nails clinking as she hammers her hand against the wood.

"Belén," she calls, "I gotta get ready, hurry up."

We only have one bathroom, and it's usually not a problem until Ava has a date with Matías. She'll be in there late at night, puffing mousse into her hair and slicking mascara onto her eyelashes. I don't know why—Matías is not worth all that effort. He usually strolls into the house desgreñado, his pants down to his ankles.

I wipe down the mirror and begin rubbing lotion onto my face. Most days I do this, it's not a big deal. But when I'm not feeling good, I look down at the sink. And after hearing my tía Myrna going on and on about everything with my pa, I'm not feeling good.

Everyone, especially Ava, is always telling me how much I'm like my pa.

It makes it hard for me to look at myself.

There are days where I'd rather look at the dried-up blobs of toothpaste in the sink basin than look at my own reflection and hear everyone's words rattling in between my ears. Everyone saying—you and your dad, always the same, those big brown eyes and that milky skin and that hair like a lion's, and that mouth, olvídate, you two with those full lips and always something to say—have you heard from him, mija, do you know where he is, how he's been doing?

It makes me paranoid.

People are always saying this is the age where you figure out who you're becoming. But how can I see myself in someone else's shadow?

How can they compare me to someone who leaves their family?

How can you be like someone who isn't even around to compare yourself to?

I look at Ava with jealousy.

She takes after my ma, with eyes the color of honey and upturned noses and dark hair that slips down their backs. It's strange looking at myself, seeing my pa in all my features, wondering if he left me or wanted to leave a part of himself.

I finish rubbing lotion onto my face and change into a T-shirt and a ratty pair of sweatpants. It hasn't been two minutes and Ava begins pounding at the door again. When I open it, I see her there, examining her split ends.

"Where's he taking you?" I ask her.

"Why's it important?"

"Cuz don't you get all dressed up for the drive-thru with him?"

She shoves past me and into the bathroom, then locks the door behind her. Not my fault I told the truth.

I walk to my room and kick the clothes on the floor away to form a path to my bed. My room is never dirty, but there are heaps of clothes and books everywhere. They usually form after I try on old pairs of jeans, realizing they no longer go up past my hips, or reread sections of my favorite books.

I flop onto my mattress and look outside at the limp phone wires, then search through the piles of books I keep in milk crates behind my bed. A bunch of them came from garage sales or the library's "free" bins. I keep them for emergencies when I'm out of things to read. Like today.

Sometimes I get so bored that I begin to think about how different my life would be if I had someone to talk to. When Jeveón was around, things were so much easier. It was like the feeling on my chest just evaporated.

I met him at a college fair Leti had dragged me to. I liked that he went to a school across Oakland. I liked the cologne he wore. I liked that both of our names had accents.

By the time we met, my pa had been gone for a few weeks, replaced by heaviness harboring in my body. But when Jevón and I hung out, everything felt lighter. Nothing mattered.

He was smart and respectful enough that I thought that he was it—the gateway to feeling normal. Since my pa left, everything felt so backwards. I just wanted what everyone else, even Leti, seemed to have—parents, boyfriends, sex.

I'd been trying to lose my virginity for forever.

I'd often lie in my bed and wonder if I'd ever be having sex there. If I'd be looking up at the same ceiling as somebody crawled atop me. It seemed so far away, like something that was never going to happen for me. Everybody had always looked at my body, but nobody wanted anything to do with it. And the people who did were disgusting, like the men on the street.

With my pa gone, I knew I couldn't have it all. But with Jeveón, I thought maybe I could have something.

When I wasn't cutting class to sweep hair at Güera's, I'd cut class to go see him at his school. After a few weeks, I invited him over to my place. I deep-cleaned my room, lit a candle from Ross, and made sure my sheets were fresh. He would be the first guy who would ever be on my bed. The first guy I'd ever have sex with.

I could've met Jeveón at the front door and kissed him in the living room. Nothing would get my ma's attention away from the TV. But for the drama, I asked him to come through the window so we could mess around secretly.

But he never wanted to mess around.

We kissed for what felt like hours. I guided his hand to my body, starting with safe spaces like my arm or my stomach. But when I pulled his fingers toward my chest, he shook his head. Then he told me he didn't plan on having sex until he was married.

And after that we didn't talk.

I kept my routine of cutting class and coming home, but the heaviness quickly returned. I lay in bed for weeks, feeling the weight of the sky press onto my body. But in August, when Leti found out she was pregnant, I was relieved. I knew helping her through it would distract me for a while. But sometimes, I just wish my distraction was more fun. More fulfilling.

I still haven't had sex, and it's upsetting. I think about Leti and how it happened for her, so quickly and so fast, with someone upright and nice.

Why can't it just happen for me?

I bet if I could just find someone half decent to date, I could forget about all the other shit happening in my life. About my pa's absence and my ma's silence and this feeling on my chest all the time.

But, while I wait for it to happen, I guess I'll just do this.

For a while, I felt guilty about masturbating. My ma sat me down for "the talk" about sex and birth control, but she never, ever mentioned an orgasm or masturbation. Somewhere in my gut I felt she'd think it was abnormal and gross. Every time I'd finish, I'd feel impure somehow, cleaning myself up with baby wipes and wiping wet shame from my skin. But lately I feel okay about it. I mean all the guys at school are always talking about doing it, so why shouldn't I?

Sometimes I'll pull up porn, but most times it makes me feel confused. I've never even had sex and I can see the way the men fuck the women is aggressive and uncomfortable. And in some strange way, I still long for that.

I pull my curtains closed and turn on my back. I don't even have my sweatpants off when I hear knocking at my door. I quickly sit up in bed. This never happens.

"Mija," my mom says, "can I come in?"

"Um, uh-huh?"

She's never asked to come into my room before. She used to just barge in and tell me to clean my room or do my homework. But after my pa left, she hardly bothers me at all.

She walks inside and looks around as if it's some place she doesn't even recognize. She looks down at the piles and piles of stuff on the floor. Jeans and bras tangled into themselves, covering piles of overdue library books. I wait for her to complain about the tiradero, almost hope for her to, but she looks at me with emptiness. In the darkness of the evening, the bags stamped beneath her eyes look more purple.

"Do you have any clothes that don't fit you anymore? I'm sending them to your family in México."

I squint. "Um, yes."

"Can you put them in a box and leave them in my room? I want to send it to them by this weekend."

"Okay," I tell her.

This is the longest conversation we've had in months.

Most days that I get home from school, she's gone. I figure she's working late after school, but it's never been this severe. It's almost like she's doing it on purpose, like she's avoiding me. But when she is home, it's no better. She locks herself in her room, listens to Rose Royce, and cries.

My ma stands there for a moment. I know this conversation was probably sparked by my tía's visit. I can say whatever I want about my tía Myrna, but Veronica and Valeria aren't walking on eggshells around her, worrying she'll burst into tears at any moment.

I know that this isn't what she came in to talk about, but by the way she keeps looking toward the floor, I'm not even sure she knows what she wanted to say.

"Okay, mija," she says gently. "I'm going to fold laundry."

She leaves, quickly darting down the hallway, passing Ava and the sound of her blow-dryer whirring. As soon as she passes, Ava opens the bathroom door and cranes out her neck to peer down the hallway, turning to my ma, then back at me. My ma goes into her room, closing the door behind her. Ava stands there, giving me a knowing look.

We know Ma is going to sit on the edge of her bed and weep, letting the blue of the evening sift through the window. We know she will sleep on my pa's side of the bed, which is steep with her weight every morning. And I know Ava will come home late after seeing Matías, and I know we will walk past each other, and I know we will keep our gazes straight. Both almost comfortable with the feeling, both pretending it does not exist.

FOUR

ON THE WALK BETWEEN THE BUS STOP AND SCHOOL, LETI TELLS ME she's eating lunch in Ms. Barrera's classroom. I might as well just turn around and go home. Eating lunch indoors with a teacher is sacrilegious, and I don't even go to church like that.

We walk down the block, the gray slate of the early morning sky cloaking our school in the distance. We're on time, but there's already a crowd of our classmates pooling at the front steps for the morning security check.

Every morning, we all put out backpacks on fold-out tables to be searched by the campus police. Then, we walk through a row of metal detectors set before the front doors, security guards patting our pockets after the machine has cleared us. On Fridays, there are even dogs sniffing through backpacks and lockers to catch any drugs coming through campus.

"She's helping me with my personal statements for college applications," Leti says, lining up with everyone else.

"Why are you being hella excessive?" I ask her, setting down my backpack. I walk through the detectors, arms spread, and wait for the security guard to pat down my pockets. "You don't *need* help applying for college." I call from over my shoulder, "You're like a brown Sor Juana. Write them a poem or something."

She gives me a look while walking into the detector neighboring mine, her big brown eyes all squinted and slitted. "Belén, you don't know how hard it is. Every year it gets harder and harder to get into Berkeley."

"Don't they give you any sympathy points?" I ask.

"Like what?"

Campus security gives us a thumbs-up and an all clear, so we grab our bags and head inside. The main hallway smells musky and damp, the overhead lighting shading us both a gross green. We push past the sea of people in the hall, elbowing our way to Leti's locker.

"Like, I don't know, maybe cuz we go to this shitty school in Oakland and nobody in your family has ever been to college and cuz you're brown and bilingual and pregnant and everything they might give you a booster point or two to make shit fair. Like that."

She shakes her head. "They don't do that anymore. And I don't want to get in because of that. I want to get in because I deserve it."

"You think people get in because they *deserve* to?" I click my tongue. "Damn, here I was thinking you were smart."

She rolls her eyes. "Stop, Belén. That's why I need to make my

35

statement perfect. Ms. Barrera went to Berkeley for undergrad *and* graduate school."

"That sounds terrible," I say. And it does sound terrible to me, but Leti has been dying to go to Berkeley since I met her. She was the only sixth grader I knew who was talking about college. Her binders were decorated with pictures she drew of the Cal logo, her handiwork protected behind the sheet of plastic. I thought she was ridiculous—who makes fan art of a university?

We stop at Leti's locker for her to trade out her books. When she pops off the lock, pieces of peeling green, rusted paint flutter onto the floor. While that's disgusting, everything inside of her locker is sterile and organized. No more fan art binders, but instead, textbooks that are alphabetized by subject, study materials arranged in order of importance, a modest sweater hanging from a Command hook she installed last week.

I tap my foot and look around the school. Even though Leti is in the AP track, her locker is at the crossroad between the AP section and my College Prep section. And in that small walkway, everything is different.

The AP hall constantly reeks of floor polish and stress, but they seem to have it better over there. Desks with storage compartments for books, bright overhead lighting, air ducts that don't have mold. My section of school isn't even in the school building, but outside in the portables by the football field.

Out there, everything sags with sadness. Wood panels bloated with water damage and lights that flicker on and off. Last year, I saw a mouse in the corner of my math class. The year before that, a trail of roaches on the windowsill of the bathroom.

Leti shuts her locker, and we start down the hall.

She turns to face me, her braid snaking around her neck. Her eyes are wide like quarters, the expression she makes when she wants something. "You should come today. Ms. Barrera invited you."

I raise my eyebrows. "Oh, this is invite-exclusive?"

She shrugs. "I don't know, she just said she thinks you should come, too."

I stop walking. How does Ms. Barrera even know who I am?

"Quentin is coming too," Leti says.

I roll my eyes. "Oh, so now I *have* to go?"

"You're gonna go because Quentin is coming and not because I'm there?"

"Well, if you both go, I won't have anybody to talk shit with at lunch. I'm not sitting with anybody else, everyone else is disgusting."

During lunchtime, Leti, Quentin, and I sit on the big steps by the gym. Quentin hangs out with us and eats his lunch before going to chess club or robotics club or whatever other club he's a part of. Sometimes we share a bag of Flamin' Hot Funyuns and talk while Leti studies. I like hanging out with Quentin because he's never made me feel like he was just Leti's boyfriend. He feels like my friend, too.

"So, you're coming?" Leti coaxes, gently nudging me.

I sigh. "Yes, I guess. But I'm not gonna do any work."

She snorts. "Oh-kay. Do whatever."

We get to the water fountain in the hallway where we split off. She goes left to the AP hall, and I weave through the double doors to walk to the portables.

I have to make sure to get to my math class early to get a desk of my own. While the AP classes have those nice desks, my classes are so overcrowded that people have to share table space. Last year in physics, I had to sit on the counter by the faucet and take notes on my lap.

I know it's my own fault for being here, but sometimes I blame my ma. When Ava was in high school, my ma sat down with her and pored over her school schedule. My ma never forced college onto either of us, but she wanted to be sure we took the right classes and made the grades so we always had the option. Together, they met with guidance counselors, my ma's ego all inflated with her teacher-expertise to ensure Ava had "choices."

By the time I was a freshman, my parents were beginning to disappear. My pa was around, but never home. My ma was always home, but never around. My pa began coming home later and later, sometimes not at all, and my ma devoted most of her time to waiting by the door.

The spring I was supposed to ask for help picking classes, my ma and pa were going at it multiple times a day. It always started the same way, like a waltz where the missteps were choreographed: she'd ask who he was with, he'd say he was working late, she'd say she hadn't seen the money to trust that, and then he'd yell.

My pa had always had a temper.

During traffic jams or lost poker games or bad service, his temper built and built until it demolished. It was like a sunburn, felt only slightly until the sting of the aftermath.

Ava says I get it from him.

And once my pa started yelling, I could forget about sleeping.

While Ava was out with Matías, I was stuck in my room, listening to arguments seep through the paper-thin walls. My ma and pa would go at it until they physically couldn't anymore, until one of them fell asleep and we all awoke to an air so thick with tension, it felt impossible to breathe.

Despite my ma not even sitting down with me to ask about my school year, let alone helping me select my courses, Leti kept urging me to sign up for AP classes with her. But I couldn't. I physically felt like I couldn't. The sensation of heaviness pulled at my chest even when my pa was still around, and instead of lying in bed and feeling the weight in his absence, I felt its pressure in his presence.

I know that cutting class and taking these "College Prep" classes won't even let me come close to apply for college. Most times I can't bring myself to care. I just want to find something that makes me feel normal.

But other times, like now, I wish I was with Leti. Because my math class looks like a fucking zoo.

The portable smells like pee, and students take up every inch of the room. I pass the turn-in tray for my homework. It reminds me of the church basket the altar boys pass around on Sundays. I never drop anything into either of them.

I miraculously get the last desk in the back of the room, open my math textbook, then prop it up so that it stands to blocks my face. After, I nestle my book, *The Poet X* by Elizabeth Acevedo, in between the textbook covers and begin reading. I do this every single day.

There are so many people in this class that my useless precalc teacher, Mr. Kluger, does not notice. He has a lazy eye that wanders and he cannot catch people sleeping in class. Or, worse, he doesn't care to.

I know I could be doing better in school, but how does anyone expect me to learn like this? Mr. Kluger lectures by an ancient overhead for thirty minutes, then sits at the front of the room eating barbecue Lay's and drinking coffee.

I read for the entire class period. I'm turning a page when I feel a piece of paper skip over my shoulder and land on the top of the textbook.

I sigh and pick it up.

Usually, when people flick notes at me, they're comments about my body.

I like to throw them into the homework basket on my way out to give Mr. Kluger something nice to read at the end of the day.

I unfold the paper, which says: *You got a FAT ass.* Typical. It's a short sentence, but somehow they still managed to make it almost illegible, like it was written during an earthquake.

I slowly turn my head to see who's written it. I see this guy named Ali, wearing a printed sweater and a pair of small, gold hoop earrings. He came late, so he's stuck sitting on the ledge of the sink in the back of the portable. He's squinting at the board, then taking notes in his binder, when he looks at me.

I must be glaring hard because he glances at the note and begins shaking his head. He arches his thumb to a group of guys sitting on the floor beside him. I shift my gaze to them, and they give themselves away. They're red-faced, holding in their laughter by biting down on their lips.

I roll my eyes and crumple the paper. I shove it into the pocket of my sweatshirt and flip to the next page.

The bell rings. Mr. Kluger begins handing out the homework I'll never do. I grab the note and toss it into the homework bin, then stand in line waiting to exit the room. That's how overcrowded our class is—you have to wait in some fire-hazardous mob to exit the classroom. While I wait, I feel Ali standing behind me. I peer over at him, and it looks like he wants to say something. But I push on. I'd never be caught dead making small talk.

FIVE

MS. BARRERA'S CLASSROOM FEELS LIKE AN ENTIRELY DIFFERENT world. The floors aren't scuffed black with dirt, the lights remain lit, and the air smells faintly of cinnamon. There's bright-colored paper on the bulletin boards and portraits of famous writers tacked to the walls. I recognize most of them, but I don't tell anybody that.

Ms. Barrera is younger and more polished than I expected her to be. She eats salad out of a Tupperware container and drinks some shit called LaCroix. I look at her desk, where I see a jar of freshly sharpened pencils, labeled for "student use." My mouth nearly drops. Last year, I made the mistake of asking Ms. Foley for a pencil. She laughed in my face.

The only reason I'm looking around so much is because I don't know where else to look while Leti is sobbing.

Quentin is sitting next to her, an arm wrapped around her shoulders. Ms. Barrera is in front of them, with her listening face on. Since she's so young, she's easy to read. Her eyes are soft and wide with sympathy, and she nods understandingly each time Leti gasps for air. She has dark skin and big, black curly hair like mine. She's kinda pretty, but I am never saying that aloud.

The whole meltdown started almost as soon as we walked in. Leti and Quentin sat up front and I took the row behind them. Ms. Barrera started asking them about how their statements were coming along when Leti rambled about how she was stuck on the prompt about overcoming an obstacle. Like, what kind of dumb shit is that? *She* can't think of overcoming an obstacle? Leti's family lives in a tiny duplex. Her pa might be an alcoholic. Her ma would rather convince herself that Jesus was white than look her daughter in the face. Leti is fucking pregnant. I thought that was the stupidest thing I'd ever heard.

But then, Leti just emotionally vomited.

She hasn't told anyone other than us and her ma about the whole thing. And once she started, she couldn't stop.

Rattling on about the first time and how he finished early and how I went with her to a Planned Parenthood to get a pregnancy test for her because she was afraid to tell Quentin that her period wasn't late it was just really light and she read on WebMD about something called "implantation bleeding" and how she took the test in the bathroom of the Wendy's on International on our way home and how she took the other one in the bathroom at Güera's and how she made me keep both of the pee-saturated sticks because

God forbid if her ma ever found them and how I held them at an arm's length complaining that I was holding her pee and how I had to dump them in a garbage can on East 13th and how she threw up from panic in a garbage can on East 17th and how she got slapped across the face when she told her ma because how could her own daughter go behind her back and God's back and betray God in such a disgusting way and how she's been wondering the same thing if she loved God so much why did she do this and now she's scared because she's gonna go to hell but before even getting to hell she's wondering how she is supposed to go to college and how she doesn't even know how to afford that and how even though she's applied for scholarships even if she got the money she wonders how she will survive academically while caring for a baby if the baby will only be maybe three months old by the start of the first semester if she goes to a semester-based school and only four months old if she goes to a quarter-based school and she wants to go to a semester school because Berkeley is a semester school and what if she wants to do a summer bridge program what will she do then?

I don't really feel like I belong in this conversation.

I've heard it a lot.

On the bus, in the hall, on the street, on the phone.

So, I'm sitting here and rereading the ingredient list on a mustard packet for my spicy chicken sandwich from the cafeteria. It's one of the only tolerable things this school provides.

"So, your dad doesn't know?" Ms. Barrera asks.

"No," Leti says. "My mom knows, but not my dad."

Quentin nods. "Her dad would not approve."

"What does that mean?" Ms. Barrera leans back in her seat. "Like, he would ask you to terminate the pregnancy?"

"Like, abort the baby?" Leti sniffs.

Ms. Barrera nods, pushing the tissue box closer to Leti. "Yeah, like that."

Leti shakes her head. "No, my family would never let me do that. They're too religious."

"You'd be surprised," Ms. Barrera says, her eyebrows raising gently. "So, what would he disapprove of? That you're too young, that you had sex before marriage?"

Quentin scoffs. "I mean I'm sure he'd be upset about all that, too. It's mainly because I'm Black."

Ms. Barrera sips her water and lets out a deep sigh, her chest deflating. "Oh, it's about blanqueamiento."

It's bizarre to me how much shit teachers can keep in their brain. It's like an accordion file in there that they thumb through to prove how smart they can be. Quentin lets out a breath and reclines. He looks almost calm this way, leaning back and extending his legs before him. Complete opposite of Leti, in her Sunday-school posture with her braid tight behind her back.

"What does that mean?" Quentin asks.

"Lightening a race," Ms. Barrera replies. "There's a lot of pressure for people to reproduce with white or lighter-skinned people to diminish the Black or darker-skinned population. They think it's a way to better the pool of ethnicity. It's completely immoral, but lots of people believe in it, unfortunately."

"My *ma* doesn't even know Quentin is the father," Leti blurts.

Quentin turns to her, as if this is the first time he's hearing this. His relaxed posture turns upright, matching Leti's. I see his back stiffen, his jaw clench.

I can't see Leti, but even from back here I can sense her cheeks flushing. She hangs her head low and looks down at the glossy linoleum floor.

I begin eating my lunch, chewing slowly, wondering why Leti is so comfortable telling Ms. Barrera her problems. Leti talks to her like she's known her forever, like she's some kind of therapist. I don't think I've ever spoken to a teacher like this. But maybe I just don't understand, because I'm stuck with teachers like Ms. Foley who keeps calling me *Buh-leen* instead of Belén. Like, isn't she a teacher? Hasn't she ever read a Bible?

"Do you have any kind of plan on what to do if you tell your parents about Quentin and they react negatively?" Ms. Barrera asks.

Leti leans over and buries her head into her arms, like an ostrich stuck in sand. Sometimes, when I see her like this, I wish I could give her a piece of myself. I've known Leti for almost six years, and she's always making herself smaller than she already is. At times I imagine crawling into her mouth and prying her jaw open with my hands, making her say all the things I know she's thinking. Things she tells me in private. I don't think it'd fix what's about to happen with her family, but it could help get that weight off her back that keeps making her slouch down when she's upset.

But Leti is no good at defending herself.

When we were in middle school and girls would make fun of her, it was always me sticking up for her. But I just couldn't understand—who lets someone call them flaca, flat-chested, and fea? Leti would just hear it and hang her head lower. Like, what kind of response is that?

Regardless, I've learned if your mouth is strong enough, your hands don't have to be. Do I fantasize about fighting? All the time. You only hear Señora Barragón ask Jesus to narrow your hips so many times before you imagine mopping the floor with her hair. But Leti just lets people walk all over her. I keep telling her that Beyoncé is also a Virgo, Beyoncé would never let people talk to her that way.

But Leti is terca, too good to shift her way.

"I don't think they'll let me live there anymore. I won't have anywhere to go," Leti says.

Without thinking, like an idiotic reflex, I smack my lips. "God, Leti, shut up. You can stay with me."

I don't even know if that's true.

Our house is big enough to house one more, or two more I guess, but with all these late notices for the electricity I don't know what my ma would say. But you know Mexicans, always offering what they don't even have. Ms. Barrera perks up and smiles at me—it's the first thing I've really said all lunch period. But what was I supposed to do? I didn't know Leti thought she'd be homeless if she told her parents the truth. It's not a bad guess for what might really happen, but I'd never heard her say it aloud before.

"That's really kind, Belén," Ms. Barrera says. "How are you navigating all of this?"

Navigating? Teachers always use the same kind of language. Next she's gonna tell me my problems are "valid."

"I'm fine," I respond.

She nods encouragingly. "And what about you? Are you thinking about college?"

"No," I mumble, then take a bite of my sandwich.

"Why not?" she asks.

"Jesus, Leti, pick your head up. Everything is gonna be fine."

I'm trying to change subjects. The last thing I want is for this already corny-ass meeting about my pregnant best friend turning into a cornier meeting about me shifting onto the "right path" in school.

Besides, I've heard it so many times before.

Leti sits up and turns to look at me. It's always me picking her up from a slump.

"Leticia," Ms. Barrera says, "it looks like you have a very strong support system here. And if things don't work out for you with Belén's family, there are many other resources I can think of to help you."

Leti wipes her eyes.

Ms. Barrera continues. "Most importantly, you still want to go to school. This is a great topic for overcoming an obstacle for your personal statement."

"But I don't want to get in because I'm pregnant," Leti says. I wish she'd shut up with that shit. "I want to get in because I'm smart."

"You're very smart, and you're very deserving," Ms. Barrera tells her, smiling with sympathy, like she's looking at a limping dog. "But most admission systems are unjust, even toward smart people like yourself. They want to read about trauma and struggle—it's almost like you have to sell yourself."

Leti sniffs. "Can't it be bad enough I've already gone through it? They need me to write about it, too?"

Ms. Barrera shakes her head slowly and sighs. "Unfortunately. We get in by writing about trauma—the rest of them get in by donating libraries."

I start picking at my nail polish, bits of dark red paint flicking onto my cardboard lunch tray. I'm praying Ms. Barrera doesn't turn to ask me about school again. I already know I'm failing—being reminded of it makes my heart race.

The bell rings.

Thank God.

I jolt up and grab my lunch tray. Leti and Quentin thank Ms. Barrera and walk to AP Calculus together. Quentin usually wraps his arm around Leti's shoulders as they walk, but today he trails behind her, his posture stiff.

I pick up my backpack and Ms. Barrera stands up. She's wearing black slacks, a T-shirt, and a pair of Nikes. A "cool teacher" outfit.

"So, Belén, who is your English teacher?" she asks.

I roll my eyes at the thought of her. "Ms. Foley."

She smiles. "That's great. How is your personal statement coming along for her class?"

"It's fine," I lie, my body tensing up a little.

In reality, I don't know what the fuck she's talking about. It's the second week of school and I still haven't gone to sixth period. It's not that it's Ms. Foley's class specifically—even though I think I truly do hate her. It's that it's the last class of the day. All the heaviness on my chest accumulates from first through fifth period. By sixth I want to be in bed, reading, trying to get the feeling to evaporate from my body.

But I don't say any of this to Ms. Barrera.

"I'm here for you if you need help," Ms. Barrera says. "I do an after-school workshop sometimes."

I open my mouth to respond, but then watch her fourth period class trickle in from the hall. I overhear their conversations, tainted with stress from SATs and ACTs and all sorts of other acronyms. But when I look over at them, I don't recognize anybody there. Without Leti or Quentin, being here is like being in a different country, where I don't speak the language and don't know anybody.

Instead, I mumble a thank-you and push past her and her AP students, finding my way back into the CP hallway. There I am met with faces I do recognize, and language I can understand. Our principal yelling down the hallway, her voice bouncing off the lockers as she's like—*get to class, Saturday school is at capacity, the next group held in the tardy-sweep will receive an in-house suspension.* I move my shoulders past people with ease, curving around the parts of the floor that are scuffed and chipped, understanding every bend and loop of this side of the school where I've told myself I belong.

SIX

ON SATURDAY, LETI SNEAKS OUT OF HER HOUSE. I WAIT FOR HER around the curb, tugging my jacket tight over my tube top.

Yesterday, during passing period, Quentin invited us to a party at UC Berkeley. As soon as he said it, Leti's mouth dropped. I could see the excitement in her eyes. But quickly, it dissipated.

"My cousin is on the track team there," Quentin said, leaning against Leti's locker. "Come on, it'll be fun."

"It's so far," she said, turning away from him to organize her books.

"It's not," Quentin coaxed, squeezing Leti's hand, "it's, like, fifteen minutes, max."

I didn't know how to explain to him that everything outside of Fruitvale felt far for Leti. As soon as the billboards stopped being in Spanish, she'd freak out. She often talked about going to Berkeley as if it were some cross-country move, and not three BART stops away.

"I *can't*," she said, poking her chin down toward her stomach.

"You'll be fine," Quentin said, "I'll be there to take care of you."

Leti shot him a look, her brown eyes narrowed beneath her brows.

"Belén, would you come?" Quentin asked me.

I'm always the glue in their arguments: *If Belén goes, we go. If she doesn't, we don't.*

Going to a party has never been a problem for me. I like to drink, I like to dance, but mainly, I like to meet new people. But when Leti comes, it's a different story. I never get to meet *anybody* if Leti's around.

Especially not guys.

We've never gone to a party with Quentin before, but if she'll be anything like she was when just the two of us would go to a Quince in somebody's garage, she'll grip on to me, her stubby nails somehow finding a way into the skin of my arm. Anytime anybody approaches her, not just guys, she'll dart her big eyes over at me in some cry for help.

"Depends," I told Quentin. "Are you babysitting, or am I?"

Leti smacked her lips and started for the hallway. "Belén, stop. I'm not going, no matter what you say."

I rolled my eyes at her. No matter how cool Quentin and I were, I knew that without her, I couldn't go. And I was *dying* to go. Even though I thought tagging along to that college fair was pointless for me, at least I met Jeveón there. If Quentin could keep Leti occupied, I'd bet it'd be the same thing here. Despite me not having plans to go to college, let alone *Berkeley,* there'd have to be someone at this party who was half decent to kiss.

I glanced at Quentin, whose eyes were similarly dissipating into disappointment.

"Leti," I told her. "This is your chance to see Berkeley's student life. Not those tours they take you on. Like, the real thing."

Leti turned to me, her eyes softening.

Behind her back, Quentin gave me an exaggerated smile and a thumbs-up. One of the best things about Quentin was how he never tried to meddle between me and Leti. He didn't stick up for her when we were just playing around, and he seemed to know his place instantly.

"I'll be there to help," he chimed in. Then, he looked over at me. "Does she dance?"

I snorted. "Just with her chambelán at her Quince. And even that took all of God's will to get done."

"Who was your chambelán?" Quentin asked this in his best Spanish, but the word still clunked around in his mouth.

"My cousin, Manny," Leti said, rolling her eyes slightly.

I smiled, remembering the ugly lilac dress Señora Barragón forced Leti to wear. While Leti two-stepped around the makeshift dance floor of her backyard in kitten heels and a ridiculous sash that said "MIS XV AÑOS," I danced with one of her family friends. He was tall and wore a corny-ass vaquero hat, but he had nice shoulders. Later, we made out in the alleyway by the garbage bins while the crowd danced El Caballo Dorado.

I realized then that Quentin and Leti had probably never danced together. They probably had never even gone to a party together. Because of her racist parents, all their dates were in secrecy. And even in secrecy, with the mounds of studying the AP teachers assigned, their dates were all academic, all the time. I wondered how wild they could get in the library, but then remembered the baby kicking around in Leti's uterus and figured there were things about both of them that I didn't know at all.

Leti looked at me. "Just cuz I don't dance like you doesn't mean I don't dance at all, Belén. I don't have to be all bent over to have fun."

"You sure bent over with him." I pushed Quentin ahead of me. He bit his lip, holding in his laughter.

Quentin's car idles behind me with its headlights off. I lean against it, bringing my freshly ironed hair up to my nose to check if it smells burnt. I spent the entire hour and a half it took straightening my curls on the phone with Leti, giving her the pep talk she needed to convince her to sneak out.

Now, I see her head bob up from the windowsill. Her hands carefully jimmy the window open. It shouldn't be very hard for her to sneak out. Her ma and pa hover like nobody else, but when they're asleep, they're damn near dead. I've never heard anybody snore like her ma. Señora is real uptight till you hear those wet grunts come out of her mouth.

Leti's family lives on the top section of a duplex. So, when she slips out through the opening of the window, she has to climb down a fire escape. Her whole maneuvering feels theatrical to me—when I need to go to a party, I just go right through the front door. Ava is usually out with Matías, and it's a miracle if my ma even looks at me on my way out. Today I pulled on a too-tight tube top, a pair of ripped jeans, and my nameplate hoops, an outfit that would've sent my pa into hysterics. But when I walked into the living room tonight, my ma said goodbye to me without ever taking her eyes from her novela.

As Leti climbs down a flight of rattly stairs, Quentin turns off his car to help her down. She walks toward me wearing a large, black hoodie and a pair of jeans that are ripped at the knees. I swear it's the most skin I've ever seen her show.

"Ready?" I ask her.

She shrugs her shoulders. "I guess."

Quentin's car is a two-door, so he has to slide the passenger seat forward to make room for me to get inside. I crawl in carefully. I hate narrow shit like this—it makes me feel huge. My hips bump and scrape against the seat-belt buckles and headrests, and I land on the back bench with a thud. While Quentin adjusts Leti's seat, I breathe in the car's smell of spearmint gum and stale French fries. I look at the seat covers beneath me, realizing I'm sitting in the exact spot where their baby was conceived, and wince.

Leti settles into the passenger seat, her right knee bouncing the entire time that Quentin gets adjusted. He plugs his phone into a cassette adapter, then starts playing music. As he drives down Foothill, we maneuver past families walking down the street, swerving around sex workers standing on curbs. The streets are lit with the neon haze of liquor store marquees, the dark of the sky interrupted with helium balloons tied to the memorials on intersections.

But when we inch farther and farther away from Oakland and

into Berkeley, things are much different. The streets are tree-lined and wide, and never once does Quentin's car dip into a pothole on the road. We snake our way through suburbs, approaching a row of houses with Greek lettering lining each awning. Quentin turns past the frat houses and onto another street, each house somehow wider than the last.

At a stop sign, I watch him reach over and plant his palm on Leti's leg, settling her knee. I smile a little, then feel something in my stomach twist.

Quentin announces that we're here, pointing to a brown, shingled house. Its windows are lit, the yellow light spilling onto the lawn. There, people stand in groups, drinking and smoking and laughing. Quentin pulls over and parks, then asks if we're ready to go. Leti sighs deeply.

"Hold on," she says. I think she's going to begin praying once she reaches for her purse—she keeps a spare rosary everywhere she goes, it's concerning. But instead, she pulls out a powder compact and a sponge. My jaw drops to the floor.

"Makeup?" I ask her.

"Stop," she mumbles, then turns on the overhead lights.

I pull out my lip liner and begin curving it over my lips carefully, using a button mirror I got from the flea market to clean up the edges with the tip of my fingernail. When I'm done, I catch Leti's reflection and squint.

"*That's* not your color," I tell her. She's spackling this tan, sand-colored shade onto her skin, streaking it over her cheeks.

"This is what my ma has."

Señora Barragón is lighter than Leti.

This is probably the biggest reason she resents that Leti is dark.

She's always coming up with the most ridiculous rules for Leti to follow to try to mask her backwards shame. Like how Leti is never allowed to wear her hair in two braids, because Señora Barragón is afraid she'll look too "India."

I always tell Leti not to trust her, because apart from the racism, Señora Barragón doesn't know what the fuck she's talking about. She still has those highlights that are the width of a bra strap, and her faja is always showing around her waistband. Who is she to give advice on how to present yourself?

Quentin looks back at me, then darts his eyes over to her, looking unsure of what to say. He digs through the center console of the car, handing her a wad of napkins from Wendy's. Leti picks one up, pinching it between her fingers, and rubs it over her chin.

I lean back and grab my makeup bag, then hand her my lip liner. "Try this instead."

Her face washes with relief. "Thank you."

While she finishes, I use a spare safety pin I keep in my makeup bag to separate the clumps in my eyelashes. Quentin studies me carefully, squinting his eyes tightly, as if he's the one concentrating.

"That's so unsafe," he tells me. "You could hurt yourself."

I shrug, then glance outside at the groups of people making their way down the block. They look so much older, each guy sporting facial hair that isn't a shadowy disaster like the guys at school. I adjust my top to make my chest look better, then lean forward.

"Are you ready?" I ask Leti.

She finishes swiping the pencil over her mouth, lets out a breath, then nods.

Outside, it's unusually warm. I leave my jacket in the car and watch Leti unzip hers. Beneath her baggy hoodie is her "going out" top—a simple camouflage T-shirt.

"At least undo your braid," I suggest.

She blinks at me and pulls her braid forward. It's so long and wide that it almost conceals the cross around her neck. She tugs at her hair nervously, snapping the elastic band at its end.

"Maybe we shouldn't go." Leti nearly pants. "We can still go home."

"Leti," I whine. "We're already here."

She peers over at Quentin, her eyes wide and glossy, already on the brink of tears. I feel annoyance splintering inside of me. All I want to do is find some guy in that house who can keep me from going home and feeling heavy on my bed. I know Leti doesn't get it because she already has a boyfriend, but she's never understood why I want to meet someone so badly to begin with.

She's never even bothered to ask.

"Look, keep the braid in if it makes you feel better. You look great," Quentin reassures her. "We can leave if you want to, but I really want you to meet my cousin."

Leti grits her teeth, her palms forming fists in the pockets of her jeans.

"Come *on*, Leti. We can leave early, I swear to God," I plead.

She shoots me a look. She hates when I "swear to God."

"Okay, I *promise* we'll leave early," I say.

"Fine," she mumbles.

I smile and flip my head down and back up, trying to give my hair volume, and look over at Quentin. We're both trying to conceal our excitement, playing it cool as we walk down the block. But my excitement fades when we get to the porch, quickly replaced by embarrassment.

I tried to pick an outfit that would make me look older, but I feel painfully overdressed.

The girls on the porch wear regular shirts and jeans, their hair tied into sloppy ponytails, suggesting this is just any other Saturday for them. They move fluidly from group to group, cigarettes dangling between their teeth and sweaty beers in their hands. They completely ignore us. Their relaxation makes me envious, and shame pinches my cheeks.

Quentin leads us inside. The house is old, with walls paneled in dark wood and crumbling brick. The living room is four times the size of my own, but as we step farther and farther inside, everything feels smaller. There are people everywhere—crowding the kitchen, dancing in the foyer, sitting on the staircase.

Just when I wonder how we'll be able to find Quentin's cousin in the crowd, a slender figure approaches and taps him on the shoulder. Quentin spins around, his face glowing with familiarity. They embrace warmly in the crowd, while Leti fixes her posture and stands straight. Quentin turns to her, the tips of his lips upturned in a smile.

"This is my cousin, Najia," he says loudly, over the music thumping from a speaker in the kitchen.

Leti extends her hand, but Najia pulls her into a tight hug. Leti's eyes bulge at the affection. From here, I study Najia. She looks like Quentin, with matching deep-set eyes and high cheekbones. Both of their smiles are broad and inviting, an easiness I've never seen Leti share. When Najia pulls away, she studies Leti at an arm's length, her eyes fixating on her stomach. Leti nervously sets her arms in front of her, wringing her hands together.

"It's so nice to finally meet you," she says to Leti, her voice smooth and sincere. "How far along are you?"

Leti turns bright red, matching the cups everyone in the crowd is holding. She mumbles something none of us can hear over the music. Najia cups her palm to her ear, asking Leti to repeat herself, and I watch Leti shrink.

"Around two months," I chime in. Najia turns to me and smiles, her teeth immaculate.

"This is Belén," Quentin says. "She's Leti's best friend."

Najia hugs me, her smell of sweat and vanilla coursing into my nostrils. As we embrace, I look at Leti from over Najia's shoulder, widening my eyes with urgency for her to speak up.

"Thanks for inviting us," Leti says, just barely audible.

"Of course!" Najia singsongs. "I've been dying to meet you. I was so sad I wasn't there when Quentin broke the news to his parents."

Leti slumps at the memory. A few weeks ago, after ten pregnancy tests and the weight of acceptance, Quentin told Leti he needed to tell his parents about the baby. After Mass one Sunday, she took the bus to Quentin's church. She found Quentin in the large, after-sermon rush in the parking lot of St. Columba, where he was surrounded by his family.

I didn't go with her, but she called me afterward in tears. I was home alone and lay in my bed, grateful she called to distract me from how awful I felt.

As soon as I heard her sniffle on the line, I sighed. "That bad?" I asked.

She didn't say anything for a while. I just listened to her cries, even and thick.

"They were disappointed." She breathed. "Everyone was there, aunts and uncles and cousins. We told his parents privately, and they gave Quentin this huge lecture about responsibility and told him they still expect him to go to college."

She paused. I heard the noise of traffic zooming around her at the bus stop.

Then she sobbed.

I sat up in bed, ready for the next blow. To me, their reaction sounded reasonable. I knew Leti was bursting with shame, but her sobbing was heavy with something other than embarrassment. It was like someone had died.

"But then they were happy." Her voice cracked and broke, the feeling matching the one in my chest. "That they were having a grandchild, they took it as some miracle. They invited me to stay for lunch."

"Did you?" I asked.

"No." She panted. "Cuz, you know."

And I did know.

I was watching it happen in front of me.

Najia smiling, and Leti's face twisting, the reminder of her reality so tangible. She knew her parents would never welcome her baby as their grandchild. And though Quentin's family's warmth was better than their denial, it was hard to be reminded of what she would never have. What her parents would never give her.

Najia begins peppering Leti and Quentin with questions about college. This is where my brain tunes out. I elbow my way into the kitchen to grab myself a drink, finding a warm carton of orange juice and a bottle of tequila. I splash each into a cup and grab a few sodas for Quentin and Leti. But by the time I turn back into the crowd, they're gone.

I steer through throngs of students, sipping my drink as I head toward the front of the house. On the way, I see Najia is in the living room, sitting with a crowd of girls whose legs are so mile-long, I figure they must be her track teammates.

Back on the porch, I see Leti and Quentin leaning against the wooden railing of the house. I want to announce myself, but Quentin's brow is furrowed, his frustration palpable.

"Leti, she was just being nice," he says, turning away from Leti.

"I know she was being nice. And I'm sorry, but it just reminded me of my ma—"

"This is messed up," he says to Leti, "I thought you'd already told your mom."

"I *did* tell her," Leti says. It's the loudest I've heard her speak all night. "I just didn't tell her it was you."

"It?" he repeats. "You mean the *father*? Is that supposed to make it better? What if I told my parents I was having a baby, but I didn't mention you were the mother? How would you feel?"

"It's different for me." She breathes. "Your parents were so happy when we told them."

"They weren't over the moon, Leti." He snorts.

"So?" she says. "They were upset about the impact this will have on your future—not because they think you're disgusting. They still loved you after it."

I know how this is going to end. I can tell by the way Leti is wrinkling her nose. She's about to start crying, and when Leti begins crying, she can't stop. And then we'll have to leave. Before I even had the chance to meet anybody.

I bolt away from the porch.

I push my way back into the house, stumbling past a keg, and into a crowd of people dancing.

Their bodies angle together, the bass thumping in the floorboards, making the walls rattle. I scan the crowd to see if there's anybody good-looking enough to dance with, but with so many people, everyone blends together. I walk around the perimeter of the crowd and through the kitchen, where there's a door leading to the backyard. There, I see a couple kissing by the brick fencing, and a bong being passed between friends.

But farther down the yard, I see someone sitting on the stoop of the back porch.

I step through the patchy grass and peer through the fog of the bong—it looks like a guy reading something thick, like a Bible. I kill my drink as I approach him. I hope he's not one of those Bible-preaching, repent today people that stand on street corners with megaphones.

"What're you reading?" I call out.

A guy somewhere a few years older than me turns around. His dark, curly hair hangs low over his eyes, which are framed in thick reading glasses. He smirks upon seeing me, the ends of his mustache trailing upward. He wears an oversized sweater that looks second-hand, with those tiny pills my ma is always complaining about when I put the wrong things in the dryer. As I move closer, the sensor light of the backyard flickers on, casting him in a divided yellow haze. He's half lit and half in the shadows.

When he looks up at me, he looks me straight in the eyes. Something guys never do—especially when I'm dressed like this. "Oh, I'm just waiting on someone."

"Okay," I tell him. "I asked what you were reading, though."

He closes the book and flashes me the cover. I can't read it in the semidarkness, so I squint hard. I must look ridiculous, because he scoffs a little.

"You've never read Neruda?" he asks me.

I sit next to him. He smells good, like fabric softener. I clear my throat. "No, it looks boring, though."

He smiles, his cheeks curving into soft dimples. "How can you tell?"

"That cover is just, I don't know, words. Like, no spice."

He cocks his head back. "It's plenty spicy. Chilean romance poetry? Nobody does it like this anymore."

I feel my face redden.

"Why aren't you inside?" I ask. I pass him one of the sodas I've been babysitting, trying desperately to change the subject and gain control of the conversation.

He shrugs, rolling the can of soda between his palms, the sweaty aluminum dampening his skin. "It's boring. I'm at one of these every weekend."

"With your friends?"

He chuckles a little, his Adam's apple bobbing. "Something like that."

"So, you come all this way just to sit outside and read?" I arch an eyebrow at him.

He shakes his head. "It's never my intention. But when things get too chaotic, I try to find a space for myself. I always try to keep a book on me in case I get bored."

"I do that too," I tell him. "Just not with boring books."

He smiles again, the skin around his eyes crinkling tightly. "Okay, so what do you read?"

"Depends. Sometimes poetry, sometimes novels, sometimes short stories. Whatever sounds good."

"Well, I wish I could read more of that. But I have to read for school."

"You go here?" I ask.

He nods, coolly blowing away the curls cascading toward his lashes. "I'm in my second year."

I calculate in my head. He must be nineteen, twenty at most. He gives me a nearly imperceptible smile, the fullness of his lips sloping only slightly. "What about you?"

I bite the tip of my tongue, thinking of the most ambiguous way to answer his question. "I'm about to graduate."

He laughs with his whole body, like this is the funniest thing he's ever heard. His chin tips back, almost parallel to the moon, and his shoulders round. "From *where*? Berkeley High?"

I wonder if it's that obvious. Maybe I should've dressed more like

Leti, like those girls on the porch, like I couldn't care less about where I was. Instead, I wore a tube top I'd outgrown in middle school. It seemed to be the perfect tightness when I left the house, but now, I feel it constricting my breathing.

"I go to International High, actually." I say this lightly, as if I'm in on the joke, even though it's probably the most embarrassing thing I could've said. *No, I don't go to this high school, I actually go to* that *one*.

"Ah, in Oakland," he says, popping open the can of soda and taking a sip. He hands it to me after. I mimic his movements, trying not to think about how both of our lips were just on the same can. It's like we kissed.

"You know where that is?" I ask.

"I'm from Oakland," he explains.

I squeeze my fists, feeling my nails pinch against my skin. It can be easy to flirt with guys who are gross. But he feels so familiar, so genuine. My body is overwhelmed by warmth.

He smiles. "Are you excited to be finished with high school?"

I nod, grateful that he doesn't ask any follow-up questions about my plans after graduating.

"I'm excited to not be told what to read. Everything my classes offer is so boring." I sigh.

"I remember that. I mean, it was just a few years ago for me. But if you think those were bad, wait till they make you read books with 'just words' on the cover."

I feel my face grow hotter, but he laughs and gently nudges me. It's pathetic how I'm immediately overcome with relief when I feel his skin on mine. Before I can look over at him, I hear someone calling my name. It's Leti, standing by the side gate leading to the backyard. Her arms are folded across her chest, and she cocks her head sideways, letting me know it's time to go home. She fixes her eyes on this guy, taking him in with a squint.

Quickly, he stands, extending a hand to help me up. When I take it, he laces his fingers into mine as he pulls me forward. After I'm up, I measure myself against him. In my perfect posture, my hairline only skims his chin, nearly touches the fullness of his bottom lip.

I wipe the dirt off the back of my jeans with my palm, trying to point his eyes toward my hips. But even then, he doesn't look at my body. He looks me dead in the eyes.

"I'm gonna get going," I say.

He nods. His gaze slices into me, almost cutting me in half. His eyes send a coolness over my chest, a lightness I welcome after months of dragging around all this weight.

"I'm Alexis." He extends his hand. When I shake it, something like electricity surges between our palms. I move to pull away, but he curls his fingers into mine. My heart thrums in my chest—we're so close I can see the pores in his cheeks, the wetness of his lips.

"Belén," I say, trying to stand beneath the glow of the sensor light. This is my attempt to look poised and effervescent and completely casual the way I'm sure most college girls do.

"Nice to meet you, Belén. We should meet up sometime—I have lots of less-boring books at my apartment that you can look at," he says. "Can I give you my number?"

I hand him my phone immediately.

SEVEN

"IT'S THE *WAY* HE ASKED, LETI," I SAY ON THE PHONE. "HE ASKED IF HE could give me *his* number. Nobody ever does that. They're always asking me for *my* number."

It's eleven a.m. the next morning. I'm lying stomach-down on my bed with my phone pressed to my cheek. Leti only ever calls me. She says texting stresses her out, that she feels her ma might figure out how to translate it. I keep having to remind her that Señora Barragón doesn't know how to use Google, let alone their translator, but it's Leti. Her rules, her way. I look out the window at the telephone wires striping the sky, imagining our conversation stretching between them, spiraling from one mouth to the other's ear.

Last night, after I met Alexis, we were quick to get home. I practically floated toward Leti, feeling Alexis's eyes beam into my back as

I walked away. But once we found Quentin on the porch, my bubble burst. The tension between him and Leti writhed midair, like thick smoke after a fire.

We walked down the block wordlessly. Inside of Quentin's car, Leti sat with her knees pointed toward her door, and Quentin gripped tightly at the steering wheel. The thought of Alexis was the only thing keeping me calm. Without it, Leti and Quentin's demeanors would have reminded me of my ma and my pa.

I was relieved to be dropped off at home, where I held the memory of Alexis to my chest. I was cherishing it privately up until now, when Leti sounds unamused.

"I don't know, Belén." Leti sighs. "Isn't he kind of old?"

"He is *not* old. He has to be, like, twenty at most. But it doesn't matter, Leti. You don't get it cuz you've got Quentin, but good guys are so hard to find."

"But Belén, you *have* been out with good guys. What about Jeveón?"

"Jeveón was nice, but I'm not trying to die a virgin," I say. "I want to have sex with the person I'm with."

"Hmm," she says. "What about that guy at my Quince?"

I roll my eyes. "Right, him. Remember when he just straight up stuck his hand down my dress with no announcement?"

She pauses and exhales. "Oh, yeah. I guess you're right."

"It's impossible, Leti. Sometimes I don't even think good guys exist."

"They do." Leti sighs again. "But I don't know. I think I saw Alexis with some girl at the party."

I turn onto my back, my chest alleviated from the weight of my body. "Well, he mentioned he came with a friend."

"Yeah, but—"

I groan. "But what?"

"She was just, I don't know, close to him."

"Okay, so maybe they're best friends. Who cares?"

"I'm just saying." She exhales, the whiny sound almost crackling on the line. "I don't know why he's talking to you if you're still in high school."

I roll my eyes again. "Okay, Saint Leticia. I get it."

She's quiet for a second. Those jokes about her sainthood used to be funny before she got pregnant. Now she takes them backhanded, which they never are. No matter what is growing in her uterus, she's still Leti. Having sex didn't make her stop doing her homework. Going to the party didn't make her stop going to church. But things are different now—whether it's the hormones or other changes, she's more sensitive.

"Sorry," I tell her. "I'm just joking around."

"It's fine," she says quickly. "You should meet up with him if you want to. I guess he sounds nice."

"Really?" I ask, sitting up.

"Yeah. I mean, he can't be worse than anyone else you've dated."

I haven't dated many people, but my rap sheet is not nice.

There was Mario, from Leti's Quince. That short-lived romance started from our initial meeting, when he asked me to dance a que-bradita with him, and ended while we were making out. We had been kissing for maybe five minutes when he just shoved his hand down the collar of my dress, pulled my boob out of my faja, and squeezed at it like he was picking ripe fruit.

"They're huge," he said, eyes wide.

I pushed him off so hard that his head dipped back and hit the pole of the streetlight. He stared at me for a second, then opened his mouth and started rattling off. I didn't listen. I just walked back to the party and found my place beside Leti.

And then there was Jeveón, who was almost respectful to a fault, saving himself for marriage and shit.

With these opposites constantly on the table, I don't know what to do. I don't think I need to be in love with the person I lose my virginity to, but I don't want to fuck just anybody. It's confusing.

But I hope with Alexis it will be different.

Maybe because he's in college, he knows how to do both. Maybe he'll want to get to know me. Maybe we'll go on dates. Maybe I'll be his girlfriend. Maybe we'll have sex. And maybe then, this feeling on my chest will finally go away.

"I just feel like"—I tell Leti on the phone—"guys either want to date me or have sex with me. Never both. I just want to feel distracted."

"Distracted from what?" She sounds preoccupied, her voice distant, like she's out of reach.

I look out at the phone wires.

As much as I've been there for Leti since she became pregnant, she's hardly asked me anything since my pa left. I know she can't relate, because her parents are always hovering around her, but I wish I didn't have to lay it out for her all the time. She's never had to do that for me. I can always tell when she's upset or stressed or about to cry—I don't know if she knows that about me.

Sometimes I feel like she doesn't know me at all.

"I don't know," I tell her. "Sometimes I just don't feel good."

"Well, if you want to distract yourself, maybe you should do your homework. That'll keep you busy."

I wait for her to say something else. She doesn't.

We're both quiet, my disappointment stretching between our breathing.

I break the silence. "What about you?"

"What about me?"

"What's up with you and Quentin?"

She inhales. "Nothing."

"I heard you two on the porch."

"It's fine," she says, her tone clipped.

"Leti."

"What?" she snaps.

It has always been a challenge telling Leti when she's wrong.

She takes after her pa in that way—shielding her ears and shutting her eyes to ward away criticism. On the rare occasions I do tell her, the aftermath is tension so dense I feel like I can touch it. Most times it's easier to say nothing. Especially since she got pregnant, when her temper has been even shorter.

But sometimes it's worth it.

"He's right," I say.

Her sigh is staticky on the line. "I don't want to talk about this right now."

"Your stomach is going to do the talking for you if your mouth doesn't start. Your Ma is too afraid of your pa to tell him, but you can't hide this from your pa forever."

"But Belén, my pa is going to be so upset." I hear a waviness to her voice, the threat of tears. "It's too hurtful to even think about sometimes."

"Okay," I say. "But by not telling him, you're also hurting Quentin in the process."

There's a beat of silence.

"I have to go," she says.

And, like that, she hangs up.

I know she has things to do. It's after church on a Sunday, which means that between homework and college applications, she has to fold her pa's work shirts, iron his slacks, wash his dishes, and help cook his dinner. Having to baby her pa is the perfect excuse to avoid telling her pa about the baby.

Regardless, at least she has *something* to do. My Sundays used to be busy—before things got so complicated, my pa would take us out to get carnitas at Jalisco's on International. We'd spend the rest of the afternoon being dragged from Home Depot for my pa and Ross for my ma.

Later, it became watching as he and my ma got into it over breakfast. It got so bad we stopped going out so that they could argue in the comfort of the house. Ava would try to look busy while they went at it, expertly studying her cuticles, while I felt like I was following a Ping-Pong match, my head turning with every one-liner.

I'd even take that over what I have today, which is nothing.

Ava is out with Matías, and my ma is somewhere, anywhere but here.

I set down my phone and feel heavy. Sunlight slants through my blinds in even, straight lines, painting my skin in stripes of dark and light. I look at the phone wires and think of how I have so much to tell someone and no one to really tell it to.

But the thought of Alexis is there to keep me company.

I lift my phone back to my face and begin looking up Neruda collections to find the exact one Alexis had been reading, when I hear the sound of a car door slamming. I sit up, my chest swelling with hope, thinking maybe my ma might be home. But then, I hear a second slam. I groan.

Before I can even think of being too annoyed that Matías has played tagalong with Ava, Ava shouts my name into the house so loudly I think the walls might vibrate.

"Belén!"

She sounds angry.

I grab a pillow from beside me and slam it over my head again and again. It's always some shit.

I roll out of bed and head toward the kitchen, where Ava is standing with a hand on her hip. So predictable. I peer behind her, at the digital clock glowing green on the stove. It's been wrong since daylight savings time started, and the only person who ever knew how to reset it was my pa. Since March, it feels we're immobilized by time, frozen in place.

The sight of Matías snaps me out of it. He's sprawled on the couch with his feet kicked onto the coffee table. With one hand, he tips a bag of Hot Cheeto fries toward his mouth, red crumbs cascading onto his T-shirt. With the other, his fingers are contorted to wrap around the TV remote and a can of Arizona. It's not even a good flavor either, but the gross watermelon one.

"Belén, this shit is not cute anymore," Ava calls.

I peel my eyes from Matías's crusty hair, caked with day-old Moco de Gorila gel. I swear, he looks like the duck on Lucas candy. I turn to Ava, her dark eyes squinted, brows pinched together, nostrils flared. It's the most she's ever looked like my pa.

"What's not cute?" I ask. "Me? I'm plenty cute."

She pulls her phone from her back pocket, flashing the screen to show me an email.

"Your school sent me a message. Apparently, there's this big fucking paper due in your English class, and you haven't started because you've never fucking gone. You think it's not important, huh?"

I knew the "huh" meant I shouldn't answer.

I knew it meant I should just listen.

But who was she to care all of a sudden? She's the one who let me sweep the floor instead of sitting around, listening to Ms. Foley.

"Since when do you get school emails?" I snort. "You're not even a parent."

"Belén, answer the question."

I lean against the kitchen counter, the tile cool against my skin. "Well, if you're asking, no. I don't think it's important."

"So, what's the plan then, huh? Are you just gonna freeload around here? I am not looking after you and neither is Ma."

"I mean—"

"Shut up, this is serious." Ava runs a manicured hand through her hair. "Belén, what the fuck are you doing? You don't have a *plan*. I tried cutting you some slack last year. I tried being nice last week. But what do you think you're going to do *next* year? Or the following year? Or with your life? I am not here keeping shit afloat for you not to have a head on your shoulders," she fumes.

I roll my eyes. She acts like she's suddenly my ma, like she's sacrificing her whole life to give me this lecture. Meanwhile, her useless boyfriend is doing everything I'm being accused of. Ava doesn't know anything about me, especially not that I don't have a *plan*-plan, but I have a plan. I know Leti would need help taking care of the baby once it was born. It wouldn't pay, of course. I'm not gonna charge her for being a tía. But when I tell Ava an iteration of this, she scoffs at me.

"Belén, you're not that naive," she says. "You cannot plan your life around your friend or her baby. What about *you*?"

I blink at her, confusion warping my vision. I didn't think the plan was naive at all—Leti and her baby affected me, too. Maybe it wasn't college, but it was *something*. I'm about to say this when Ava shakes her head at me, the disgust in her gaze almost palpable.

"I didn't even want to tell you, but it looks like you don't even care." She practically flings her phone at me, and I roll my eyes again. I know I haven't gone to class, but all of this is painfully dramatic. Ridiculously excessive.

But then, I look at the screen.

The letters mirror the ones on our past-due electricity bill, bold and red. I silently reread the words. The only thing audible amid the tension is Ava rhythmically tapping her nails against the counter.

"Read it right there," Ava says. "'Grade point average at risk of detention.' You've flunked so many classes that you may not even graduate high school. How pathetic is that, Belén? We have a mom who risked everything to go to college, and you really want to be that much like Pa?"

76

And there it was again.

My pa dropped out of high school his junior year. He had never been good at school and felt too discouraged to finish. He became a construction worker instead, a job he grew to hate. He resented how much it physically weighed on his body, spitefully reminding my ma that one college degree allowed her to make more money by doing, what he believed, was "less work."

That was one of their favorite things to argue about.

But I never thought that not going to college meant I wanted to be anything like him.

I always thought not wanting to go to college meant that I just didn't want to go.

Really, I thought it meant that I didn't know what to do. Nothing about college sounded interesting to me. But looking at this email makes my stomach twist in embarrassment. I knew I wasn't going to class, and I knew I wasn't doing my work, but I didn't think anyone was keeping track of what I was doing. Since my pa showed me he didn't care about what happened to me, I didn't think anyone did. *I* didn't.

Looking like my pa was one thing. But not being able to graduate was something else. How was I behaving like him without even knowing it? The thought of that made me paranoid. I didn't want to be anything like him.

But that's my own shit to deal with.

I'm already forced to think about college every day at school and with Leti barking in my ear. But now, when Ava brings it up like this, it doesn't feel like the usual nagging, which I usually try to write off as somewhat caring.

It feels personal.

"Cool," I say. "I'd rather be him than date him."

She put her other hand on her hip. Big move. "What the fuck is that supposed to mean?"

I roll my eyes. "It means your boyfriend is a loser. Maybe I'm fucking up in school and don't know what to do, but isn't he, like, thirty? What's his excuse?"

Matías glares at me, Hot Cheeto bag suspended midair. When I turn back to Ava, she has her arms resting at her side. She curves her neck down and looks at the floor, her shoulders falling in exhale—a stance of defeat. The same one my ma did when she got tired of arguing with my pa.

The symmetry makes me feel heavy.

It was worth it, though. I know I have a big mouth. It's what got my pa in trouble, and by Ava's logic, it's what gets me in trouble. But I am not going to stand around and get criticized without anybody drawing any connections.

Ava and I have never physically fought, but I thought this comment might be it. She gets close to my face, close enough that I can see how much she takes after my ma. But if she were really like her, she wouldn't even care about me cutting class, she wouldn't even know. She would disappear right now, evaporate until there was nothing in the house but silence. Instead, she looks me dead in the eyes, her pupils striking something deep in my stomach.

"Go to class," she says slowly, "before I go with you."

EIGHT

MS. FOLEY IS AT THE BLACKBOARD—YES, A BLACKBOARD—WRITING something in her illegible cursive with a thin piece of chalk. The sound scrapes against my ears, and it only gets worse when she starts talking. Ms. Foley sounds like she swallowed one of her lungs. Like she's perpetually in an asthma infomercial. I wish she'd just die. No, I shouldn't say that. I wish she'd just retire.

But once Ms. Foley opens her mouth, I'm pretty good about tuning her out. I'm sitting in the back of the portable, and when I slump forward, it's like I'm not even there at all. I look at the backs of the heads of my unrecognizable classmates, who look just as disinterested as I do. The one person I do recognize, though, is Ali. He sits in the front row, way too close to Ms. Foley for my comfort.

I know I should be listening, but Ms. Foley is always going on about something so fucking boring. The only thing keeping me from falling asleep is the thought of going to the library after school. I want to find the book Alexis was reading at the party today, that way I can text him about it tonight.

The thought of him is the only thing keeping me afloat.

After Ava and I fought yesterday, I lay in bed and felt the worst I had in weeks. Like the phone wires that were pressing against the sky began to press against my skin, ready to snap at any moment. But it's okay, because as long as I find this book and can text Alexis, I know I'll feel better.

I have the whole thing planned out: the photo I'll send of the book cover, strategically taken in front of a mirror that reflects a glimpse of my face and a good view of my chest.

I'm deep in that daydream when I hear metal scraping against the floor.

I look up and see that everyone is turning their desks. They pair up in twos and threes, and because I wasn't listening, I'm left in the middle of the room like I'm on an island. Ms. Foley nods approvingly at the rest of the class until she looks at me.

"Oh, Ms. Del Toro. Thank you for gracing us with your presence," she says, walking closer to my desk. From here I can smell her old-lady scent of potpourri and mothballs. Or is that weed? Who knows? "Ms. Del Toro, had you been listening, you'd know you're supposed to find the partner for your assignment."

Oh great. Group work. I fucking hate group work. Not because I'm the reliable one who is left with all the work—that's Leti—but because I have to hear somebody nag and nag and nag about how I never showed up to class or didn't turn in my part on time.

I'm not reliable. But at least I know it.

I'm about to argue with Ms. Foley, who I haven't seen since May, and tell her I'm going to work alone. But I listen as Ava's words circle in my head, spiraling tighter and tighter about how I'm so much like my pa. My pa, who argued with every teacher, who flunked every class he attended, who I see every time I look at my report card, and every time I look in the mirror.

I have to learn to pick my battles.

Yesterday was heavy enough with Ava, but today is a new day. I look at Ms. Foley dead in her face, in her wrinkly eye sockets that seem to deepen each hour, and wonder if it's worth it.

"Who's my partner?" I ask, my teeth near gritted.

Suddenly, Ali stands up.

I look up at him, his eyes already on mine, the same sharp precision he had when he attempted to talk to me after Mr. Kluger's class. He walks to the desk beside me and shoves it against mine with a thud.

Ms. Foley gives me one of those tight-lipped white people smiles. "Great. Get to work."

For the first time since she started vandalizing the blackboard, I look up to read what's written on it. It just says: *Personal Statement*.

Great teaching.

"That's it? That's all the directions?" I ask, but Ms. Foley ignores me and goes to sit behind her desk.

"Well, you missed the instructions. And the lessons leading up," Ali says, pulling a binder from his backpack. "I got you, though."

"You take notes?"

He wiggles his eyebrows. "I take notes? In school? Yes."

He sets the binder on the table. It's like Leti's old one, but instead of college fan art behind the sheet of plastic, it has a collage of album covers and quotes that have been taped down. On the bottom, I see a photo of him as a baby with an older woman, who I'm assuming is his mother. He opens the binder and pulls out a sheet of paper—the kind that's laminated on the hole-punched side to prevent ripping. The kind Leti would kill for.

"That's fancy paper," I tell him.

"My mama gets it for free," he says. "She works at an OfficeMax."

He pivots his desk so it's right across from mine, then looks directly at me.

"Where are you applying?" he asks.

"Nowhere," I say. "I'm not going to college."

"That makes sense."

I raise my eyebrows. "Yeah?"

"I mean you're never here. If you don't wanna come here, why would you wanna go to college?"

I nod. "Yeah, exactly." I feel relieved he understands, like maybe that'll make working together easier.

Then he looks at me, his brown eyes deep. "Well, listen. *I* want to go to college. That means if you don't turn in your feedback on my essay, I won't get full credit, and my grade will drop."

I roll my eyes. "That's stupid."

He snorts. "This whole application process is stupid. Listen, I tried talking to you after Mr. Kluger's class, but you left so fast. I know you haven't been here, but I *really* need you to do your work."

"All I have to do is mark up your essay in a red pen, right? That's easy enough."

He shakes his head. "This is a peer editing assignment—so, you have to write your essay, too. If I don't turn in my notes on your assignment, my grade will still drop. You gotta do your work so I can pass on my work, too."

I roll my eyes so deeply I feel it in my ears. "Got it."

He nods and looks down at his paper, then begins writing. Since I didn't expect to come into this class to actually work, I don't even have a notebook in my backpack. Not that I would normally, but you know how it goes.

I can't go up to Ms. Foley and ask her for paper. Her laughter when I asked for a pencil last year still echoes in my head. And this isn't like Ms. Barrera's room where kids are welcomed to available supplies. I am here, on the other side of campus, where everything is different.

Ali pauses from writing, opens his binder, and hands me a sheet of paper. After a moment he says, "Please tell me you at least brought a pencil."

I pull my backpack onto my lap and pull out a pen. It has Liam and Lauren's real estate information on its side. I lick the tip of the pen, rub it on the soles of my sneakers to get the ink flowing, then wiggle it near his face. He looks at it, sighs, then keeps on writing.

"There are eight prompts you can pick from for your personal statement. Ms. Foley will give you a printout of them, if you need. But if you don't wanna talk to her, which I assume you don't, the guidance counselors keep them in the paper organizers outside their office. They're printed on yellow paper."

"Next to those pamphlets about birth control?" I ask. I only know this because Leti frantically stuffed her backpack with both once she realized her period was late. I didn't get either.

He smiles. "Yeah, but those are in pink. Kinda sexist, I think."

He looks back down and continues writing. He has neat handwriting, some of the best handwriting I've ever seen, all small and right-leaning, the words perfectly spaced out. He catches me staring and glares at me.

"You have pretty handwriting," I tell him.

"Thanks."

"My ma says you get nice handwriting if you work with your hands a lot. You ever sewed?"

He shakes his head. "No. My mama just made sure my letters were neat when I was younger. We didn't have TV, so she got me those practice workbooks from OfficeMax."

He goes back to writing.

This whole situation reminds me of what it's like hanging out with Leti when she's studying. I'll say something, she'll say something back, and then she'll immediately look at her books to keep working. It's like a tennis match that's always getting interrupted. Sometimes I feel like I'm bugging her, but she's told me before that she's learned to work with my talking. She's even said it helps her focus. But with Ali, I can't tell.

In just under ten minutes, he's managed to fill half of his sheet of paper. I wonder if he's been working on drafts, if the class has been working on drafts, in my absence. I open my mouth to ask when the bell rings.

It's sixth period, so everyone turns their desk to their original spots and hops up to stack their chairs. I pack up, then follow Ali out the door. Ms. Foley glares at me the entire way out.

"Ms. Del Toro, I expect to see you tomorrow," she calls as I exit.

And, unfortunately for both of us, I know coming to class tomorrow is a sure bet.

Because Ms. Foley's class is in the last portable in the very back of the school, the walk to the main building is long. Ali and I walk past the track, past the basketball court, past the gym, and past the locker rooms before hitting the sad square of brown grass people call the quad. It's central to the school, like a fork in the road, so while I head left to meet Leti, he veers right.

As we separate, I notice he stops to unzip his backpack. He pulls out a beat-up pair of headphones and pulls them over his ears.

I look toward the windows of the main building, where the slate sky stands still. Everyone is pushing quick to get out onto Foothill to catch the next bus, and soon, if the Neruda collection isn't in our school library, I'll be there with them.

When I meet Leti at her locker, she's stuffing all her books in her backpack. Because the SATs are coming up, she totes an additional stack of review books in an extra bag. It droops down at the bottom, threatening to rip with the weight.

"You're *here*?" She arches an eyebrow at me. "You went to class?"

I nod and help her sort books into her bags. "Ava gets emails when I cut class now."

She raises her eyebrows. "Oh, wow. She must've gotten a bunch of them when she logged in."

"Shut up," I mumble.

I haul her extra bag for her while we walk down the hall together. Leti spends seven a.m. to seven p.m. at school, from zero period until sundown. After sixth period, she and Quentin find a spot around school to do their homework. Today, she's meeting him in the library. I hold the door open for her, then follow her inside.

"Are you staying?" she asks, somewhat eagerly, while giving me a pointed look. "To do homework?"

I beam at her, exaggerating a smile. "No, I'm just here to see if we have a book in stock."

She pauses for a moment, then shakes her head as realization overcomes her. "I can't stand you sometimes."

NINE

THE NERUDA COLLECTION ISN'T AT THE SCHOOL LIBRARY. I TELL LETI I'm leaving. She calls out after me, her tone whiny and nagging, but I duck out the door before I can listen.

I take the bus to the César Chávez branch of the library in the Fruitvale Village, where I find the book nestled in the poetry section. But when I bring it up to the front desk, the librarian tells me I have too many overdue books to check it out. She writes down the long list of past-due titles on a fluorescent Post-it, hands it to me, and takes the book from my hands. I crumple the note and throw it away on my way out, feeling determined to get this book today, determined to text Alexis tonight.

I decide to BART to Berkeley to go to their public library. I pass the Oscar Grant mural, hop the turnstile, and wait for my train at the top of Fruitvale Station. It feels strange standing here, knowing an officer murdered the innocent man painted onto the mural right on this pavement. I think about it every time I have to wait for a train.

It's early enough in the afternoon that there's hardly anyone else on the platform. It's just me and the sun illuminating the sky, bold and bright and bleaching. I'm grateful. Sometimes, when more people are out, guys lurk on the platforms and follow girls onto the trains, masturbating in their jeans, or worse.

I get on my train and settle into my seat. I like riding older BART trains because the seats are soft and cushioned like a couch. They remind me of before, when my family would take the train to the city. When I'd try to lie down and nap on the seats, Ava would scold me and say someone had probably peed on them. Then my pa would sit beside me and let me sleep with my head on his lap, his body a buffer. I stare at the seats ahead of me, plush and blue, trying to remember what it was like to be held.

I shift my gaze forward. I pull my headphones out of my pocket and slip them on. I never listen to anything when I wear them. I mainly use them so men don't approach me, or, so if they do, I can point to my headphones and pretend I can't hear them. It's the same reason I still wear my Quinceañera ring. If men approach me, I just point to it and say, "I'm married."

It never works.

It's just worth the try.

When I enter the Berkeley Public Library, I shoot straight for the poetry section. I scan the titles on book spines but have no luck.

Fuck this damn book.

Out on the sidewalk, I groan in frustration. I pause for a second, thinking maybe not finding this book is a sign from God or the universe or whatever, like maybe I shouldn't text Alexis.

But then I think, nah.

I hold my phone up to my nose, checking the bus schedule to route me to the other library branch across Berkeley. The next bus isn't for twenty minutes, so I wander into a coffee shop on the corner of Shattuck to kill time.

Inside, college students hunch behind sleek computers, their fingers clouded blurs as they type. I slip past them and line up, glancing at the menu overhead. Sometimes, when Leti and I have the money, we walk to the Starbucks near the laundromat and split a Frappuccino—decaffeinated, of course, because she's Leti.

But I don't see any Frappuccinos on this menu. Just a bunch of coffees and teas with names almost as stupid as Frappuccino. I feel the only five-dollar bill I have burn in my pocket as I begin calculating the prices on the menu. I can afford a small iced coffee—no added syrups or flavors or creams.

I hand the barista my five, which is creased and waxy from going through the wash.

When my order is ready, he shouts into the shop.

"Buh-leen!"

My face gets hot. It sounds like he was saying "balloon" and "spleen." I know my name has that accent or whatever, but it's short and easy enough to pronounce. I don't know why people make it hard.

He hands me a sweaty plastic cup and a straw that he explains is biodegradable. I sip the coffee, feeling the bitterness coat my tongue, and try not to gag.

You'd think I like coffee now since every Mexican family practically bottle-feeds their children with it. Every morning, every dessert, every night, it's the same thing—pan y café, pan y café, pan y café.

And it *was* that, before my pa left, but my ma never made coffee like *this*. Her coffee was made in a clay pot with canela and piloncillo, then served with milk or Coffee-Mate.

This shit tastes like rubbing alcohol, and the biodegradable straw gives it the aftertaste of paper. I try to play it off and look cool, then carry my cup to the bar with cream and sugar.

I take off the lid and douse the coffee with half-and-half and this powdered vanilla shit they have in a shaker. I sip it, wince, and add more milk. When it's finally drinkable, I snap the lid on and walk to a small, empty table in the corner of the shop.

I put my backpack on the empty chair across from me and kick myself for not packing at least one of the books from my room. I was so sure I'd find this book at the library that I didn't pack anything else. All that's in there is my near-empty wallet, Liam and Lauren's pen, and a bag of Sabritones. I set them on the table and consider opening them, but read the room and decide I probably shouldn't.

"Buh-*leen*," I hear someone call. I look up, then blink in disbelief. In front of me is Alexis, wearing a pair of thick-framed glasses and a dark gray shirt. My face immediately gets warm again, and I begin to panic. I wonder if he's been watching me this whole time.

"What're you doing here?" he asks.

"Huh?" I ask, hastily shoving the Sabritones into my backpack.

He gestures his arms widely. "*Here.*"

I let out a breath. "Um, I was, um, at the public library."

I wonder if college students even go to the public library, or if it's a tragically high school thing to do. He gestures to my backpack. "Can I sit down?"

I nod and sip my coffee. I wonder if I prepared it right, if it makes me seem older and cooler that I'm sipping iced coffee, or if it makes me seem younger and immature since I drowned it in milk.

"What were you looking for?" he asks.

I get nervous. Would it be pathetic to admit I was looking for the book he'd been reading? So that I could text him a sexually suggestive photo of me reading poetry? So we'd start talking? So he'd ask what I was up to? So he'd come over? So he'd ask me to be his girlfriend? So we'd have sex?

I'm quiet for a second too long, and the silence gets stiff.

I try to be cool, taking another sip of coffee. "Um, this collection of poems by this Chilean poet named Pablo Neruda. Have you ever read him?"

"Yeah," he says, smiling, "I'm familiar. Did you find it?"

I shake my head. "No, it was checked out."

He nods. "I heard it's assigned to this Latin American Literature class at Cal. Someone must've borrowed it." He smiles again, his dimples pressing against his skin. "You wanna read it today, though?"

I let out a breath. "Yeah, that was the plan."

"Let's go get it then. There's a bookstore a few blocks down. I have a break between classes, so we can go now. Unless you're busy?"

"No," I blurt quickly. "Let's go."

Alexis packs up his things. He'd been sitting on the opposite side of the coffee shop, hidden behind his computer screen. He folds his laptop into a case, stuffs his books into his backpack, and slides it over his shoulders. Seeing him with all this stuff reminds me of what it's like waiting around for Leti. It makes me feel more directionless than usual.

Alexis walks the streets so calmly, like he knows every pocket and curve of town. He makes sure to walk on the street-side of the sidewalk and cautions me as we circle around the earthquake cracks that have risen the pavement. Being next to him and his confidence makes me feel like I also belong here. Like maybe I belong here with him.

We approach the Half Price Books right near a BART entryway. We walk through the low awning, where I'm overcome with the stale smell of dust and ink. It's strong enough to cover up the smell of Alexis's deodorant, which I've been trying to ignore this whole time. Some winter pine shit they bottle up and sell to guys to make them more attractive to women. I hate that it's working.

"This place is really good," Alexis says as we enter. "They have new and used books. I get a lot of books for class from here for really cheap. Way better than supporting Amazon." He scoffs. "God, I hate Amazon. Don't you?"

I don't know anything about Amazon.

I nod fast. "Oh, yeah, totally."

Alexis looks at me, and then winks. *Winks.*

He guides me down the stretching aisles of the bookstore. The lights overhead remind me of the porchlight Alexis sat under when he was outside the party. I thought I could see him well then, but now, in the light of the afternoon, I can see him so much better. His brows are thick and expressive, his lips pout, his facial hair looks rough against his soft skin.

I wish I wasn't so attracted to him.

I know I'm always whining about not having anybody to mess around with, but I really thought I'd be in control of the situation when it finally arrived. But looking at Alexis makes me feel like I'm being pulled outside of my body. Like I'm not even real.

We snake around aisles of textbooks until we get to the poetry section, the brown bookcases high above our heads.

"This will be here," he explains.

He reaches for the top shelf. He's tall enough that he doesn't have to use the step stool at the end of the aisle. He brings down two books with him, each with opposing covers.

"You have options," he says. "More modern blue, or more nineties yellow."

I feel impressed by his attention to detail. But I'm quickly humbled by looking at the price tags of each of the books. They're both marked used and both cost less than five dollars, but I can't afford it. The pocket of my jeans that burned with the five-dollar bill now rattles near empty. I don't know what to say.

"Which do you want?" he asks, holding each book up. "I think the yellow one has someone's notes in it, so that's cool if you like reading them. But the blue one looks newer and can give you room to write your own notes in it."

I don't tell him I've never written in a book before.

Ms. Foley and the rest of the English department have made it very clear that we aren't allowed to, not that we'd have the room over the penises people draw on every chapter anyway. At the public library I can't either, unless I want to pay fees for "vandalizing" the book.

"Th-the blue one," I stammer, swallowing the dryness in my throat.

He smiles. "Cool. That's the one I would've picked too."

We walk around the bookstore, looking at the small section of novels in Spanish. Alexis browses the titles, telling me about how he's majoring in Latin American Studies. He says it makes him feel closer to his culture, since his family is from El Salvador.

"Have you ever had a pupusa?" he asks, passing a display of wall calendars.

"No."

He smiles softly. "There's a really good place around here called Café Plátano. I'll take you to get them sometime."

I feel the blood in my body rush to my toes.

He shows me a section of something called readers, pointing to the ones he's been assigned for class.

"They're just a bunch of articles professors put together and get bound to look like books," he explains.

They look disgusting. They have thick bands on the spines and covers made of construction paper. I'd rather stab my eyes out than read something like that.

We keep circling around the store. I'm trying my best to focus and enjoy Alexis's company, but I can't stop thinking about what I'm going to say when it's time to pay for the book.

The more I think about it, the more nervous I get.

I begin cursing my pa in my head for leaving, for taking all our financial wiggle room with him. He's probably using it to take women out on dates, and probably ruining this kind-of date I'm on.

I'm not even listening or looking at Alexis as we walk around, even when the backs of our hands brush together, even when I catch him eyeing my body. I can't focus on anything but the sweat pinching in my armpits. By the time we approach the front of the store where the registers are, I open my mouth and stammer again.

"I—I, uh—"

Alexis blinks, unaware of my panicking. "I'm gonna pay for this. Do you want to wait for me here?" he asks.

"You're gonna what?" I blurt.

"I'm gonna buy it for you, well, I mean, if you let me."

I stare at him. The corner of his mouth twitches, teasing a smile. His brown eyes meet mine, melting against my gaze.

He looks at me in a way nobody has before.

"You don't have to do that," I tell him.

"I know," he says, "I want to."

We stand awkwardly near the register. I stuff my hands into the pockets of my jeans, where the change from the coffee shop jingles mockingly. He rocks back and forth on his heels.

"Um, okay," I say quietly.

"Cool." He nods. "I'll be right back."

No guy has ever bought me anything before.

I never wanted anyone to say they had done anything for me, the way I'd heard my pa say when he and my ma would get into it during fights. I never wanted to feel indebted to them somehow.

But Alexis approaches everything so much better.

He's so much smoother and softer.

I watch him pay for the book and wave his hand when the cashier offers him a paper bag. He crumples the receipt into the back pocket of his jeans, picks up a free bookmark, then tucks it behind the book's cover. When he returns, he hands me the book.

"Ta-da," he says, then winks at me again.

I fiddle with my hoops and look at the floor. "Um, thanks."

"No problem."

We walk outside, met by a rush of people loading off and onto the BART entrance. In the blur of bodies passing by, Alexis still looks sharp and vivid, my eyes completely focused on him.

I don't want to go home.

I want to stay here with him.

But I'm prepared to turn around and board a train if he mentions he has something collegiate to do—a study group, a library session, a date.

"You need to get going?" he asks, gesturing to the BART map beside us. I glance at it, and when I turn back, Alexis is smiling at me.

In the fit of everyone else's movement, he steps toward me. He brushes his fingers over mine, the space between our palms tense with anticipation, leaving us both still.

"I was just thinking that maybe I could show you those books at my place," he says.

TEN

I roll my eyes. "No, Señora Barragón. He did not deflower me. I'm still with God."

She smacks her lips. "So, what happened then?" she asks, closing her locker. It's passing period between fifth and sixth period, which only gives me the length of the hallway to fill her in on what happened with Alexis. I rush to tell her about how we took the long way to his apartment—a two-bedroom near College Avenue.

The inside of it was small and humble, clearly shared with a roommate, but Alexis was quick to tell me he had his own room. His mattress was on the floor, topped with pink, patterned bedsheets and yellowed pillows. There was a desk pushed into a corner, every inch of it covered in books, and as I reached to pick one up, he approached me from behind, wrapping his arms around my waist.

Our first kiss was slow.

I wanted to remember everything about it, how he tasted like coffee and Altoids, how his lips felt buttery and plush. But things picked up quickly. He led me to his bed, where he lay atop me and kissed me. That weight on my chest dissipated, evaporating as he kissed the skin exposed from my T-shirt. We continued for a while, until the sun completely set, until the room was clouded in darkness, until a vibrating sounded from his desk. It was his phone buzzing, an alarm reminding him about his last class.

Alexis paid for my Uber home. We waited for it to arrive together, standing on the curb, our tongues dancing between our lips. When I got home, I swear I floated from the car to my front door.

"So, you only kissed?" Leti asks. She is the only person who could ask this with relief instead of pride.

"For now." I sigh, nudging her side.

When I tell Leti this, she doesn't seem amused.

"He didn't ride in the Uber with you?" she asks.

I smack my lips. "It was late, Leti. And he had class."

"At night?"

"Yeah, at night," I say, rolling my eyes. "Maybe it's different in college. Wouldn't you know about that?"

"Yeah, but it was too late for you to get in an Uber alone. Something could've happened to you—haven't you heard of all those rapist-murderers-sex-traffickers that pose as Uber drivers?"

"Whatever, at least he paid for it." I shrug her off, brushing my hair over my shoulder.

She looks at me with her Leti-concern. A pious look drilled into her during Mass mixed with her ma's constipated expression. I worry for a moment, thinking she's judging me or something, but then I remember the fetus kicking it in her uterus. I calm down.

I look at her stomach, which curves just slightly over the fabric of her jeans. She's beginning to show a little. It's not too noticeable, though—she looks like me after I've eaten too many frijoles. But in a few months, she'll be popping out, and then she'll have no choice but to tell her pa. Leti catches me staring and holds her binder over her stomach. She picks up her pace, splits off to the AP hall, and disappears into a classroom, not even turning around to say goodbye.

Nobody gives a fuck about this assignment but Ali. Not even Ms. Foley. She's sitting behind her desk, sipping tea while online shopping. The rest of the class is in their assigned pairs and groups, texting beneath their desks and looking at the clock nailed above the door.

I glare at them with envy.

I slump down in my seat, stare at my blank page, and begin cursing my pa, cursing Ava, cursing Ali, because now *I* have to give a fuck about this assignment.

I look over at Ali, the only person in class who is writing anything, his pen moving miles a minute. He catches me staring, pauses, and pulls a yellow personal statement pamphlet from the plastic sleeve of his binder. He side-eyes me as he hands it to me, and I roll my eyes, annoyed that he knew I wouldn't go grab one myself.

All the prompt choices are so dry—most of them are academic based. A bunch of bullshit about a thesis I'd write in the future or a positive contribution I'd make to research. Like, who thinks about shit like that? With my grades and truancy, I don't have much to offer there. So, I pick the one Leti picked, about some challenge you've faced.

It can't be that hard.

I can't remember the last time I wrote an essay. Maybe last year, *maybe*. But this prompt seems more like writing a journal entry than a big paper.

I came somewhat prepared to work today, milagro, so I pull out a notebook and a pencil, date and label my page, and stare at the pamphlet. I reread the prompt, glance at my page, reread the prompt, glance at my page.

I try to start writing, but I can't.

Nothing comes to me.

And worse, the things that *do* come to me I would never want to think about, let alone write down, in a million years.

Ali glances at me and clicks his pen. "Writer's block?"

I look over at him. He sits up, adjusting the earbud hidden into the long sleeve of his shirt. Ali is perpetually listening to music. It's almost obnoxious. Outside of class, he's always wearing his bulky headphones. But during class, he sneaks an additional pair of earbuds into the left sleeve of his shirt. That way, when he rests his hand on his fist, the music filters through the fabric and to his ear. When it's quiet enough, I can hear a skeletal beat whispering through the classroom.

"Kind of," I tell him, flicking my pencil against the spiral of my notebook.

"What prompt did you pick?"

"The one about the biggest challenge."

He nods. "I picked that one too."

"How'd you start it?"

He shuffles his papers. "My first line goes—"

I shake my head, my curls bouncing over my shoulders. "No, not like that. Like, how'd you pick *one* challenge?"

He pauses and then looks at me. He tilts his head, his earrings reflecting in the fluorescent lights above. "I talked about it with my mama."

Oh great.

I can't ask my ma or Ava or even Leti about the assignment without feeling the weight of their judgment. And I'd die before asking Ms. Foley. So, I stare at the ruled paper of my notebook, its straight lines becoming mazelike.

"I also go to these after-school sessions with Ms. Barrera that Quentin told me about."

I raise my eyebrows, remembering Ms. Barrera's offer last week. "How do you know Quentin?" I ask.

"We used to be neighbors, lived in the same apartment complex." He pauses. "He's with Leti, right? How's she doing?" he asks, adjusting the collar of his sweater.

"Good," I say. "Coming along."

"I'm happy for the both of them."

I nod, and he nods. This is the way most people ask about Leti's pregnancy—in some suggestive secret language.

He clears his throat. "Yeah, anyway, Ms. Barrera was really helpful. I've never been in Honors or AP, but she offers help for students whose parents can't sign them up for those application classes. It's like tutoring on the low. You should come."

I glance at his page—he's so far ahead of me, almost four pages in. Just the thought of staying at school past three makes my stomach hurt. But I know if I don't, I won't pass this assignment. And then, I'll be more like my pa than I already am. I'll be just like him.

"When is it?" I ask.

"Next week." He pauses, putting on his best convincing tone. "She's really nice—when we stay late, she'll buy us Chinese food."

"Chinese food?" I repeat, like this is supposed to impress me.

"I know you probably don't want to come, but the statement is due right after Thanksgiving break," Ali says, eyes darting to my blank page. "It sounds like a lot of time, but it isn't. I've been working on my statement since the summer, and it's not even done."

"You're not even *done*?" I echo. "But your pages are always full."

"I mean I'm trying to make mine *good*-good, you know? But we can figure yours out."

"Don't diss me like that." I roll my eyes.

"It's not a diss! But what can I assume if you're never here?"

I nod, understandingly. "That's fair."

"You read, though," he says, smiling. "That'll count."

"How?"

He laughs. "Damn, you really don't listen in class. Ms. Foley says all the best writers are good readers first."

"I don't really trust Ms. Foley too much."

He nods, mimicking me. "That's fair." He pauses. "Are you gonna work on it over the weekend?"

I raise my eyebrows in disbelief. "Do my homework? On the weekend? No."

He smiles. "Well, if you need to catch up, I usually go and finish my homework at Oakland Grill on Saturday mornings."

"You just stay studying like that? After-school sessions, *Saturday* morning homework?"

He shrugs. "I told you. I'm trying to go to another school." He pauses. "I have to do better for myself."

I blink. "You have a top choice?"

"Look at you with that college language!" He nudges me.

I roll my eyes. "Six years with Leti and it rubs off."

He shakes his head at me. "Give yourself some credit. But yeah—I wanna go to Howard."

"Howard? Where's that?"

Nobody here talks about anything that isn't a UC. And even then, it's all about UC Berkeley. It's like getting into the Harvard of the Bay Area—that's why Leti's been on it for so long.

"It's in Washington, DC—it's an HBCU, Historically Black College and University. What about you?" he asks.

I snort. "I already told you. I'm not going."

He shrugs again. "Yeah, but you can always change your mind."

I scoff. "I'm not getting into a UC."

"So? That's the problem. People think you have to go somewhere fancy to go anywhere at all."

"You sound like this brochure," I say, shoving the pamphlet near his face.

He waves me off. "Whatever." He pauses. "So you're down?"

"For what?"

"For the workshop. I'll tell Ms. Barrera to save a seat for you."

I let out a long sigh, then I look at him. He's wearing a pair of wiry round glasses that make him look like a young librarian. From behind the frames, he darts his eyes from me to my blank page, then back to me.

"Fine," I say to him. "But I'll ease into it."

ELEVEN

LETI CALLS AND ASKS IF I CAN TAKE HER TO A CLINIC. I WALK TO HER house, on the corner of Foothill and East 17th. I look up at her duplex, at the million red stairs leading up to her front door. I wonder how she gets up and down with all those books on her back and a baby in her stomach. I sit in my usual spot at the bottom step and wait for her. I used to sit up higher, but the higher you sit, the more you can hear the tenants below. They host cockfights on weekends and once, I swear, I heard blood splattering against the windows. Never again.

I look at Señor Barragón's truck parked in the driveway. It's an ugly rust-red with a bumper sticker that says "Hecho en México." Then I glance at the car wash and the liquor store across the way, sandwiched on either corner of the intersections where the sideshows drag when it's hot out. I pull my phone out of my pocket and nestle it between my legs. I've been waiting for Alexis to text me since we hung out a few weeks ago.

He hasn't.

I listen to the front door creak open behind me. I turn to see Leti wearing her usual uniform: a plain T-shirt, jeans, her backpack, and a braid. Her ma trails behind her.

If you couldn't already tell, I'm not Señora Barragón's biggest fan.

She's like the worst telenovela villain you could imagine but with zero of the glamour. Her hair is clipped up on the crown of her head, her cross is shiny around her neck, and her wedding ring is modest on her finger. She waddles down the steps. When she's close enough, I catch her signature Latina mom scent—Suavitel, manteca, and lots of immigrant nostalgia.

She doesn't say hi to me.

This isn't unusual for our interactions.

"Leticia is not allowed to go to a clinic in Fruitvale." Her tone is firm, already scold-like and accusatory. She stands on the step above mine, hands on her hips, her wide shadow shielding me from the afternoon sun.

"Sí, señora," I say. To anyone else, I'd just give a nod or an "okay." But Señora Barragón has made it very clear that when I answer her, I say, "Sí, señora."

"Belén, if I find out, if *God* finds out you took her to a clinic here, you will be very sorry."

Imagine if *God* found out Leti got pregnant in the back of a car.

"Sí, señora," I say.

"The people at the church cannot know until I am ready to tell them."

"Sí, señora."

"The clinic you are going to is free?"

"Sí, señora."

She nods, and then she does what she always does when she needs Leti, she shouts her name loud enough for all of Oakland to hear. Her voice bounces off the cars blocking the driveway and off the liquor store marquee and off the freeways.

"¡Leticia María!"

She yells even though Leti is right behind her. I swear for whatever drama Leti lacks, her ma makes up for it tenfold. Leti stands in front of her with her head bowed and her eyes closed as her ma conducts her fingers in front of Leti's face, dousing her in bendición.

After slipping Leti money for BART fare, Señora Barragón gives Leti a hug so tight I think the baby might pop. I feel like a weird third wheel, so I look away. It feels like I'm intruding.

She levels it out fast enough. Once they've pulled apart and I stand up, she gives me the same up-down she's given me since my hips widened in the sixth grade. She watches as Leti and I hop off the steps and onto the street, her eyes burning into our backs until we round the corner, completely out of her view.

"¿A dónde?" I ask Leti. She's been researching clinics in the area forever.

"This clinic downtown."

And then she books it ahead of me.

Damn near runs.

I squint at her—she's never done this before. Ever since we met that day in sixth grade gym, she usually uses me as a guard and walks behind me.

That day, like today, it was hot out. All the girls were hiking up their gym shorts, revealing their freshly shaved legs, until Marta López caught sight of Leti. Leti, of course, was wearing sweatpants. Marta approached Leti and kept asking her why she was wearing her sweatpants instead of her gym shorts to run. Even in the shade of the locker room, I could see Leti's cheeks turning red. When Marta kept bugging her, Leti loosened her braid to cover her face.

But when we started running laps, Leti ran circles around everybody. Ran with real grace too, jumping over the dips in the grass with ease. I figured maybe that's why she was always looking at the floor, cuz she had to know what would be in her way.

When we were done, there were sweat rings staining Leti's shirt collar. Marta and her friends began pinching their noses, gagging and saying Leti smelled like mierda. Leti pulled at her hands. Marta got in her face, pressing her about how come she didn't just put on the shorts, she wouldn't be so sweaty if she'd just shown her legs, she bet her legs were hella hairy, your ma probably doesn't shave, so I bet you don't either, hahaha what's with that smell from your sweat, how come you smell like when my ma makes fajitas for dinner?

Leti just took it.

No spine.

Marta went on and on, her green eyes getting bigger and bigger while Leti got smaller and smaller. So, I got in front of Marta and said that Marta wouldn't know what fajitas smelled like because Marta's ma couldn't cook to save her life. That at Marta's tenth birthday party her ma burned the rice, so how would her ma know how to make fajitas if señora couldn't make a simple pot of rice, that if Marta's ma's life depended on cooking, her ma would probably be dead by now.

Marta didn't think it was clever. Nobody really did.

But later, when we were away from everybody, Leti, quietly, privately, between just us two, thanked me in the locker room. She talked like a little mouse, whispering like she spoke in all lowercase.

We've been good since.

It's like that now. But instead of hiding behind me, she rushes ahead and mumbles out into the air. I keep leaning forward to try to hear her, and even pin my hair behind my ears to try to listen better. But with the cars passing, I can't hear anything. I speed up to meet her at her pace, when I see her face is wet with tears. I pull at her shirt-sleeve to slow her down.

"What's wrong?" I ask. The question itself is dumb, like there aren't a million things that are wrong.

She stops and catches her breath. Her shoulders heave up and down, her bottom lip quivering like she's a little kid. "I just don't want to be doing this."

"No mames, Leti. You can't be pregnant and not go to the doctor."

"No," she says. Her shirt collar is damp from tears, almost like it was all those years ago. "I just don't want to be doing *this*." She gestures to her stomach.

My eyebrows raise. "Oh."

"On Saturdays, Quentin and I used to go study at the library, and then I'd watch him shoot free throws afterward at Dimond Park."

Gross, I hate hearing about their dates.

"But I mean *that's* what I'm supposed to be doing. I have a huge AP Chem test on Monday, and I'm supposed to be at the library with him and he's supposed to be helping me with my flashcards. But instead, I have to go to the clinic, and Quentin can't come because he's working to save money for the baby, and my ma won't come because she's embarrassed of me, and my pa doesn't even know."

When Leti begins rambling, it's usually bad. No one that quiet can just naturally spew out so much. I grab her shoulders and pivot her forward. "I know. But we have to go. What's gonna make you feel better?"

She doesn't say anything.

She stands still, wiping her tears with the back of her palm. I look ahead, squinting at the sunlight that slants against the sidewalk. I can see the bus stop we meet at in the mornings hovering in the horizon. Anything south of that I know like the back of my hand. I tug Leti's wrist and pull her forward, through International in all its smog and car exhaust, to the fruit stand next to the Bank of America.

Leti and I have been going to this frutero for forever.

We don't know his name, but he knows our orders by heart. He looks like my grandpa, with dark skin and white hair, and takes care of us the way most grandpas would. He usually gives us a two-for-five deal when we come together, and when one of us is having a notably bad day, he doesn't charge us at all.

People say a lot of things about immigrants, but if there's one superior trait of them all, I'd say immigrants have some voodoo shit on fruit. They just always know how to pick it. We've come here in the dead of winter when nothing is ripe and somehow this man's fruit is always sweet and soft.

As we get closer, the frutero squints at us in the distance. He's sitting on a milk crate, holding a knife in one hand and a mango in the other. Even from under the shade of his baseball cap, I can see his eyes fill with worry. When he sees Leti crying, he stands and speaks softly.

"¿Qué te pasa, mija?" he asks Leti, who is heaving now, thick, guttural sobs coming from her throat. When she doesn't answer, he looks at me. I'm not in the business of outing Leti's pregnancy to anyone, not even the frutero we've been faithful to for years, so I just shrug. He drops the mango and begins expertly preparing Leti's order—pepino with limón y sal. Leave it to Leti to get pepino at the fruit stand.

He hands her the bag, and she takes it wordlessly. And then she just stands there, cemented to the pavement, crying quietly. The frutero hands me my order—sandía with chile, limón, y sal—and a wad of napkins. When I fish for money from my back pocket, he shakes his head and looks over at Leti.

"Mija," he says. "Cuídate."

We sit on a bench in Fruitvale Village, BART trains passing overhead. The sun beams bright on the Oscar Grant memorial mural behind us, and Leti sits there crying with a bag of pepino balancing on her lap. If she wasn't pregnant, I'd think it was pathetic.

I wait for a while, hoping she gets it together soon. I pull out my phone again, checking to see if Alexis has texted.

Nothing.

I unzip my bag of watermelon and fish out a piece. Between bites I say, "If we wait like this long enough, you'll end up missing your appointment."

Nothing.

Instead, Leti stares down at the pepino and kicks her sneakers into the air. I look at the time on my phone.

"Leti," I say, my tone even. "You're going to miss your appointment."

Nothing.

I get up from beside her, take the pepino off her lap, and pull her up. As I drag her through the plaza and to the entrance of the BART station, I think about how Leti would probably never do this for me. Physically pick me up from a slump, carry me to where I'm supposed to be. According to her, I should just do my homework to distract myself. And she doesn't even know what I need to be distracted from.

I push away the thought.

Truthfully, I'm grateful she asked me to come.

Alexis clearly hasn't texted me and being at home makes me feel like dying. Especially with this personal statement shit on my neck. I haven't started it yet, because needing to write about the things I never want to think about makes me feel like I'm choking. And being at home to do it is like reporting from the scene of the crime.

I pull Leti in through the emergency fire entrance to the BART station. If I was by myself, I'd just hop the turnstile. But since I'm with her and she's pregnant, I gotta go a different route. White people look at us with squinted eyes as we avoid the fare, but the person at the customer service kiosk looks like they couldn't care less. No alarms sound off, so I push past with ease.

"Belén," Leti says, "we have to pay our fare."

I knew that would get her.

"We have one minute to get upstairs and to our train," I urge her. "I know you hate being late. You better hurry."

We stand on the brown tiles of the station, the damp smell of the concrete walls filling my nose. Her eyes begin to brim with tears, but I hear the whirring of the oncoming train above us. I grab her arm and pull her up the escalator, climbing two stairs at a time.

We slip through the doors of the train with just enough time. The train is mostly empty, so we sit in the four-sectioned seats that face each other. I sit on the left side, and Leti sits across from me on the right. She sets her backpack beside her and leans back.

"You should eat that," I say, handing her the bag of pepino. "It's gonna get soggy."

She's silent.

She peers out the window, through all the graffiti etched into the plexiglass, watching Fruitvale pass beneath us. I sigh. Cheering Leti up is hard because once she's in a mood, she's in a *mood*. But she doesn't even seem upset. She just seems defeated.

I lean forward and grab her backpack. She's too sad to even protest—I'm never allowed to touch it. But I dig through the pockets until I find a wad of flashcards held together by a binder clip. It has a bunch of words that I don't understand, so I can't even tell if this is AP Chemistry or AP English or AP whatever, but when I see one with a periodic table that's been trimmed and glued to fit the card, I smirk a little. Leave it to her to haul her ass to the library, resize a periodic table, print it, cut it, and glue it to a flashcard.

I unclip the cards and clear my throat.

She looks at me, then at the card in my fingers, and smiles for the first time in an hour. Then, because she's Leti, she perfectly recites the definition on the back. We move on to the next one.

*　*　*

The waiting room has no windows.

We sit on an ugly, lime-green couch that's so overstuffed it feels like it might burst. A watercooler sweats across from us. Nobody is here except for me, Leti, and the receptionist behind the front desk. She keeps glancing at us with pity, as if she should feel bad for us. Really, I feel bad for her with that terrible fucking perm on her head. I'd give her Ava's card if I wasn't still mad at Ava.

Leti balances a clipboard on her lap and holds a pen in her palm. She taps her foot, her leg bouncing up and down like she's taking some kind of exam. I keep telling her to relax, it's just a questionnaire about her "reproductive health." But she's hella deep in test-mode. She writes neatly on each line, marks every box with a symmetrical tick, and double-checks her spelling before presenting it to the receptionist.

A few minutes later, a nurse appears from a door. She calls Leti's name, butchering it the English way of *Luh-tish-uh*, and Leti jolts up.

"You want me to go with you?" I ask her.

She shakes her head, which is surprising. I held her hand the whole way here. But I nod and watch her go. She lugs her backpack with her, like she's gonna study while they do an ultrasound.

I check my phone again to see if Alexis has texted.

Still, nothing.

I groan and pull the Neruda collection out of my backpack. I'm only a third of the way in, but reading it is beginning to feel like a chore. I know romance poetry is literally supposed to be romantic and whatever, but after reading Sor Juana's poems, this shit feels so corny to me. Like, how many times can you talk about the fucking stars? Still, I flip to my dog-eared page and begin reading. I want to be able to talk about it with Alexis the next time I see him.

I'm midway through a poem when I hear someone enter the waiting room.

I glance over and see Quentin standing by the receptionist's desk, still wearing his polo shirt from the shoe store he works at part-time. His head drops when the receptionist says Leti is already being seen.

"Can I go back there to see her?" he asks. After a moment, he adds, "I'm the father of the baby."

The receptionist's eyes harden. "I'll call to make sure that's okay."

Quentin turns toward the sitting area, where I greet him. He slumps down in the chair beside me, then lets out a long exhale.

"Hey," I say, closing the book. "I didn't know you were coming."

"I didn't either. I asked my manager to let me out early to try to be here on time. But even then, I'm late."

I read the wary expression on his face. "Long shift?"

He nods. "Long shift, then this. *And* I have an AP Chem test coming up."

"Yeah, I just helped Leti with her flashcards."

He puts his head between his knees. "God, everything feels like it's piling up. Normal things, and then this."

I put my hand on his back, trying to offer comfort. "I'm sorry. You're here, though."

"I'm late."

"But you're here," I say, thinking of my pa. "That counts for something."

He lifts his head up, then buries his face into his hands. "I guess so. I'm just so stressed."

I nod, because what else can I do?

Quentin continues. "There's all that and then there's telling her parents. I keep telling her it's gonna creep up on her. But I really feel like it's gonna creep up on me."

"What do you mean?"

"I mean, you know her family. Her pa."

The Barragón family presents themselves as perfect and pious—attending church fundraisers, volunteering at Sunday school, and planning community events. But behind closed doors, it's a different story.

Most people think they are just like any other family. A pa who lives, sleeps, and eats on his recliner. A ma who is cooking, cleaning, and catering to everything around the house.

But I know Leti, so I know the truth.

I know that the scar on Leti's face came from the time she was warming up her pa's food too slowly. I know Leti stays at school until sunset to avoid going home. I know that she used to be yelled at so loudly that the neighbors would call the police.

And I know it only stopped because Señora Barragón grew embarrassed.

She said if Leti arrived at church with more scars on her face, people would have too many questions. If the police kept coming, he could get deported.

And then what would the ¿qué dirán be?

The Barragóns only relaxed to protect the smoke and stained-glass mirrors, to present as a perfect Catholic family. But any time Leti has tried to tell them how backwards they can be, she has been met with the same lecture, the same violence.

Sometimes, it almost makes me understand why Leti would wait to tell her pa about her pregnancy. But when I look at Quentin now, his face worn and weepy, it makes my chest hurt.

Quentin lets out a long exhale, leaning back in his seat. "This whole thing is never going to work."

"You and Leti?"

"No, me and her family. They're never going to approve."

I know this is probably the part where I'm supposed to pat his back and say it'll be okay. But I don't think it'll be okay. I think he's right. No matter how extreme it sounds, Leti's family would never approve of Quentin. Even though he's smart and hardworking and kind, all they will see the inevitable moment they have to meet is his race. All the comfort in the world can't pad the truth of the situation.

I stare at him for a moment, waiting for him to elaborate. But the same nurse from earlier stands in the threshold, holding a clipboard to her chest, interrupting us.

"Bailen?" she calls, like my name is a verb.

"*Belén*," I correct.

She glances at her clipboard. "Leticia requested you and Quentin come see her."

Quentin and I stand and start toward the nurse, but she stops him, holding her palm up.

"You're the father?" she asks Quentin, an accusatory finger pointed at him.

He nods, and she fishes a clipboard out of a plastic bin. "You need to fill out this questionnaire before you can head inside."

I turn to him. "Want me to wait for you?"

He shakes his head. "No. I need a minute anyway."

The nurse leads me down a hallway of closed doors, doors, doors. I glimpse through the few that are open—cramped rooms with long examination tables and monitors snaked with wires. I wonder if Leti is plugged up that way, with some television beeping beside her, and realize she's probably panicking. The one time we went to a blood drive at school, she looked at the needle and legitimately fainted. I don't know why she didn't just ask me to go with her in the first place.

When I get to her room, I see her lying on an examination table, her T-shirt lifted to reveal the small curve of her stomach. A different nurse hovers beside her, using a gloved hand to rub this thick gel on Leti's skin.

"I need you here," she tells me, her brown eyes big with worry.

"Why didn't you just ask me to come when they called you?" I ask, sitting beside her on a chair.

"I thought I could do it by myself," she replies, her voice flat.

"Quentin is here. Do you want to wait for him?"

She shakes her head quickly. "He can come later. I need to get this over with."

She turns her head and looks up at the tiled ceiling. The nurses are beside her, their noses and mouths covered by thin surgical masks, their blue eyes piercing above them. As I settle next to Leti, I catch them sharing a pointed look, and then glancing away.

I can already hear it—them taking their coffee break after we're gone, talking about how tragic it is that so many of these Latina girls are getting pregnant, that their mothers should talk to them about birth control options, that they'll have no future after the baby is born. They'll go on and on talking about how these Latina moms need to do a better job of raising their daughters, that their moms did such a good job with them, and it's such a pity that other girls don't have that chance.

I don't think anybody gets it.

Not even me, really.

I can say what I want about Señora Barragón and some of it will always stand—she is rude and sexist and racist and her highlights are too yellow for her skin tone. But she never finished elementary school. She doesn't have a lot of money. She crossed a border while pregnant with Leti and came here with what she could bring. For most traditional Mexican women, they don't have a birth control lesson in their bag. They have a Bible.

Then there's me, with my ma who went to university and had the whole birth control talk with me. And me, who has never had sex in my whole ass life. There's Leti, who has memorized her AP Chemistry textbook front to back all while researching how to raise a baby in university housing. And there's me, who got a truancy letter from the school district last Friday. It doesn't add up on paper. There is no paper. White people created the script and get confused when we don't follow it. But still, their judgment remains.

I move over and hold Leti's hand. The nurses sit beside Leti on tall, computer chairs and look over at her. Leti doesn't say anything, just keeps staring at the ceiling.

I learned about pregnancy in Sunday school and in health class. In Sunday school, under the "appropriate" conditions, it was described as a miracle. In health class, it was described as a consequence. Either way, I did not think this shit would go like this. Nobody mentioned racist nurses who cut through your name. Nobody mentioned waiting rooms with uncomfortable couches and sad, blue paint on the walls. And nobody mentioned the ultrasound process.

I glance at the curve of Leti's stomach, slick with gel, and I squint with questions. Like, how is this gel working on her stomach and showing a picture? Is this an X-ray? Doesn't that have radiation? Isn't that bad for babies?

Suddenly, there's a grainy, black and white image on the screen.

Listen, I do *not* think babies are cute.

No matter how much I love Leti, her baby will be no exception. From the image on the screen, her baby looks like every other baby. A tiny little alien with fragile features and a fat ass forehead.

Leti grips my hand and slowly turns toward the monitor. The nurses continue sliding their tools on her stomach, giving us a view of the head and the feet.

"Do you want to know the sex?" one of them asks Leti.

Leti is wordless. After a moment of strained silence, the nurses look to me. I wish we'd just waited for Quentin.

I look over at Leti. She shakes her head, and I look at her face. Her cheeks are wet, her tears dripping down from her chin to the thin tissue paper lining the examination table. I worry for a moment that she's going to start sobbing the way she did on the sidewalk, that there's no frutero or flashcards I can pull out at a time like this, and that we'll all drown in a pool of her tears in this examination room.

But she pulls at my hand and brings me closer to the monitor, smiling in miraculous disbelief at the image of her child.

TWELVE

"WE NEED A PLAN," QUENTIN SAYS.

His arm is outstretched, the printout of the ultrasound held between his fingers. We're sitting on the steps of the clinic, Leti sandwiched between us, heads tilted as we stare at the image.

I twirl the free lollipop I got from the receptionist's desk around my mouth, listening as it clicks against my molars. Quentin looks at Leti, his eyes red-rimmed and pink. He cried the most during the ultrasound, plucking tissues from a box in the examination room.

"I think we should tell them during Thanksgiving break," Quentin offers. "That will give us some time to mentally prepare."

Leti pulls her knees up to her chest, resting her chin atop them. After the blur of her tears during the ultrasound, she began to see the situation clearly. The baby was coming, and we needed a plan on

121

how to tell her parents. How to tell her pa. Just the idea of it caused her to revert to her pre-appointment disposition—quiet and stuck in place.

"He's right," I say.

Leti buries her face into her thighs.

"You have to prepare for the worst with your pa," I tell her. "You know that."

"Will you come?" Leti asks, her voice mumbled behind her legs.

"Will *I* come?" I repeat, almost choking on my lollipop.

She lifts her face, her cheeks imprinted with the creases of her jeans. "Yeah. I was thinking maybe if you were there, they wouldn't explode as much."

I snort a little. "Yeah, okay."

"I'm serious, Belén," she says. "You know how my family is. If you see my pa explode or my ma get hysterical, they'll both be worried you'll tell other people."

"I don't know," I told her. "When your pa is mad, he's *mad*."

I think about the time Leti caught her pa messing around with a sex worker she recognized from the neighborhood. She had been walking home from the bus stop when she saw her pa's truck parked around a corner. When she approached, he looked at Leti with such disgust—as if she was the one who should feel shame. Leti turned around immediately, got back on the bus, and came over to my house. We sat on my bed, watching the phone wires dangling above us, because Leti was too afraid to go home.

"I don't understand," I remember her saying, "I can't go out with a guy, but he can do something like that?"

I shrugged in response. Nothing about Señor Barragón surprised me anymore. After my pa had left me so abruptly, nothing about fathers did.

For a moment, she lay on the bed and stared at the ceiling, then tried to pin it on the woman. I turned to face her, shaking my head.

"You're smarter than that," I said.

Leti goes back to crying, pressing her palms to her lids, as if the pressure from her hands can mimic a floodgate. These tears are different from the tears she'd shed before the BART ride, of fear and hopelessness. They're even different from the ones shed in the clinic, of amazement and joy. These are stained with something heavier—disbelief, or maybe even despair.

"I'm just worried," she breathes. "He's just so terrifying."

I look at her. I hate being around her parents, especially her pa. I knew him well enough to understand what he was capable of in a state of semi-sobriety. I don't have to stretch my imagination to wonder what he would be like under a fit of rage.

I know that whenever Leti decides to tell him about the baby, her pa's rage would expand in a way neither of us had experienced before. It would reach everything it hadn't.

For a moment, I wondered if Señora Barragón would be helpful. But then I remember the leaps and bounds she'd gone through to stop her husband from hitting Leti—and not because it was the right thing to do, but because it avoided the embarrassment of accountability.

I sigh.

As much as I want to support Leti, I'm praying Alexis will finally text me and want to hang out over Thanksgiving break. The holidays were already bad enough when my pa was around. But now, with him gone, I can't imagine how depressing they will be. Being with Alexis would be the perfect escape route.

But when I look at Leti, her damp cheeks are oppressive mirrors, my own face reflected against the wetness of her skin. At least being there when she breaks the news, like being here today, is a definite way to escape home.

I nod.

"Fine," I breathe. "I'll go."

"I don't understand," Quentin interjects. "Your parents are more worried about being embarrassed in front of people than they are about our safety?"

"Yes," Leti and I both say, our voices in unison.

I wrap an arm around Leti, trying to offer some comfort, but Quentin shakes his head and stands, pacing the gum-covered sidewalk.

Leti decides to tell her pa at the end of Thanksgiving break, hoping that time with their extended family can soften her parents, can weave her a safety net. She wipes her eyes with the hem of her shirtsleeve and looks at Quentin.

"Maybe you shouldn't come," she says, "for your safety."

I can see Quentin's eyes widen at the suggestion, the disrespect strained in his stare. "I'm the *father* of the baby," he says, "whether they like it or not. It's my responsibility to be there."

Leti takes a deep breath. I dart my eyes from the tears pooling in Leti's palms to Quentin's expression, pained with incredulity. I stand up.

"Maybe Quentin's parents should come too," I suggest. "That way there's more support for him."

Leti nods, but it seems like she's not listening. Like she's not here. Quentin exhales, his breath tainted with disappointment. "We should get back. Your ma is probably wondering where you are. I can drive us."

Leti shakes her head, eyes fixed on the ground. "I think I need some space."

Quentin looks up at the sky, clouds taunting us in the distance, approaching slowly with the earth's tilt.

"Belén," he says. "Let me drive you home."

Quentin has been silent the entire car ride. I lean against the passenger-side window, watching as the sun curves behind Lake Merritt. I glance at the apartment complexes between the arms of trees, their windows lit like yellow eyes. I wonder what conversations are being housed there, if they are anything like the one we just had.

"I'm sorry I got tense," Quentin says, finally breaking the silence.

I look at him. "Why would you be sorry?"

He stretches his palm over the length of his face, his shoulders swooping with exhale. "I just get worried, you know? Like, if Leti's parents give her all this shit for being dark, what are they gonna do when our baby pops out and it might be darker than me? I'm proud to be Black, my parents are proud to be Black, and I would want *my* kid proud to be Black."

He sighs. "I don't think her parents would be proud at all—they'd be ashamed. I don't think it'd be good to raise a baby with her family. They've really messed her up, you know? Can you imagine what they'd do to a Black kid?"

I don't say anything. There isn't much advice to offer when you agree with someone. I don't know what Leti's parents will do with the baby, apart from traumatize it the same way they traumatized her. Maybe even worse.

Quentin shakes his head. "I knew this was already going to be hard. But even my parents are stressing out. They warned me about dating someone Mexican—they know how things can be with y'all. That's why I think we need to leave."

I take a breath. Clearly, this has been on his mind for a while. "For school, right?"

He nods. "Yeah. But I mean, *far*. If her parents talk to our kid like they talk to her, *I* couldn't take it. But I tell her this, and she doesn't listen. It's like she lives in her own world—it's so frustrating."

I look ahead. Quentin turns off the 580. Cars braid around traffic, zooming in and out of lanes, while I feel like we're stuck, centered by gravity.

"Like, how come *you* have to be the one to bring up the idea about bringing my parents? Why would she ask you to come before suggesting bringing my parents?" He scoffs. "Why isn't she thinking ahead—about telling her parents, about my safety, about the reality of having a Black child? I keep telling her we just need to leave but it's like she won't listen."

"I've asked Leti about that," I say. "But she's set on going to Berkeley, and I know she'll get in."

He shakes his head again. "I know. But that can't be it."

"What can't be it?"

"The end of the conversation. But it always is with Leti. Every time I mention moving away, we get into an argument about it."

I lean back in my seat, watching as Quentin pulls into my neighborhood. I can't imagine what it's like arguing with Leti about this.

I just look at her stomach and she bolts away. But hearing him say all this reminds me of how he doesn't know Leti like I know her.

They only met last year—he wasn't there when she was drawing college fan art, or bombarding counselors with questions, or stargazing at the Campanile. He has no idea how long she's been fantasizing about going to Berkeley, how it has become her beacon of light at the end of her parents' tunnel. Neither her pregnancy nor her parents were enough to deter her. Only the admissions office had that power.

But I don't say any of that. It doesn't feel appropriate.

Instead, I guide Quentin farther down the street, where he double-parks in front of my yard. There are no cars in our driveway, and when I look up at the house, I know it promises emptiness.

"I didn't mean to spring all that on you. I just don't know who else to talk to about this with," Quentin says, then pauses. "Thanks for listening."

"Of course," I say. Then I hug him from the passenger seat, the center console pressing against my rib cage.

For the first time since he saw the baby on the monitor, I see Quentin smile a little.

I hop out of the car and close the door behind me. Quentin idles, waiting for me to get inside safely. As I turn my key into the lock, I feel that heaviness creep from my toes and nestle in my chest. It had been gone all day—so distracted with Leti and Quentin and the baby, I had no choice but to forget about it. But without Alexis calling, without anywhere else to go, without anyone inside, we both know we have to find ourselves at home at the end of the day.

THIRTEEN

"IT'S WEIRD SEEING YOU STAY AFTER SCHOOL," LETI SAYS, CLOSING her locker.

It's Monday, the start of Ms. Barrera's personal statement workshop.

"I've stayed with you before, pre-Quentin," I say, which is true.

Before she met Quentin, before my pa left, I would sit with her in the library, feeling my eyes roll to the back of my head as I flipped through flashcards with her. I'd hear her recite Latin roots, biology vocabulary, dates of wars. You'd think, by now, I would've picked up some of it on some osmosis-shit. *Osmosis* is one of the words I learned through her flashcards, though.

"Yeah, but you're staying for *you* this time."

"Technically it's so that Ava gets off my back," I say. I haven't told her I may not be able to graduate, just like my pa. I don't think she'd understand—I don't think she'd even care.

I sigh. "If it were up to me, I'd be on a BART train to see Alexis right now."

Leti looks toward me, but not at me. She quickly veers farther down the hallway, as if she's suddenly going to be late.

"I should go," she calls from over her shoulder, "I'll see you."

The library doors thud behind her.

I walk down the AP hall to Ms. Barrera's room. Her door is fully open, the honeyed light of her classroom pooling on the linoleum tiles. When I enter, I see there are a few students scattered around the room, sitting at random desks. Ali is in the back, headphones on, head down as he scribbles in his binder. Behind him are yawning windows that stretch from the ceiling to the floor, encompassing the entire wall. They give view to Foothill outside, the November sky gray and dampening with rain. I look to my right, where Ms. Barrera is behind her desk. When she sees me, she almost jumps.

"Belén, it's nice to see you," she says, standing. She smooths her palms over her slacks and adjusts her Berkeley crewneck. I'd say it was another "cool teacher" outfit, but the sweater is a little try-hard for me.

"Where do I sit?" I ask.

"Anywhere," she says. "Do you want something to drink?"

"Huh?"

"I buy snacks and drinks from Costco for the program. They're lined up by the textbooks." She looks eager, like a dog in a pound.

"No, thanks," I say.

I pick a desk close enough to Ali, but a few seats over. I want to give him space to work without me distracting him. It feels strange sitting in here to work. Knowing it's an AP class makes everything seem more luxurious. And not even luxurious, just functioning.

I pull my notebook out of my backpack along with the pamphlet Ali gave me. I date and title my page, reread the prompt, but feel nothing. I tap my pen against the pad of paper. I reread the prompt three times. Then a fourth.

Nothing.

It had been so easy to tell Leti what she could write for her statement, but she's pregnant. That's gold right there.

I try not to think about things that are hard in my life.

Every time they come up, I end up in my bed. That's why I like helping Leti and being with Alexis and reading—especially reading. The more I read, the more immersed I am in someone else's life, someone else's thoughts, someone else's problems. It's the easiest way to push down my own.

I imagine it's like when Ava asks me to take out the trash, and instead of doing it, I just grab a paper towel and stuff the garbage farther down until Ava gets frustrated and takes it to the curb herself.

I look up at the whiteboard, where Ms. Barrera has written "Personal Statement Study Crew" in thick, purple marker. How corny. Suddenly, I hear her stand from her desk chair and walk my way.

I knew I shouldn't have looked up.

"You need help, Belén?" she asks.

I shrug. "I guess."

She pulls a chair from another desk and sits across from me, close enough that I can smell the gardenia scent of her perfume. I hate that she's young and pretty. I wish she looked more like Ms. Foley, that way I'd have an excuse to hate her.

"What prompt did you pick?" Ms. Barrera asks, smiling.

I point to it on the pamphlet. "The one about a personal challenge."

"Good choice, that's usually the most profound. How much do you have done?"

I hold up my blank paper.

"Where are you applying?" she asks. "Some schools have later due dates, so we may be able to stretch our time working on it."

"I'm not applying anywhere," I say. "This is for Ms. Foley's class."

She nods, waiting for me to say something next. When I don't, we sit in a lengthy silence.

"Let's do a graphic organizer to get some ideas down," she offers, ripping a page from my notebook. She grabs my pen and draws five ovals.

"Off the top of your head, name five challenges you've had in your life."

"Off the top of my head?" I snort, like it's an easy question.

She nods again. "Just the tip of the iceberg."

"Uh . . ." I look around the room.

A spiral begins churning in my chest, tightening with every passing cycle. It's followed by dampness along the nape of my neck. A dryness at the base of my throat.

Usually when this starts, it's hard for it to stop.

It's what ties me to my bed on bad days, what propels me to

distractions on days that are in between. By the way my heart's beginning to pound, I know this is the start of a bad day. But in this classroom, with this essay, with this teacher, there are no distractions. I'm stuck.

I regret coming here.

I want to leave.

Even if Ali suggested it, even if Ava lectured me, even if I flunk out of school and am exactly like my pa. All of that might be better than feeling this way. I close my eyes, imagining I am at Leti's ultrasound, imagining I am with Alexis, imagining I am anywhere but here.

I open my eyes when I hear Ms. Barrera stand up. She goes to her desk, grabs a manila folder, and turns to set it in front of me. She sits down again, looking right at me, her brown eyes firm.

"Belén," she says. "I know this is hard. I hope you don't feel your privacy has been invaded, but I looked up your student file when Ali told me you'd be coming."

She hands me a thick packet of paper, a silver staple in its corner. I thumb through my student profile, my ma's name and phone number printed in bold letters beneath the emergency contact section. My pa's information has been removed, Ava's name in his place. I flip past it and see my records all the way from ninth grade.

I feel my brows sloping together. "And what?"

She takes the packet from my hands and rifles through it, stopping at my records from my first two years of school. I shrug at her—I did decently enough.

But then, she flips to my records from last year. A row of Fs line the sheet.

They're accompanied by bright red flags that mark each of my absences. She points a finger at my grade-point-average, hovering just over a 2.0, the bare minimum needed to graduate. "You're too smart for this."

I stare at the page, the only thing keeping me from looking at her. It's embarrassing, because it's true. I know it isn't even all my fault—but somehow, it's all my responsibility to fix it.

"I talked to Ms. Foley," she announces. "This paper is a large percentage of your final grade. If you do well, it'll hold you over enough to graduate. You can fail literally every other class, you just need to do this," she says, holding up my notebook.

Silence stretches between us. After a moment, I say, "I know."

"You know?" she asks, a little surprised. Maybe she had expected me to come in here with motivation. I kind of expected that too. But just the thought of everything made me feel terrible.

I nod at her. There is so much I could say. I could tell her what I'm really thinking: that this is the only thing I have in my control to prove that I won't end up like my pa. And that even then, I don't know if I can do it. That the thought of it is enough to make me feel like I am hovering outside of my body. That maybe failing and being just like him was better than this feeling.

But instead, I say, "Yeah."

She looks at me a while longer, the sincerity of her stare making me squirm. I turn back at Ali, who is still scribbling away, the music in his headphones seeping a beat out into the room. I look beyond the windows at the pale gray sky, the rain that's drizzling, the Mac Dre mural, and cars trailing along the street like colorful ants.

"Belén," Ms. Barrera calls.

I whip my head around to look at her. I feel my eyes mirror the sky, damp and wet, and blink so she doesn't notice.

"I know this is probably not what you want to be doing," she says. "But I'm here to help you."

I look down at the floor. "I was just thinking."

"Have anything?"

She presses the tip of her pen against the paper, ink seeping onto the white like blue blood, ready to take notes at any moment. She looks at me, her eyes wide with wonder.

I can't look at her when I tell her.

I look beyond her, like Leti had done to me a few minutes earlier, at the whiteboard with the purple writing.

The last time, and only time, I told someone about this was the day it happened. And I only told Leti. After my ma picked me up from school that day, she drove us straight home. I didn't look into her and my pa's room. I didn't want to see if he'd taken his things. Still, when I walked inside, I heard an echo in the house. Everything felt emptier and lighter. Hollowed.

I couldn't call Leti for a few hours because she was in class. So, I sat on the steps of the house and looked at the driveway, at the earthquake cracks on the concrete where my pa would park his truck. The sagging phone wires dangled above me, their weight oppressive. After a few hours, I dialed Leti's number. She picked up on the first ring.

I told her the way my ma had told me—my sentences short, my breath caught.

I felt like I was underwater.

I felt like I was drowning.

We had all been expecting it for some time, but I was still in shock. After a long, thick silence, Leti said that she was sorry, and asked if there was anything that she could do. I said no, then quickly hung up.

I didn't know what else to say.

My pa hadn't died, but he was gone. We couldn't do what most do after a loss—have a rosary or a burial or a wake. I was mourning someone who was alive, but who willingly chose to be somewhere else, apart from me.

About thirty minutes later, Leti showed up at my house with a bag of sandía from the frutero. She got it just how I liked it, in spears instead of cubes. She handed it to me and sat beside me on the steps to my house. I leaned my head on her shoulder, my curls cascading down her back and the watermelon juice dripping onto the sidewalk. We ate in silence.

I didn't cry.

I didn't hug her.

I didn't say anything.

After we were done, she gave my shoulders a squeeze and took the bus home.

We haven't really talked about it since because I haven't talked to *anyone* about it since. No one asked me about it, not even Leti, and sometimes I was grateful for that. It was so embarrassing—to be someone who had been left.

Although I only told Leti, the news traveled quickly. My pa's family whispered and gawked when we'd show up to Sunday menudos— so much so that we just stopped going altogether. Señora Barragón looked at me with a mix of judgment and pity. And my ma stopped looking at me at all.

Now Ms. Barrera sits across from me, looking at me with her resting expression that still manages to be both patient and kind.

I swallow and take a breath so deep my chest fully swells. "My pa left last spring."

She pauses, then writes it down. "How was that impactful?"

I look around the room, eyes fixated on a poster about class requirements for college. "It just is."

She nods, takes notes, and keeps going.

"Okay, what else?" Ms. Barrera asks.

I look up at the ceiling, counting the water-stained tiles as I think. This room has eight. Ms. Foley's has twenty-seven. "My ma is, like, not around."

"She left, too?"

"No," I say. Then, I pause. I recount the tiles. Still, eight. "Kind of."

"She's different?"

I nod.

"How is she different?"

"Since my pa left, she's, like, I don't know." I feel stupid. Me with my big ass mouth at a loss for words—and in front of an English teacher, no less. "Just different."

Ms. Barrera writes. "What else?"

I hear rain hit the windows. I turn to look at it. With the warmth of our bodies, the windows have fogged up—instead of seeing the street, I just see a clouded reflection of myself.

I wish I could stop telling Ms. Barrera things. I wish I had a different partner for this assignment. I wish I looked like my ma. I wish I took after her. I wish I wasn't so much like my pa that I had to go out of my way to be different. I wish things weren't so heavy.

But wishing has never made anything easier—if it did, my pa would've come back months ago.

I look at Ms. Barrera.

"Everybody says I'm so much like my pa," I tell her. She nods, thoughtfully. "But it's like, how can you be like someone you don't even know? Like, he's not even there for me to compare myself to. I don't know what I'm supposed to be like."

I can feel Ms. Barrera looking at me, so I fix my gaze on the space behind her desk. There's a bulletin board that's covered in senior portraits of former students. She's one of those teachers—the kind who you give your portrait to. I'm sure Leti's will be there, big and huge, next to Quentin's.

Ms. Barrera is still looking at me. She does this for a long time, until finally I hear her write down what I've said.

"Anything else?" she asks.

"You mean, my fourth biggest challenge?"

She shrugs. "You've got some good material here. But, if you have more to share, I can write that down."

I look at the floor. I don't think I can physically think of anything else. The heaviness in my chest has traveled into my brain. Everything is dreamlike, the edges of my memory foggy and blurred.

I shake my head. "So, now what?"

"So now, you pick one."

I look down at her paper, at her bubbly handwriting. A real contrast to the content.

"To make it easier," Ms. Barrera says, pulling out a highlighter. "I've found some large consistencies in your examples."

She swiftly swipes the highlighter over the page, then turns it back to me. She's highlighted the word "dad" like, a million times. The spiral in my chest twists tighter. Everything that had been tugging me onto my bed was now written in beautiful handwriting, streaked in yellow. I look back at Ali, who is looking at me for the first time since I've been here. He slips off his headphones, hanging them loosely around his neck. His music echoes into the classroom, the bass thumping like my heart.

Then he glances at the sheet of paper.

My face gets hot.

I know he's my partner for the assignment, but this feels humiliating. I turn back at Ms. Barrera with my eyes wide.

"Don't worry," she tells me, like she's read my mind, "you're gonna read about some of his shit, too."

Ali gives a coy smile, then he shrugs and slips his headphones back on. He hunches his head and continues writing. That makes me feel better.

Ms. Barrera places the sheet of paper back on my desk and looks over at me, a hopeful smile on her lips. Then she grabs her phone and begins dialing the number to a Chinese food restaurant.

FOURTEEN

I AM GRATEFUL WHEN ALEXIS CALLS.

I didn't remember what it was like being in a school so late, where I watched the sun set from a desk, where the only light came from the overhead buzzing of bulbs, where the hallways were silent. The only other time I'd done this was when I stayed with my ma at work, so comfortable with her company that I'd fall asleep on the floor of her classroom library while she made copies in the staff lounge. But tonight, when the janitor came in to do her nightly sweep, my feet tapped against the floor, ready to leave, feeling I had overstayed my welcome.

I looked down at the first page of my draft. My handwriting was sloppy and uneven, the type of handwriting found in emergencies. I stared at it. The page itself was full, but inside I felt the ache of emptiness.

I forgot what it was like thinking about it.

About my pa, about before.

Now I had to write about it so vividly, it was hard to move. My fingers felt like they were full of sand, the pressure in my palms parallel to the churning in my chest.

Ali stood up from behind me, carrying his paper plate to the trash can, where he scraped leftover bits of fried rice into the bin. Then he turned to me.

"I gotta get home," he said. "You need a ride?"

We stacked our chairs. Ms. Barrera held the door open for us as we slipped out of her room.

"Belén," she called out after me. I turned to her, her back lit by the distorted haze of her classroom light. "I'll be here if you need anything."

I know she said it in support, but it only made me feel worse.

Ali and I walked to the student parking lot together, hoods tight against our heads as finishing rain fell. With every move forward, I felt the weight in my chest grow heavier. Every step was a step closer to home, a permanent absence promised behind its doors.

"You good?" Ali asked, turning past a portable.

And then my phone buzzed, and I was good.

I held it in my palm, staring at the glowing screen, seeing Alexis's name stark and bold. He hadn't answered my texts in days, and I had to constantly remind myself that he was in college and I was in high school, that he was busy. That things were different. "Sorry," I breathed, "gimme a second."

I ducked into a bathroom, still staring at the screen. Alexis had

never called me before, and I wondered how he would greet me—
hello? Or *hi*?

When I picked up, he didn't say either.

"You finish the book yet?"

I let out a breath, winded from moving so fast. "Yes, this morning."

I looked at myself in the mirror, my reflection warped by the etched graffiti in the plexiglass. I squeezed the phone tighter in my palm, feeling my knuckles bend against my grip.

"What'd you think?" I heard wind whip around him, like he was outside. I wondered if he was walking where we'd walked a few weeks ago.

"I don't think I've had enough time to sit with it," I said, racking my brain for an ambiguous way to say I thought it was boring, "but it was interesting."

"Yeah, I think so too. My Latin American Poetry class is doing a section on it next week."

I was quiet. Sometimes when he talked like that, about college, I felt like a wall was being built between us, brick by brick.

The pause on the line grew bigger. "Yeah, um, sounds cool," I blurted.

"Well, I want to hear more about what you thought. I'm craving Plátano—maybe we can get dinner and talk it over. Are you free now to hang out?"

I cocked my head back. It hit the door of the stall behind me, and I winced. "Like, *now*?"

"Yeah, now."

Sweat pricked at my palms. I could feel the itch of anxiety scraping at my throat, but I couldn't be a fucking coward like that. I had to seem down.

"Now's good," I said.

I could sense him smiling. "I'm excited to see you."

When I stepped outside, the rain had stopped. I told Ali I'd be heading to the BART station. He grimaced. "You need a ride? It's dark."

"I'll be fine," I called from over my shoulder, shooting straight for the gate. The damp pavement beneath me became a blur as I ran toward the bus stop, the heaviness in my chest evaporating with wetness of the downpour.

When I arrive at Alexis's apartment, we don't go to dinner.

We don't talk about any books.

He opens the door and immediately pulls me into his room. He kisses me quickly and gestures toward the bed. I look around for a moment, confused. In the quickness of it all, I don't know what to do. I don't know if I should take off my jacket or my backpack. I feel too embarrassed to even ask. When Alexis flops onto the mattress, I throw them both to the foot of the bed, then feel Alexis grab at my hand, pulling me down beside him.

He crawls on top of me, the weight of his body pressing onto my chest. He kisses my neck, his lips grazing my skin when he says, "By the way, I only have, like, an hour."

I stiffen.

He invited *me* here.

For dinner.

I wait a beat, thinking he might still invite me. Thinking he meant to say *we* only have an hour.

My mind stops when he starts touching me.

I've been touched by other guys, whether I wanted them to touch me or not. But because they knew they didn't totally have my permission, their touch was fast, like they were playing with fire. But Alexis's hands feel different. His skin is soft. His nails are short. His fingers are long. And he touches me slowly, which makes my skin feel like it's melting.

With his narrow mattress, we have to stay as close as physically possible to prevent from rolling off the bed. But despite being so cramped, Alexis hardly fumbles. He comfortably manages to prop up on an elbow and feel my chest. He slides his hand below my shirt and under the thick wire of my good bra without ever losing rhythm. He doesn't pause to consider the closeness of the ceiling, or how thick my breath is becoming, or the warmth of my skin. I would never be able to make such careful, calculated moves like this.

This makes me realize he's probably done this before.

With his weight pressing against my body, his fingers feeling my chest, I open my eyes and look around the room. I peer at his desk and wonder where he keeps his condoms, or if he even has condoms, or if he's ever even used a condom, or if he's ever had sex.

But, by the ease of his touch, it's clear he has.

His hand slips down the waistband of my jeans, and I feel hair that I never knew existed rise along my skin. My joints stiffen.

I didn't think this would happen.

If I'd known, I wouldn't have worn underwear my ma gets in the plastic value packs at Ross, the kind with floral patterns and the big "HANES" embossed on the elastic. Had I known, I would've swept hair at Güera's and saved up for the seven-for-thirty-five sale at Victoria's Secret, hand-washed the lacy thongs, and left them on the bathroom towel rack to dry like Ava does.

But I didn't do that.

Alexis pulls away from me. "Are you okay?"

"Yeah," I blurt, "why?"

"Because I keep kissing you and you're not really kissing me back."

"Oh," I reply, the syllable cutting my mouth. He rolls onto his back, and we cramp together side by side like sardines.

"Is something wrong?" he asks.

I wonder how honest I should be.

I haven't told Alexis anything.

Not about never having sex or about my pa or about Leti. I worry he'll think it's too young, too high school for him. But there's no use in lying. If I want him to see me naked, he should at least know the truth. "No, not really. I just didn't think we'd be moving so fast tonight."

He stares at me, like I'm speaking in a language he can't understand. "You think *this* is fast?"

I roll my eyes in my head. I knew I should've just shut the fuck up. I knew I should've just kept going, pretending to know what I was doing. "No, no. Not fast," I blurt. "I just, I don't know. I just didn't expect it, I guess."

"Expect what? Kissing?"

"No, like, all the touching."

144

His face twists up in confusion. "You didn't expect me to touch you while we kissed?"

I pause.

I want to say what I'm thinking: I expected to go get pupusas and talk about this corny poetry collection. I expected to kiss but not to, like, *kiss*-kiss. I expected to move slower.

Instead, I say, "I guess so."

He's silent.

I stare at the ceiling and feel my chest rise, waiting for him to say something else. But the only noise I can hear comes from the traffic outside, sirens wailing below us.

When he finally does speak, all he says is, "Would it be, like, your first time?"

"Yeah," I say flatly.

"Oh."

And then there's silence. Lengthy and strained and longer than the last.

"It wouldn't be your first time, right?" I ask. I feel my voice stretching, reaching for anything to fill the quiet.

He sits up as far as he can, his curly hair centimeters from the low ceiling. "No."

I blink. "Um, would it be a problem that it'd be mine?"

He shakes his head. "I don't really care if you don't."

"Oh," I croak, "um, okay."

This conversation feels so offbeat, so crooked.

Right after I say that, silence returns to nestle between us. I want to ask him what we're really doing—who I am to him. A few weeks ago, he'd bought me a book and held my hand, telling me how beautiful I looked under the streetlights near Sather Gate. Now I'm here, with whiplash from how quickly this is moving. I half expect him to say something else to alleviate the tension, but he just shifts on the mattress and says, "I should get going."

Before I can respond, he gets up. He stands in front of the mirror nailed to his door, adjusting his clothes and fixing his hair. I catch a glimpse of myself behind him, wondering how many other people have looked at themselves in this same reflection—if they felt as confused as I do.

I pull down my T-shirt and button my jeans, shame warm in my chest. Alexis side-eyes me, and when I turn to meet his gaze, he thumbs through a book instead.

I know he's kind of being an asshole. But, still, I really want this to work with him. After things with Jeveón ended, I felt so terrible. Everything felt so inescapable—but now, with him, there is the hope of release. What am I supposed to do if I lose that?

I slip on my jacket. It's still warm from my ride here.

Alexis begins ordering my Uber while I bend down, my knees pressed against the carpet as I fumble beneath the bed for my backpack. I peer underneath, where I grab it, and immediately see a bra behind it. It's lilac and lacy and small.

I jolt up quickly, hoisting my bag over my shoulders, beelining for the door. I stand at the threshold for a moment, waiting for Alexis to walk me out. He stays put by his desk, still thumbing through the same book, his shoulders pinched in annoyance. I walk to the sidewalk alone, waiting on the curb, enveloped by darkness. My neck is bent as I study my sneakers. I keep my gaze low, worried that if I look up, the swelling disappointment in my stomach will spill out of my mouth.

The headlights of the Uber pierce through the darkness, and I climb into the back seat.

I watch Alexis's apartment pass by in a blur, the glow of his window almost as taunting as Leti's voice in my mind. The girl at the party, his age, her judgment. I press it down, trying to silence it. Leti has no idea what it's like—finally meeting someone that makes everything else feel lighter, even if only for a little while.

She doesn't even know I feel this heavy to begin with.

She doesn't even care.

So, I compress her voice in my mind, folding it tightly until it is the quiet of nothing.

The driver pulls into the night, setting his radio to 102.9 KBLX. The Isley Brothers are on, reminding me of my ma. I know she won't be home when I get there. The memory of her, along with the heaviness finding its way back onto my chest, are my only company the entire ride home.

FIFTEEN

THE FIRST REAL DAY OF THANKSGIVING BREAK, AVA DRAGS ME TO the laundromat. My ma would usually come with us, but she went to school today—on her first day off during a week-long break. Anything to be away from us.

Ava and I sit on the tall, bar-like chairs of a table and gaze at the box-TV suspended in the corner of the ceiling. Reruns of *Caso Cerrado* are playing, and we listen to judge Ana María Polo give verdicts. The closed captions are delayed and out of sync.

Ava helps me organize the laundry into piles. She's more specific than Leti is with her system—with piles for warms, whites, darks, and delicates. I usually just throw all my clothes into one machine, cross myself, and leave it in God's hands.

While we organize, the woman who sells tamales in the laundromat comes over to us. Ava buys us four tamales—two sweet ones, two spicy ones. The tamales lady, who we've known most of our lives and still call the Tamales Lady, also throws in a cup of atole for free. It's steamy and makes the Styrofoam cup feel like it's melting.

"For breakfast and lunch," Ava explains, handing me a paper plate.

I groan, realizing we're gonna be here forever. I look across Fruitvale Station Shopping Center, wishing I had enough money to go to the Donut Star on the opposite side of the parking lot. There, you can buy donuts and Chinese food all in one stop.

Ava dumps a pile of socks in front of me. I pair them, almost thankful I'm occupied with something that can stop me from staring at the washing machine across from me. It's cycling some woman's bras. My eyes strain at the swirl of colors, trying to make out a swatch of lilac in the pool.

I can't get the thought of Alexis out of my brain.

Every time I'm too still, the memory of him sinks my stomach, plummeting further every time I think about the bra beneath his bed. I keep telling myself that it's probably a mistake. I haven't cleaned under my bed in years. There are probably lots of things down there I don't remember.

I look outside, toward the overpass of the 880 against the sky. I bet he's back in Oakland for Thanksgiving break. Every time my phone buzzes, my arms lurch to see if he's texted me.

He hasn't.

I ball socks into puffs, watching as Ava walks to the cash-to-coin machine to exchange a five-dollar bill to quarters.

"Did you bring your Thanksgiving dinner outfit to wash?" she asks.

I sip the atole. It burns my tongue. I don't know which is more painful—having my tongue scalded by atole, or remembering we have to go to Thanksgiving dinner. "No," I tell her.

"Oh, so you're gonna wear something dirty then?" I can hear her hand moving to her hip.

"*No*, that's not what that means. Jesus. It just means I didn't bring it."

"Well, you know Mamá Tere always likes when we all dress up."

Mamá Tere is my ma's ma. Mexicans always come up with nicknames for their grandparents. It makes shit confusing. "I know that. I can figure it out."

She pauses. "Are you going to wear jeans?"

I smack my lips. "No, I'm not going to wear jeans. I have a dress."

"Where is the dress from? You can't rewear something to her house, you know. She remembers everything."

That was true. Mamá Tere is nowhere near as bad as Señora Barragón, but she has her señora mindset. If we show up anything less than perfect to her house, it would be the talk of the town, here and in México, for weeks.

"I told you last week I got a dress. It's ugly and tacky *and* from Ross, so she'll approve."

Ava turns to me, counting the quarters in her palm. "Sorry, I've been distracted."

My ma and Ava have both been doing the I'm-not-home-right-now waltz for the last month. If Ava is home, my ma is out. If my ma is home, Ava is out. They both claim they're working, but I feel like something else is going on.

I don't want to ask them about it, though. I worry it might be about my pa. If it is, I don't want to know—hearing about him would only suck me into something I may not be able to pull myself out of alone. And with Alexis ignoring my messages, I don't have the safety net needed to soften that blow.

"Belén," Ava calls, her tone a warning.

"What?" I ask, throwing a pair of socks into a hamper.

"Ma is really excited for Thanksgiving."

I wait for her to say more. When she doesn't, I turn to her. "Okay?"

She points a finger at me, her acrylics accusatory. "Do *not* mess it up for her. Do not let this be a repetition of Easter."

I shoot her a look.

Last Easter, my pa's family had a carne asada. I told my ma going was a bad idea—my pa had left only a week earlier, and she was in shambles. But my ma said we needed to look strong. That's what she said—*look* strong, not be strong.

She picked herself out of her depression slump, caked on some makeup, curled her hair, and put on perfume. She made me wear something disgustingly festive, as if a pastel sweater would somehow shove remorse down my pa's throat for abandoning us.

But when we arrived, my pa was nowhere to be found.

In his place was a crowd of his family members, gawking at us.

We tried to ignore it, but being there was like waiting for lightning to strike.

My ma placed the flan she had spent all night preparing on the potluck table with the rest of the food. People picked at it, scraping the gelatinous mass around their paper plates.

Then they began whispering.

Whispering about how it tasted store-bought, whispering about how my ma never knew how to cook, whispering about how that's probably why my pa left.

I was watching the whole thing happen when I felt a hand on my shoulder. It was one of my tíos, asking if I knew what time my pa would be arriving.

"I don't know," I said, sipping my soda, "*I* haven't seen him."

Boom. That's all it took. After I said that, it was like the world stopped. My ma covered her mouth, in shock, and Ava glared at me with sharpness, just like she's doing now.

We left embarrassingly early. Before my younger cousins could start their egg hunt, before my pa could show up. I thought maybe he'd call my ma after to say he missed us. That he was sorry. That he was coming back.

He didn't.

We were quiet the whole way home. When we arrived, Ava started washing dishes, something she usually does when she's stressed. My ma went into her room and started blasting Rose Royce, something she usually does when she's crying. And I felt heavy and ate yellow Peeps on my bed, watching the telephone wires, wondering who they were connecting if I was so lonely.

So now, when Ava tells me this, I scoff.

"What did *I* do?" I ask.

"You know what you said."

"What? All I said is I hadn't seen him, which was true."

"Belén." She whips her head toward me, her eyes firm. "It's not the

152

things you say but the *way* you say them sometimes."

I roll my eyes, hard.

Ava shakes her head. "I knew you wouldn't understand. I knew you'd react like this."

"Like what?"

"Like this." She waves her hands toward me. "All angry."

I scoff. "How am I *supposed* to react? You're over here accusing me of saying something wrong when all I did was state a fucking fact."

"Fine." Ava holds her palms up to her chest, hands suspended in surrender. "Forget I even brought it up. Just be on your best behavior."

She turns on her heels and begins sliding quarters into the pay slot, her foot tapping in annoyance. I watch the woman unload her laundry from the machine, tongues of bra tags tangling into themselves.

I can feel Ava swelling up behind me, shaking her head. I know she's going to say something else, and I'm praying she chooses to say anything other than what comes out of her mouth next.

"You better be careful with that aggression," she tells me. "It's just like Pa's."

I look across the way at the Donut Star. It's the only thing helping me avoid looking at my reflection against the glass-paned washing machines.

I'm beginning to fear that this personal statement, this graduation goal, isn't enough.

Ava has no idea what I've been putting myself through to avoid being anything like my pa. Before break, I was staying in Ms. Barrera's class with Ali until sundown, pushing myself to feel terrible just to get something on the page. Just to try to graduate. Just to try to be different.

But I feel like it doesn't even matter, because she still says things like this.

It makes me wonder if this paper is just that—paper. It is nothing compared to the weight of my pa embedded into my body. The mask of his face that I can't peel from my own.

I look at the washing machines, at the soapy water that sloshes in cycles, the circular rhythm that drums something familiar inside of me. Ana María Polo's slamming gavel echoes through the laundromat, its boom bouncing against the walls. The finality of the sound rattles something in my stomach, making me wonder if perhaps a verdict beyond my control has already been decided.

SIXTEEN

I HAVEN'T SEEN MY MA WEAR MAKEUP IN MONTHS.

But today, a half hour before dinner at Mamá Tere's house begins, she stands in front of the bathroom mirror with her mouth agape, coating mascara over her eyelashes.

Wordlessly, she scoots to the side to make room for me. I look at the two of us standing side by side, accompanied only by our reflections, and study her face—strong lines and soft curves all in one.

She catches me staring, and I quickly look away. While she finishes her face, I run a brush through my freshly flat-ironed hair.

"You shouldn't always straighten your hair for an occasion," she tells me, rubbing a dark liner on her lash line. She doesn't look at me as she speaks. Just stares at her own reflection, turning side to side to make sure her eyes are even.

"Why not?" I ask.

She runs a hand through my hair. The intimacy of the gesture makes my chest swell, the sensation deepening when I notice small strands getting tangled on the new rings she wears on her fingers. "Your curly hair is beautiful, too."

She leaves the bathroom before I have the chance to tell her that I iron my hair to look more like her.

Ava is waiting for us in the living room, always ready on time. We're back to being tense after the laundromat argument, so when I walk into the room, she pretends she's studying her nails.

I watch as my ma stands across from us, gazing into the living room mirror, indecisively holding this pair then that pair of earrings to her lobes. I want to tell her that it doesn't matter how good we look—her family will find something to nitpick no matter what. A hole in our stockings, faja lines, an absent father.

I hope she knows that.

My ma decidedly slides her hoops into her lobes, fluffs her hair, and claps her hands together.

"Let's go," she says eagerly.

I remember being excited for things like this. I would look forward to my pa pouring apple cider into a champagne flute, telling me with a wink to pretend it was alcohol.

But now I just feel dread.

My mamá Tere lives on 35th Avenue. Her sky is striped like ours, with rays of phone wires that house hundreds of pigeons. She lives a few houses down from a Quik Stop gas station and a Chinese food

156

restaurant, so the air around her house always smells electric and fried. Like the Barragóns, she rents the top floor of a duplex, so when we arrive, we have to climb a million steps up to the door.

It's warm inside the house, a thick heat that is supposed to be comforting, but just makes me sweat. In the living room, we're met with all my ma's family. My tía Myrna and Elvira and Danna, my tío Antonio and Ángel and Berto. All even pairs of husbands and wives until my ma arrives.

All fifteen of my cousins are sprawled around the living room. As soon as we walk in, there's a shift in the air. It's our first major holiday here without my pa, and though no one stops to gawk like my pa's family had at their carne asada, I can feel eyes on us as we walk through the room.

My ma kisses everyone on the cheek. I haven't seen her so affectionate in months. It doesn't feel forced, like it did on Easter. Today she is beaming, almost triumphant. Her excitement makes Ava shoot me a warning look.

I'm glad I'm carrying a pie, because now I can avoid greeting people. It gets so tiring kissing people I don't care about. Like, I know my tío Antonio is important and that I'm supposed to love him, but I don't think I love him. I don't even know him.

Leti always gets mad when I say shit like that. Her family is all "family before everything," which is painfully ironic.

But how am I even supposed to believe anything close to that when my pa can easily walk away from me?

I guess blood is only thicker than water until you're drowning in it.

I hug the pie tight to my body, treating it like a shield, all the way toward the kitchen. There, my mamá Tere is standing over a steaming pot of tamales. I set the pie down on the table with the prepared food, and Ava ushers me to greet her.

She's the one person that we have to look amicable in front of. No matter how upset we are with one another, we stand up straight and plaster on a smile. She turns to us, wearing a large apron over her wide frame, her vast eighties square glasses fogging up from the steam of the tamales. She wipes her glasses and brings us both into a hug, her thick and meaty arms tight around our bodies.

"Mis hijas," she says before holding us at an arm's length. "Bien flaca," she tells Ava, who blushes like it's a compliment.

"¿Y tú?" She turns to me, then pauses. Her eyes scan my face. I can feel it coming—*look at Belén, look at her hair, look at those eyes, her father's twin.* I preemptively bite my tongue, afraid to say too much, afraid of Ava's accusation. But instead, she pinches at the fat on my waist. "Con lonjas como jamón."

I think for a moment about how Mamá Tere buys knock-off Lane Bryant at the DD's Discounts on Foothill, how if I tried to pinch her lonjas, I'd have to use both of my palms. But really, I'm relieved. It's the first time someone in my family sees me and the first words out of their mouth aren't about how much I look like my pa.

I walk back to the living room and sit on the couch beside my ma and my tía Myrna. They are immersed in some kind of serious conversation. Tía Myrna holds my ma's hands, which is disgusting to me. I could never touch my tía like that.

I hope she knows better than to ruin my ma's night by talking about my pa.

I hope everyone knows better.

I look over to my cousins Juan and Josué, who are watching soccer highlight reels on their phones. My tío Berto and Antonio are beside them, their spit flying when they howl at the goals.

God.

I'd never be friends with anybody in my family.

I probably wouldn't even know them if I wasn't forced to come to things like this. In the past, I used to bring books with me. But then my tía Myrna accused me of being a picuda, too stuck-up to be with the family. So, I stopped. Now I just stare at the windows, or at the shag carpeting, or at the family portraits nailed to the wall that date with time and expire with passing.

Up there are pictures of my family, my pa included. We took them at one of those tacky mall photo studios in coordinated outfits. All light-wash denim and white T-shirts and smiles. I look at my pa, displayed like a relic, a monument to a past now paneled in glass. When I glance toward his eyes and see them fixed on me, I turn away, wishing I'd just brought a book.

In the lull between dinner and dessert, I lie on the couch and look at the ceiling, counting the clumps of popcorn spackle that have been there since my childhood. I feel my phone ring in the pocket of my sweater.

I sigh, praying it's Alexis.

Then I groan, because it's Ali.

"Hey," he says, somehow already exasperated, "you haven't answered my texts."

I stand up and duck into one of the bedrooms to talk privately, Ava's gaze following me the whole way. She's been shooting me warning looks all night, especially since I didn't clean up my tíos' plates after dinner was over. But if they have functioning legs to stand around and watch soccer, they can have functioning legs to wash a plate.

I close the door behind me.

"That's cuz they're all about school," I tell him.

"Yes, because our assignment is due as soon as we go back."

I scoff. "I know. That doesn't mean I want to be harassed every minute about my fucking homework while I'm supposed to be on break. Jesus."

"Okay," he says. I can hear the annoyance in his voice. "Sorry, let me start this off better. How is your holiday going, Belén?"

"It's horrible," I blurt, the admission making me deflate inside. "How is yours?"

"Mine is fine."

There's a pause on the line, bloating with discomfort.

I roll my eyes. "We don't need to talk about our holidays. I can do my homework without you calling."

"I can't trust that. I told you, my grade is riding on this." The annoyance in his voice turns to panic, which makes me soften.

I pause. "I get it," I tell Ali. "But it's almost finished."

"You've been working on it outside of Ms. Barrera's class, right?"

"On and off," I lie. I have a first draft finished, but I've buried it into the depths of my backpack since break began, too afraid to look at it. Reading it made me feel terrible. Like the weight of my entire family was on my chest. Without Alexis calling, looking at it would force me to sit with the truth of what I'd written. And the thought of that made me feel like I was dying.

I catch a glimpse of myself in the vanity across the way. With the phone glued to my hand and my stiff posture, I look like my pa when he paid the bills. I relax my shoulders. "It just needs some final touches."

"That's what peer editing is for."

I roll my eyes again. "Yes, Ali. I understand that."

"Let's meet up and look it over. Are you free tomorrow morning?"

"You want me to go do homework on a Friday morning?" I ask.

"Belén," he pleads. "Come on."

After much protest, we agree to meet at the ungodly hour of seven a.m. He'll pick me up and we'll go sit somewhere to edit each other's paper, and then I'll never have to think about it again.

Back in the living room, my tía Myrna shoots me a suspicious look, eyes focused on my phone. The rest of my tías bring out trays of coffee. They arrange plates with an assortment of desserts and carry them to my tíos. My tíos don't acknowledge them or say thank you. They just keep watching TV, expertly talking and chewing at the same time. I maneuver around them to pick up a mug of coffee, then add powdered Coffee-Mate to it. As I stir in the lumpy mix, Mamá Tere clucks her tongue.

"Ah, look at Belén. Takes her coffee just like her father."

This is what I imagine the start of an avalanche sounds like.

The first roar before the landslide.

Within a moment of my mamá Tere saying this, everyone else seems to chime in, too.

"Her hair, so thick like his," Tío Berto says.

Tía Myrna rolls her eyes. "And that mouth—always something to say."

"Ni sabes," Ava says, "you should see her when she's upset. They're like twins."

I bite my tongue and sip my coffee, feeling it spiral down my throat, warming the racing of my heart. My ma's family keeps going. After a while, their words stop filtering through my ears and disassemble in front of me. My body feels like it's separating from my skin and looking at itself from a new dimension, dampness pooling between the webs of my fingers. I feel my pa's photographed eyes fixate on mine, firm and final. And then I feel my tío Berto's hand on my shoulder, his eyes softened with wonder.

"¿Y cómo anda?" he asks. "Is he doing okay?"

I blink at him. "I don't know."

Tío Antonio shakes his head. "He was always nice to have around."

A chorus of praise erupts. They all speak about him in different tenses—past, present, future. The shift in time makes me nervous. I don't know how to remind them that he is still alive, but has willingly chosen to be away from us. That this isn't the type of thing you mourn, it is a type of behavior you scold.

Mamá Tere looks over at me. "Have you thought about calling him?"

The weight in my chest is replaced with heat, something boiling in my lungs. I look at my ma, who is frozen in place, coffee cup hanging midair. I want to look at Ava, but her laundromat lecture has been replaced by the sting of her comment. How could she add fuel to the fire? My mouth moves before my brain has the time to settle, and the questions that have been swirling in my head since spring spill from my lips.

"I mean he left us," I say. "Shouldn't he call first? To, like, apologize?"

Everyone turns to me, eyes glossy and wide and blinking.

All their attention diverted from their phone screens and their food now centered on me sitting here, with my pa's hair and mouth and attitude and audacity. I look past all their bodies to my ma. She's slumped forward, her shoulders curved, pinning toward the floor.

And I feel responsible somehow.

Tía Myrna cuts through the silence. She shakes her head, her hair whipping across her face. "Qué vergüenza," she says, "that you do not know how to present yourself since he has gone. Suddenly you can't pick up after your tíos anymore but can take a call from a boy. What kind of wife will you be?"

Sweat begins dripping past my fingertips, dropping onto the carpet like fat tears.

I don't tell my tía what I'm really thinking—that perhaps everyone should be concerned with the type of husband my pa was, the type of father he turned out to be.

All I said was the truth.

He left us.

But people, and families especially, don't want to hear the truth. The truth will set you free until it becomes an inconvenience.

I know what types of conversations they must all have privately, echoing the ones overheard from my pa's family—surely, we must've done something wrong. Maybe if my ma had cooked better, he would've stayed. Maybe if those girls weren't such an armful, he would've stayed. Maybe if they would've all satisfied his needs, he would've stayed.

But there is no keeping someone who has always wanted to go.

Somehow, it's still our fault. My fault. Even if I'm here, some kind of spitting image, telling them what I know to be true.

My ma leaves the room, her body bent and frail, the makeup she spent hours on smearing down her cheeks. She leaves a thick absence behind her, and Ava shakes her head at me with disgust as she follows her. My mamá Tere bites into a slice of the pie we brought, the only buffer I had now settling into her stomach.

"Qué pena," she says, "a girl who doesn't even want to talk to her father. What a lonely life it will be for him."

The room feels humid, the air dense. Everyone else starts eating pie and drinking coffee like none of this happened, like it was a casual part of our holiday conversation. I set my mug down on the table and lean back, staring at the ceiling again, anchored by the irony of how heavy loss can be. Wondering how no one has considered what a lonely life it has been for me.

SEVENTEEN

THE SUN IS BARELY RISING WHEN ALI PICKS ME UP. RAIN FALLS IN sheets. When I was younger and the rain would fall this heavy, my mamá Tere would say my guardian angel Gabriel was crying from all my misbehaving. I still don't think I did anything wrong last night, but this downpour begs to differ.

Raindrops thud against the roofs of unrecognizable cars. They all belong to our neighbors' family and friends, cramping up against the gutters and crisscrossing along the squares of grass in their front yards. Our driveway remains the same, just Ava's car, my ma's already missing.

I watch Ali try to find parking, then settle on turning on his emergency lights, the yellow and red flickers becoming smudges of color in the rain.

I do not want to do this.

I want to see Alexis. I want to be at his apartment. I want to do anything to get this feeling off my chest.

But I'm here.

Ali gets out of his car and pulls the hood of his jacket over his head, walking carefully around puddles as he heads to the front door. I bolt outside before he can even make it onto the steps, shutting the door behind me.

"Good morning," he says.

"Hey," I reply, throwing my hood over my head, "let's go."

He cocks his head back in surprise. "Wait," he says, "shouldn't I introduce myself to your mom or something?"

"Everyone's asleep," I lie, too embarrassed to admit that my ma isn't home. That she's never home. "Let's go."

The inside of Ali's car is unusually clean. The carpets look recently vacuumed and a dangling air freshener suspends from the rearview mirror, the smell of artificial pine thick in the air. The car itself is old, but meticulously cared for. So much better than Ava's car, which I never want to be in again after yesterday. After my ma cleaned herself up, we left. We said meek goodbyes and limply kissed everyone's cheeks before piling into the car, where Ava laid it on me thick.

"Was I not clear, Belén? What would make you say something so stupid like that? Don't you feel any shame?" Her words weaved from English to Spanish, which told me she was more angry than usual.

I didn't say anything.

I looked out the window at guests exiting houses, standing in the golden pools of porch lights, carrying leftover trays of food into cars.

Our car, except for our crouched bodies, was empty.

"I'm talking to you," Ava warned.

I rolled down the window. It wasn't raining, though I wished it was. It seemed appropriate. The air was acidic, teetering on some strange anticipation—its lack of fulfillment made me nervous.

Then, over the air whirring through the narrow slit of the window, I heard my ma start crying. Long sobs that weighed with sadness. Ava slammed on the brakes, stopping in the middle of a residential street. She turned on the overhead lights of the car and whipped her head back to look at me.

"Do you see what you did?" she shouted. "What is *wrong* with you? Why can't you just do what people need you to do? Is picking up a plate too much work? Is going to class too difficult? Is being quiet too hard?"

My ma gently put her hand on Ava's knee—either in my defense or in her support. I'm still not sure. Ava took a breath, an inhalation so deep that I watched her chest fully rise and fall. She pressed the tips of her nails into the leather seam of the steering wheel and turned off the overhead lights, blanketing us in darkness.

"You're going to end up worse," she said, then hit the gas.

She didn't have to explain for us all to know who she was talking about.

"Nice car," I say, buckling my seat belt while Ali settles into his seat.

He blasts on the heater, unfogging the windows around us. Little by little, I can see bits of my house becoming clear amid the wash of white. I wonder if Ava is looking through her own window, watching me.

This morning, in the shower, I was beginning to fear that maybe she was right.

As I watched the steamy water run over my body, I imagined it unpeeling my skin from my flesh. I wanted to study the color of my blood, hoping that it would not be the same shade of red as my pa's.

The worries in the laundromat were now realities, a truth that pressed against my ribs: a diploma was just a piece of paper. It was nothing compared to the weight of my body.

That realization made me not even want to get out of bed this morning. I felt like I couldn't, like my limbs were bloated with sadness. The only thing that got me up was knowing that if I didn't turn in this assignment, I'd only be sabotaging Ali.

Because for me, it didn't matter anymore.

Working on this essay didn't stop anybody last night from pointing out how similar my pa and I were. Graduation was nothing compared to my biological appearance—the true mark of similarity to my pa that I couldn't scrape off, no matter how much I wished I could.

So, what was the point?

Nothing could remove that connection to my pa.

Why try to be anything else anymore?

"I worked hard for it. I try to keep it clean," Ali says, buckling his seat belt.

He veers onto the road, winding around cars double-parked along the street. "I've never seen your hair like that."

I can tell he's trying to make conversation, trying to cut through the tension my sour attitude is creating. I glimpse at myself in one of the car's side mirrors. My hair, from all the humidity of the rain, sprung up into strange waves and dents this morning. Half of it looked like my pa's hair, and half of it looked like my ma's. I pulled it into my hood to try to hide it.

I don't really know what to say to Ali. I don't really know what to say at all. So I just say, "Yeah."

It's quiet again, so he connects his phone to an adapter, the trilling start of a Patrice Rushen song sounding through the speakers. The harp-like synth syncopates with the rain falling outside.

I look out to the skyline of Downtown Oakland, which warps beneath the rain. The Tribune Tower is smears of teal and pale orange, distorted into a memory of its shape. From the corner of my eye, I watch Ali open and close his mouth, still struggling to ease the tension.

"My ma likes this song," I offer, watching as Laney College drifts behind us.

"Your ma listens to this type of music?" he asks.

"Yeah," I say. My ma had once shared with me that listening to 102.9 KBLX had helped her learn English when she first came from México.

I tell Ali this, and he nods thoughtfully. I can almost see him smiling.

He drives through Downtown Oakland, passing Chinatown and turning toward Jack London Square. With the aftermath of the holiday and the early rise of the morning, the streets are empty, spare the workers lining the produce markets. Their arms swell as they lift cargo onto truck beds.

Ali parks, and we walk through the rain toward the tall,

169

illuminating windows of the Oakland Grill. Wooden booths line the center of the room, small tables along the perimeter. The warmth of the restaurant feels admittedly nice, almost breaking the coldness of my mood. I stand by the waiting area for a table, but Ali walks directly to a booth in the center, signaling me to follow along. I give him a look.

"Trust me," he says, "my mama used to work here. Me too, a little bit."

"You used to work here?" I ask, sitting across from him.

"Way back in the day," he says, taking off his jacket, "she would wait on tables and I would help the busboys wipe them down. She'd give me a cut of her tips."

Right then, a wide man approaches our table. His name tag says Gerardo. He sets two mugs of coffee in front of us. Ali stands, his shoulders softening as they swoop down like wings of a bird in flight, wrapping Gerardo in an embrace.

"Mijo," Gerardo says, "so tall. Who is your friend?"

I introduce myself, and Gerardo smiles at me, eagerly shaking my hand.

"Belén." He repeats my name, his face glowing with recognition. "Qué nombre tan lindo. Where Christ was born."

I crack a smile for the first time all morning, and Ali shoots me a look of exaggerated shock. Before Gerardo leaves, he explains to me that he has seen Ali grow up from when he was only so high, back when he had braces, back when he wore headphones bigger than his body. Then he gives Ali a bendición, crossing his thick fingers over his face.

Gerardo goes to wipe down empty booths, and Ali and I sit and sip our coffee. I stare into the darkness against the rim, trying to drink it black, the way my pa never would. But the bitterness makes me wince. I add creamer and look at the milkiness in the mug, feeling defeated.

"Belén," Ali says.

I look up. "Huh?"

"You good?"

"Just tired," I lie.

Ali slides me a menu in a thick, plastic sleeve. "Get whatever, it's on me. Well, it's on Gerardo."

"Oh," I say, "thank you."

We both order stacks of pancakes. While we wait for our food, Ali finishes his coffee and pulls his binder from his backpack. I try to glimpse at the new lyrics behind the plastic, but he opens the cover too quickly for me to see. We trade drafts of our statements, his hand-written on sheets of binder paper, mine printed. I look over his essay, which is already marked up in purple and red pen.

"Someone beat me to it," I joke. "What colors are left for me?"

"The purple pen is Ms. Barrera. The red pen is my mama's. I brought a blue pen, just for you."

I smile because I think he's kidding, but then he hands me a felt-tipped pen. Blue, as promised.

"OfficeMax?" I ask.

"OfficeMax," he repeats, nodding.

There's a pause, and it's kind of uncomfortable.

I half expect him to pull on his headphones and drown me out, like he does in Ms. Barrera's after-school sessions. But he just looks at me.

I don't have anything else to say, so I look beyond him, at the windows that stretch from the ceiling to the floor, their transparency making me feel exposed. Ali catches the hint and puts on his glasses.

We read silently.

Ali writes about his ma and her wide hands. How she multitasks with them, using one to work and one to pray. I learn she wakes up at four in the morning to take a shower, because by five in the morning all the hot water has been used up by everyone else in their apartment complex. After, she takes the bus in blue darkness to her first job. By lunchtime, she drives to her second.

Ali's father left a few months before Ali was born, but Ali has eavesdropped enough to construct pieces of his father's history. While his ma was pregnant, his father developed a gambling habit and gambled most of his ma's money away. This happened cyclically, to the point where she became homeless during a portion of her pregnancy. She slept in the back bench of her car, housed in the parking lots of places where she would work. By the time she had enough money to build herself back up and reconnect with him, his father was nowhere to be found.

Ali describes his ma's life after his father's departure like untangling hair. Pulling and pulling and pulling until something became undone, but tenderness remained. Ali lives in the cycle of looking at his reflection, looking at other men, wondering who he is, and wondering if they are his father.

This, he explains, is why he is applying to this prestigious school, to give back to his ma for all the sacrifices she made for him and to create new cycles for him to establish. The essay is tied in a bow of optimism, a bunch of hopeful promises about the future. But instead of making me feel inspired, it just makes me sad.

I didn't know Ali at all, and now I know him so deeply and so abruptly. It feels cutting, like pulling a shattered mirror from inside my body. And it's not like we're getting to know each other normally, but because he has to grovel with some admissions office to get into school.

I don't really have many corrections to make to his essay, so I put stars next to my favorite sections and add a fat smiley face to the bottom paragraph.

Then I sit there, gently tapping the pads of my fingers onto my knees, waiting for Ali to finish reading. He takes a long time, which is surprising. He didn't strike me as a slow reader. He flicks his pen across the page fluidly, and when he's finished, he begins reading my first paragraph aloud. My face feels warm, and I'm suddenly grateful the restaurant is empty.

"'I often catch myself speaking about my father in the past tense, as if he has died. My father is alive somewhere, though he is apart from me—divided by veins of the highway, while the blood in our veins shares the same red.'" Ali takes off his glasses and sets them on the table, his eyes still fixed on my paper. "This makes sense."

"What makes sense?" I ask.

"You're a great writer. It's like Ms. Foley said, great writers are great readers. You're always reading, so it makes sense." He pauses, then laughs. "But I didn't think it'd be *that* good, no offense to you. This is great, Belén. The whole thing."

I expect Ali to slide my paper back to me, but he looks down at it, his eyes skipping across the page as he rereads. I thought I'd feel embarrassed having him read such personal details about me and my pa and my family. No one has ever read anything I've written. I've never really written anything.

"Are you sure you don't want to apply? This would give you good leverage," he says.

"It feels like you kinda have to sell your sob story to have a shot. No offense," I say.

He nods. "I understand. You're right. But I have to play the game, you know? I can't risk it."

I slide his essay back over to him, pointing to my starred sections. "You should be fine. The essay is powerful—an orchestrated sob story, just like they want."

Right then, Gerardo brings out our breakfast. I watch Ali's wrists flex as he cuts his pancakes into perfectly proportionate squares, while I cut mine into sloppy triangles. We eat silently for what seems like a long time. It's so quiet that I can hear the dishwasher humming in the kitchen.

"Do you ever worry you're going to run into him?"

I shove a forkful of food into my mouth. "Run into who?" I mumble.

"Your dad," Ali says.

It suddenly feels difficult to swallow. I look outside, at the consequence of my misbehaving persistently pouring rain into the street gutters.

"Sometimes I worry," I say. "I guess I wouldn't really know what to do. I don't know who would say hi first. But I worry more that I'll keep hearing about him more than I worry that I'll see him."

"Why?" Ali leans forward, resting his chin on the heel of his hand.

"Because people never shut the fuck up about it," I say through a sigh. "It's all my family ever brings up, and if they're not bringing it up, they're just preparing to bring it up."

Ali nods, staring down at the glossy finish of the table. "Yeah," he says. "With me, nobody brings it up. It's like a shameful secret no one wants to discuss. So, if no one ever talks about him, I wonder what it would be like to see him. I don't even know if that man would recognize me, or if I'd recognize him."

"Your ma doesn't have his contact information?"

Ali shrugs. "She says she doesn't. But maybe that's for my own good."

"You think it's best you never know him?"

Ali leans back, pausing. "I don't know. I mean, you know your pa, right?"

"I guess so," I say. "I mean, I did. I don't feel like I know him anymore."

"Do you think it makes it worse?" he asks.

"Knowing him?"

"Yeah," he says. "Or, I guess, having known him. Sometimes I feel grateful. At least when I close my eyes and imagine my pa, I can imagine him as somebody good. I don't have the real thing in front of me to prove me otherwise." He rubs his fingertip along a smudge on the table. "But other times I feel so sad. Everybody says we look alike, but how do you live in the shadow of someone who's invisible? Sometimes I think it'd be better to just know."

I feel like Ali has plucked the words out of my brain and into the air.

It makes my stomach hurt.

"I guess it can be," I say. "It's not easy. I just feel like I know the truth and nobody else does. Now that my pa is gone, everything is pinned on my family. Like if we worshipped him more, he wouldn't have left. But I can't keep thinking about any imaginary scenario. The reality is, he left. And nobody wants to call it what it is—but he left."

"At least you know the truth. Maybe it is easier then, that you know him—knew him."

I shrug. "I don't think anything will make it easier. It's a double-edged sword. You never knew him and you're stuck imagining. I knew him and I'm stuck with the truth." I take a breath. "The worst part of it is my fucking family. Things are always harder when you're a girl."

"What do you mean?"

"In my family, I'm either the devil or an abandoned dog on the side of the road or something. Either I forced him to leave or I'm pitiful because I've been left." I sigh. "A man can choose to be your father and choose to leave you and people can believe it's your fault that he left you."

"Nobody in my family blames me. I can't even imagine that—it must be hard." He pauses. "I just think people expect me to *be* like him. I hear my mama praying at night about it. I try to remind her I am half of him, but I'm also half of her. Sometimes that works." He smirks. "And other times my mama kisses me before I go to school and stops me to say how much I look like my pa. I don't even know what to say when she gets on about that."

"Does she say it spitefully?" I ask, thinking of Ava in the car last night.

Ali shakes his head. "Nah. At least, I don't think so. It's more like a matter-of-fact thing. But when I'm acting up, it's a warning."

I smirk. "I guess I'm always acting up then."

Ali smiles at me, then looks down at the table.

We're silent.

After a moment, we agree to start working on our final drafts. I pull out Ava's laptop that she lends me for school assignments and begin editing my essay. When Gerardo comes to clear our plates, he drops off a computer for Ali. It's so old that I hear it wheeze when it starts up. I don't say anything to Ali, I don't want him to feel embarrassed, but he beats me to it.

"This is Gerardo's son's old computer," he explains. "For me, it was between the car and the laptop. I use the car to drop my mama off at work sometimes. So, I got the car."

I nod.

Ali continues. "I know nobody is gonna give me any type of opportunity unless I'm some shining star." He sighs, then looks back at his computer screen. A blue rectangle reflects in his glasses. "My mama doesn't know much about school, so she didn't know I had to be in the AP track to look good on college applications until it was too late to enroll. That's why I have to do this essay so well."

I nod again, closing my computer and sliding it across the table, feeling suddenly unworthy of using it for an assignment I don't care about, while Ali is scrambling to finish his. "Use mine."

He shakes his head. "Nah, it's not like that either. I got it."

We spend the rest of the morning revising. Ali never puts on his headphones, though sometimes I catch him slapping a beat against the table. When we finish editing, we pack up our things. Ali returns Gerardo's laptop to him, and we both thank him before we leave. By the time we're outside, only a faint mist of rain hovers in the air.

Instead of going back to Ali's car, we walk through Jack London Square. We stare at boats that anchor in the bay's water, at the towering cranes that stand stiff in the sky. Some of them stretch long like bridges, while others zigzag upward—the higher they are, the more oppressive they seem. We sit on a bench overlooking the water, Downtown Oakland behind us.

Ali leans forward, setting his elbows onto his knees, watching water lap against the rocky shore of the bay.

"I know it's all rigged. I'm not stupid," he says abruptly. "I know I have to sell what I've been through to get schools to care. I know it's not fair. But what else am I supposed to do, you know? My mama never got a chance to go to school—she had me. I try hard to prove to her that not everybody is gonna be like my pa because I know she worries—but *I* worry. Like, what if I do everything right? What if I'm the total opposite of him and go to school and get a degree and show up, and then I'm still just like him?"

I wish I could say something to reassure him.

But, hearing him say that just feels like something is ripping across my chest, my biggest fears stumbling out of his mouth and circling in the air around us. I don't tell him what I'm beginning to believe, which is that we can try as much as we want, but maybe we'll end up like our fathers because of our habits, our genetics. That I worry there's no use trying. That I just want to give up. That really, I already have.

But instead I say, "Yeah."

"At least we're in it together," he says, half-heartedly, like he's just trying to fill a space too.

I nod, looking at the water in front of us, coming and going in cycles like everything else we've known. The overhead drizzle pings into the bay like marbles, like dust, like memory. As light as it is, it feels heavy over us.

EIGHTEEN

WHEN MY PARENTS TOLD ME AND AVA ABOUT THEM IMMIGRATING to this country, they described it as a curtain that divided their lives into a before and an after, change nestled somewhere at the center of that partition. Sometimes they'd tell us about what they saw, what they witnessed, but most days they'd just tell us that they just try to forget.

At times, my ma says this is where she lost my pa, someone who actively attempted to erase his memory with other things, other people, other women. My ma describes it all—coming over, gaining him, losing him—as the type of growing pain that throbs along the stretch marks of her brain.

Like my parents' story, everything I know about the Barragón family's migration is told to me in pieces of reconstructed history.

Leti heard this once, then overheard that, then was told this in spite. From what she's learned, she's explained to me that her parents' migration story is the scariest thing she's ever heard. Worse than the time in the seventh grade when Marta López told her about Bloody Mary appearing in the library's bathroom mirror. And that's saying a lot for Leti.

I remember Leti leaning her head against the bus window that was etched with graffitied initials, proving that someone else had been here before us.

"I think that's what made them how they are today," Leti said, thinking of her parents. "They think they've been through the worst life has to offer, so anything they do can't be half as bad. I don't know if that's true. I don't think it's right. It just is what they think."

That's why, when I sit on the vinyl-covered couch in the Barragón living room, I feel sweat beading behind the creases of my knees. I don't know what's going to happen. It's Sunday afternoon, right after church, and Leti, her ma, and her pa just got home. They're still dressed in their church clothes—ironed shirts, starched pants, lace-trimmed socks. Quentin and his parents are supposed to be here any minute in their own Sunday Best, to announce he and Leti are having a baby. And I'm here to serve as a mediator, or as a witness. The only thing looping around in my brain are Leti's words on that bus ride: *I think that's what made them how they are today.*

I know whatever empathy the Barragóns gained crossing the border will find its limit when they learn Quentin is the father of this baby.

Even if their racism is plainly clear, Leti's parents believe all the harm they faced in their migration somehow makes them exempt from inflicting harm on others. How could they be racist when a border denied them access? How could they make someone feel unwelcome when they were still undocumented? How could they cause pain when they are still wounded?

I fidget on the couch, the plastic liner squeaking beneath me. Leti told her ma I was coming over to help her study for a test. But when her ma notices that we aren't going to Leti's room like usual, and instead are sitting side by side on the couch, she moves her hands to her hips.

"Your pa is going to watch TV here," she tells Leti. "You and Belén need to go somewhere else."

Señor Barragón glances over at us but doesn't really look at us. It's as if our bodies are transparent, blending into the nothing of the plastic on the sofa.

He's wearing a shirt that's too tight, a midsection button almost snapping in half, revealing a slice of his skin. Though I haven't seen him in a while, his stench of cologne and Tecate are familiar to me. He stretches, his back cracking like old firewood, and then plops down onto his La-Z-Boy.

"Mamá," Leti tells her ma, "I need to tell you something."

Señora Barragón gives Leti an up-down, then fixes her eyes on Leti's stomach. Leti nods. I try to dig my nails into the fabric of the couch, but they bend against the thick plastic covering, searing pain through my palms. Right then, I hear footsteps coming from the bottom of the duplex's stairs. Señor Barragón stands, peers through the blinds, and waves his hand for Leti to get the door.

Leti moves a centimeter, her body pushing forward with the abruptness of someone shielding a passenger from the harsh stop of a car.

But after she moves, she freezes.

She and her ma stare at each other, wondering who will move first. Before anything can be said, I stand up and open the door.

Quentin stands there in a navy-blue suit, holding flowers from a street vendor in one hand and a pink cardboard box from La Peña Panadería in the other. His parents hover behind him, weary smiles on their faces. Had he been any other color, he might be praised as the boyfriend of the year. Modest clothes, nice cologne, a fresh shave, and bringing something for both hosts. An applause and a toast for a husband in the making.

But he is him. He is Black.

I lock eyes with Quentin, who doesn't say anything to me. He just flattens his lips into a hard line, takes a deep breath, relaxes his shoulders, and stands tall as he walks inside, his parents in tow.

I shut the door behind them and set the flowers and pan dulce onto the coffee table. Señora Barragón's eyes bloom into two brown moons. She snaps her head from Leti to Quentin, Quentin to Leti, and even looks at me at some point, her expression mixed with disbelief and disgust. Señor Barragón looks at me with his eyebrows knitted together in confusion, wondering what my guests are doing in their house.

"Hi," Quentin says, "my name is Quentin. These are my parents, Martin and Denisse. I'm a friend of Belén and Leticia's. Really, more Leticia's."

His words suspend in the air, arcing over the Barragón family's heads. Silence spreads among the seven of us. I see Leti open her mouth to say something, but air clogs her throat. I realize then that Señor and Señora Barragón have no idea what Quentin is saying, and I begin translating. Señor Barragón leans back in his La-Z-Boy and sips his beer, eyeing Quentin with precision.

Just then, Leti stands up and gestures for Quentin to sit beside her. He sits on her left side, and I sit on her right side. Quentin's parents say hello and remain standing. When Señor Barragón does not greet them, they look at him with concern. Meanwhile, Señora Barragón gawks at them. It looks as though she wants to leave but is held by the gravity of her incredulity. When Quentin sits next to Leti, he keeps a measured distance. My body might fit between the two of them. I scoot closer to Leti, so that she feels I am with her.

Despite Leti gaining the strength to invite Quentin to sit beside her, when it is time for her to speak, her lips can only part. I look around the living room, at the knitted doilies Señora Barragón has placed on every imaginable surface of the house. At the family pictures on the end tables. At the freshly vacuumed lines in the carpet. At the crucifix of Jesus's pale body nailed above the door, which I can feel Quentin's parents are looking at too.

"¿Y qué?" Señor Barragón grunts.

I expect us to be blanketed in more silence, but Leti speaks abruptly. "Pa, estoy embarazada."

Back when I used to pay attention in school, one of the only lessons that really absorbed into my memory was one on Spanish false cognates. Mr. Uribe wrote "embarazada" and "embarrassed" in neat print on the board. He explained to us with a laugh that while these two words sounded similar, they did not mean the same things at all.

"One is a moment of shame, and the other is a moment of joy," he said, before wiping the whiteboard clean.

I wonder what Mr. Uribe would think now, when Leti tells her father that she is pregnant, and immediately hangs her head in the type of shame reserved for the confession booth. I look at Señor Barragón, whose eyes are centered on Quentin.

In the brief moment of stillness, I remember when Leti first found out she was pregnant. We lay stomach-down on my bed, watching all sorts of movies about teen pregnancy, predicting the formulaic nature of the telling-the-parents scene: expressed disappointment, a brief lecture, always followed by concern and care—sometimes even love. Those families, like Quentin's family, would embrace and say, "This isn't ideal, but we will get through it."

But those families were not the Barragóns.

Instead of saying anything, Señor Barragón finishes off his beer in four loud glugs and sends the bottle flying across the room, where it shatters along the front door. I don't realize that I'm holding Leti's hand until we lift our arms to shield ourselves from the oncoming bits of glass.

Then, Señor Barragón unhinges his jaw, speaking so quickly that all his words slur together. He begins saying what Leti has been fearing for her entire life—that she was a disappointment to him the moment she was born, because he had always wanted a son. Because he knew women did this, open their legs and waste the potential they were given. And what a waste she was. Didn't she realize that all the weight he carried on his shoulders when he crossed a border was given to her to carry? And how useless all that weight has become—she was supposed to go to school, to pay for their expenses, to make their life comfortable. How dare she destroy all the work he put in to give her this life? Did she know he walked miles barefoot to catch a train through México? Did she know he was detained twice? Did she know he slept in the trunk of a car? Did she know women like her go to hell? Did she know men like Quentin go to prison?

Señora Barragón looks horrified. I'm not sure what she is upset about—her daughter having a baby with a Black man or her husband verbally abusing a group of kids. She answers my question by looking directly at Quentin and shaking her head. Her pale skin shades green, her hand hovers toward her mouth. She scurries out of the living room, to the bathroom.

When she first found out Leti was pregnant, her lecture really halted there. She reminded Leti of all she had done for her and all Leti was giving away. But in Señora Barragón's absence, Señor Barragón seems to multiply.

Quentin's parents' eyes are wide, their shock palpable. They study Señor Barragón closely, watching as he rises from his recliner. He begins yelling at me, blue veins bulging beneath his neck. Me and my big hips and big chest just asking for it all the time, of course I've rubbed off on his only daughter. What a shame there is no one at my house to watch me and what I do, that there was no father to raise me, because having his daughter be around me was like watching mold spread onto fresh fruit.

And then he points a finger at Quentin.

I stare at his yellowing fingernails and think of how the webbed curve between his thumb and index finger looks like a gun. His face blazes red, like summertime pavement, like the end of a hot day, like he is running out of air. He gasps for air like a fish lunging out of water, calling Quentin a mayate, calling him and "his kind" disgusting, and damns his own lack of money for never pulling his family out of an area crawling with so many people like him to prevent this from happening.

Those movies missed all the intricacies.

They missed race, migration, weight.

They missed Quentin's expression, struggling between standing up for himself and keeping himself safe. They missed Leti's sadness, the kind that does not have sobbing, the kind that is blanketed in silence. They missed Quentin's father walking toward Señor Barragón, palms outstretched in defense of his son. They missed Quentin's mother, looking to me to translate something I can't fully understand myself. They missed my heart thumping in the rhythm of what do I do what do I do?

I decide to wait until Señor Barragón is finished to say anything. It feels unsafe to interrupt him.

But then he begins pointing his finger right at Quentin's father's face with this enraged look in his eye that only comes when someone is going to do something irreparable. I stand up.

I've never been this close to Señor Barragón, I have avoided it with expertise. But with my proximity, I realize there is something amazing about him. The decibel of his voice, the candor of his yelling, the magnitude of his force reminded me so much of my pa. I haven't been so close to a father figure in so long—nothing had paralleled my pa's similarities like this, not even my own reflection. Loss panged in my chest, thrumming with the memory of what I no longer had.

And at the same time, Señor Barragón's demeanor, his disgust, his denial of his own daughter, reminded me enough of my pa that I was grateful he was gone.

I swallow the feeling, approaching Señor Barragón slowly. From here he is smaller than I could have imagined, his chin barely hovering over my hairline. He reminds me of my younger cousins, who puff their chests with pride but who never close their hands to form a fist. I look at him and gesture for him to back away, to sit down. Whatever he can say to Leti, I know he will say to her in our absence, but he cannot say those things to Quentin or his family or me.

"Señor," I tell him, "I know you are angry. But, please, calm down."

He then mimics his daughter, air lodged in his throat, his face softening from a stark red to a pale pink. I watch his eyes scan over me as he thinks of the words to say. But, instead of saying anything, he looks beyond me, eyes settled on Leti and Quentin as he shakes his head. He spits onto the carpet, walks toward his bedroom, and slams the door shut.

Leti immediately exhales, then puts her head between her knees. I wonder if the baby can feel her breathe along the curve of her stomach. Quentin sits stiffly, mannequin-like atop the sofa, his eyes fixed on the lines in the carpet. His parents stand by the front door, heads shaking. I wonder if Quentin had prepared them for the potential of this interaction, or if he had some spark of hope this would turn out better than the promised reality.

I move near Leti, sitting on the arm of the couch, and put my hand on her shoulder.

"I'm sorry he said all those things," Leti says between jagged breaths, "you know how he is. I'm not saying it's okay. You just know how he is."

Quentin stands up, walks past his parents, and exits the duplex.

I peer toward the kitchen, then look at Leti. "Maybe you should talk to him alone."

Quentin and I sit on the steps outside.

After a week of rain, it is oppressively sunny. The sunlight beats down onto us, so pure and bright and miserable. I watch through its clear-yellow rays as people pass along Foothill, washing their cars, going to church, playing soccer in the street, enjoying their Sunday of normalcy. Quentin peers toward the steps, watching his parents walk toward their car. After a long conversation, followed by a longer hug, he asked to wait here to speak to Leti alone. His parents initially refused to go, refused to leave him alone with Señor Barragón inside. They only relented when Quentin compromised, saying they could supervise from their car across the street.

Quentin watches them lean against their sedan, their protectiveness felt through the distance.

He turns to me, sadness softening his eyes. "What's all that stuff he called you?" he asks.

I click my tongue. "All sorts of things—a slut, a whore, all these comments about my body."

"I'm sorry," he says.

"It's not your fault."

He lets out a breath. "When we told my parents, they weren't happy. But this is something I wasn't prepared for. How come they're like that?" he asks, his legs stretching forward onto the steps.

"Her parents?"

"No," he says, "all of you." He shakes his head. "I mean, some of you. I don't know. Sometimes it feels like all of you. Things like this always happen—I get called all kinds of shit by Mexicans."

I turn my gaze from the car wash to Quentin. "I think they think they've had it bad. And they have, I'm not saying it's easy for them. But I think people like Leti's family, like my family sometimes, think people treat us like shit, so we can't treat other people like shit. If people discriminate against us, we can't discriminate against anyone else. It's not true, though," I say. "Obviously."

"I keep asking Leti why two things can't be true," Quentin says.

I nod. "I wish I could answer that for you."

He pauses. In the quiet, I can hear the kids playing soccer in the street shouting at each other to move, huddling their makeshift team along the sidewalk when cars pass. After the traffic clears, they keep playing. Quentin opens and closes his mouth a number of times.

Finally, he asks, "What's that word he called me mean?"

I pause.

Since our last conversation, I anticipated Señor Barragón would call him that. I prepared mentally on how to tell him what it meant, hoping Leti would be the one who would break the news, but my imagined self is so much braver than who I am today.

I almost consider lying for Quentin's sake, but he deserves to know the truth.

He deserves to know who his child's grandparents really are.

I look ahead, at one of the kids playing soccer miming a "T" for a time-out, all of time suspended around us.

I take a deep breath. "It literally means the black beetles that feed off animal feces. But people mainly use it for its slang. In Spanish, it basically means the N-word."

He lets out a long breath and sets his elbows onto his knees.

"I'm sorry," I tell him.

We're back to being quiet.

After a few minutes, we hear the door behind us close. We both jump. It's Leti, with her arms full of Quentin's offerings. Quentin takes the bouquet of flowers, the petals wilted and brown, and I grab the panadería box. The three of us sit along the steps, with me in the middle.

"What happened?" I ask Leti.

"He tried to hit me," she says, "but my ma got in the way. She said people probably already knew I was expecting, so if I got hurt, it would only be more embarrassing for them."

Quentin's eyebrows jump high, nearly touching his hairline. "She stepped between you to save your family embarrassment? Not to help you?"

"Yes," Leti and I say in unison.

"This isn't right," Quentin says. "What if you get hurt? Should we call somebody?"

"No," Leti replies. "I found out that if anybody ever called Child

Protective Services, it could risk my parents being deported. Besides, I'm almost eighteen."

"Which means what?" Quentin asks.

"Which means I won't have to be around them as much. I'll get into Berkeley and be at least twenty minutes away. I won't have to think about them."

"It's not that simple," Quentin says. I hear the rising anger in his voice. "Berkeley isn't even that far. They'll be around. If your parents call me that word, what do you think they'll call our kid?"

Leti is quiet.

Quentin looks at her. "Leti. What do you think they'll call our kid?"

I turn to look at her, but her gaze is set forward, watching as the soccer ball below us passes between traffic cones. When she catches me staring, she pulls at the base of her braid so it widens, her hair concealing her profile. Quentin stands up, positioning his body in front of Leti, shielding her from the sun.

"Leti," he says, "you are a coward."

For the first time today, she looks at him. Her brown eyes scan upward, fixing on his. She opens her mouth. I'm praying for her to say something, to say anything, but she closes her lips.

"You're a coward!" Quentin repeats, almost laughing in his disbelief. "I know this is hard." He breathes. "I know your family is difficult. I've been trying my best to be helpful—but if you're just going to sit there and not answer a basic question that affects me and our *child*, I can't even be here right now."

Quentin leans his legs forward, stretching them wide enough to walk down the steps two at a time, his grip tight around the bouquet.

I look at Leti, who is still gazing ahead.

"You should go," she says.

"Are you sure?" I ask.

She nods.

I follow behind Quentin, pastries rattling against the cardboard box in the long way down. I feel Leti getting smaller behind me as I approach the sidewalk, where Quentin is beelining toward his parents. When he senses me behind him, he doesn't turn around. He walks faster and calls to me from over his shoulder.

"Thank you for being here, Belén. I feel the least I could do is give you a ride home, but I need to be alone for a little bit."

"That's okay," I say over the noise of the traffic around us. "I'll see you."

A bus approaches right as I get to the stop. I shuffle inside and sit by a window, balancing the box of bread on my lap. I open it and see the array of pan that Quentin selected stacked in heaps, disorganized.

I imagine Quentin at the bakery, carefully using the metal tongs to set pastries onto a tray. I imagine him calculating the cost of a good impression in his head. I imagine him walking down the street amid a crowd of people who double take at him.

And then I imagine Leti cowering beneath the shadow of her pa, the box being flung at her head and crashing into the wall behind her.

I stare at the bed of crumbs in the box and fish out a cookie. It's pale yellow, a lopsided smiling face piped atop the surface with red gel icing. I take a bite as the bus depresses its brake, a loud hiss sizzling in my ears before it pulls onto the street. I look out the window.

From here, I see Quentin approaching his parents. He slams the bouquet down onto the pavement and clenches his fists. They're balled so tightly, like all of the afternoon is being vacuumed into his palms. His father steps toward him, attempting to embrace him, but Quentin shakes his head. Instead, he unclenches his hands and spreads his palms wide to grab the roof of the car. With his head craning low, I watch his chest heave up and down, weeping into the relentless sunshine.

NINETEEN

THE THURSDAY AFTER THANKSGIVING BREAK, I WAIT WITH LETI BY HER locker. I lean against a bulletin board while she dumps textbooks into one of her bags. I try to talk to her before going to Ms. Barrera's room to do my reading and hang out with Ali. I like to read there now since being home with Ava makes me want to die. She won't even look in my direction since Thanksgiving, which I'm almost grateful for. So, I stay in Ms. Barrera's room until it's dark out, and Ali usually gives me a ride home afterward.

I ask Leti what she's up to, but she gives me the silent treatment. I shift my gaze across the way, where Quentin usually waits for her in the AP hall.

But today, and for the past few days, Quentin is nowhere to be found.

"Where's Quentin?" I ask Leti.

She shrugs in response.

"I haven't seen him in a few days. Is he okay?"

She shrugs again.

I cock my head back. "Leti, stop. Where is he?"

"I don't know, Belén." She slams her locker shut. "I'm not with him every second of every day." She turns on her heels and begins walking toward the double doors that lead outside.

"You're not going to the library?" I ask, following behind her.

She shakes her head. "My ma wants me home every day after school since she found out."

I roll my eyes at Señora Barragón's delayed attempt at discipline.

Leti moves to push the door open, but I stop her. "You should talk to Quentin," I say. "He seemed pretty upset after he left on Sunday."

"I know he's upset." She sighs, setting one of her bags of books on the floor and pushing loose hair behind her ears. "He won't talk to me."

"Oh." I purse my lips.

"His mom called me. She says that he's really upset and that she's concerned. She thinks that we should try talking to my parents again. By myself, or with them."

"That does sound like a good idea," I agree.

"No it isn't, Belén," she says, her tone short. "It wouldn't help—you know how my family is."

I try not to give her a look, but my face can't help it. It twists in disappointment.

I know telling Leti when she's wrong is practically pointless, but I can't stop thinking about how she wouldn't answer Quentin's question. The entire bus ride home, I thought about Quentin's face sinking when I explained what Señor Barragón had called him. Every time I replayed it, I felt weight scrape across my chest. The denial from a family member, blood-related or not, reminded me of my pa.

By the time I got home, all I could do was lie in bed. I prayed for Alexis to call, to invite me to his apartment, to lift some of the burden from my body. Instead, the weight rose and fell as I breathed, growing heavier as I watched the black of the phone wires disappear into the dark. If I'd felt so terrible, I couldn't imagine how Quentin felt.

"Leti," I say. I look right at her, and she shifts her gaze to the floor, "what your pa said to him was awful."

"I know, Belén."

"And your ma didn't help. She didn't say anything, which can be just as bad. Maybe Quentin's mom is right, maybe—"

"I *know*, Belén," she snaps.

I hold my hands up. "Sorry," I tell her.

She picks up her bag from the floor and slips outside, not bothering to say goodbye as she slams the doors behind her.

I sit by the tall windows in Ms. Barrera's classroom. She's behind her desk, eyes squinted while she reads an essay. Ali walks in wearing a colorful sweater, his headphones tight over his ears. Before we went to Oakland Grill over the break, he usually sat at least two rows ahead of me, but lately, we sit next to each other.

Since we've been hanging out, we don't really talk about our personal statements, or any of the things we shared at the restaurant, which I appreciate. Instead, I'll read while he listens to music and does his homework.

He sits beside me and slings his headphones from his ears to his neck, a beat flowing into the room. "What're you reading today?" he asks.

I flash him the cover of my book, a collection of short stories by Kali Fajardo-Anstine that Ms. Barrera recommended to me. "This book called *Sabrina and Corina*. You?"

He flashes me the screen of his phone. "'All for You' by Little Brother. It has one of my favorite Phonte verses."

I nod at him. He slips his headphones back over his ears and pulls his OfficeMax pens from his backpack, prepared to start his homework. I turn back to my book when I notice Ms. Barrera waving her hand at me, gesturing for me to join her at her desk.

I sit across from her, my eyes squinted in suspicion as she smiles at the essay she's reading. She sets it down, caps her pen, and looks at me.

"I have some things for you," she says, eagerness ringing in her tone. She hands me the essay in her hands. It's the personal statement I'd turned in on Monday, a bright A at the top. "Ms. Foley gave this to me in the staff lounge. Congratulations, Belén. You should feel so proud of yourself."

I stare at the words on the page. I'd only written them a few weeks ago, but none of them resonated with me today. Holding them was like holding hollow hope in my hands. Ms. Barrera looks at me, waiting for me to say something, waiting for me to feel something.

But I feel awful.

Here I was, holding the physical evidence that I would graduate, absolute proof I was not going to be exactly like my pa. And here I was, looking at my own hands and thinking of how much they looked like his.

The spiral in my chest starts spinning. Ms. Barrera swivels in her chair, pulling a brochure from behind her and sliding it across the desk. It's from Laney College.

I blink at her. "What's this?"

"Belén, I was blown away by your personal statement," Ms. Barrera says, clearing her throat. "Let me be clear: I'm not telling you to apply to college. It's too late now anyway. I'm just saying that you could save your personal statement, work on your grades at community college, and reconsider next year."

"Next year?"

She nods, her curls bouncing around her shoulders. "Yeah. Many people take gap years or go to community college. I did."

"*You* did?" I glance behind her, at her framed diplomas from Berkeley, at the gilded font Leti is always talking about.

Ms. Barrera sips her coffee. "Absolutely. Most people think it's a straight shot to college, but lots of people take different routes to get there. I had the grades, but I didn't have the money. I was too devastated to even try community college, so I took the year to work and save up. But I think you should consider it."

"Community college?"

She nods again. "It's affordable, but you can get financial aid. And you can live at home to save money." She sighs. "Belén, you're *very* smart. Most people who get into school don't have half the brain that you do. If it goes well, I can help you transfer."

I stare at her.

The longer I look at her, the worse I feel. The coiling in my chest circles faster with every passing moment that I think, *Is this it?* Scaling upward in goal after goal, trying to prove I was not like my pa, only to plummet and prove something that was already decided? Something my body reminded me of every day?

Ms. Barrera keeps looking at me, and I feel my heart begin pounding. She opens her mouth to speak when we're interrupted by my phone buzzing in my pocket.

It's Alexis.

Thank God.

"Hold on," I blurt.

I rush into the hallway, staring at my phone in disbelief. Though I'd been praying for him to call, I understood why he didn't. I kept replaying our last conversation again and again in my head, kicking myself each time. I should have just played it cool. I should have kept everything going. I should have said nothing at all.

I look at my phone, then look ahead at a tall water fountain, my body distorted in its steel-paneled reflection. I feel a cooling rush of relief flood into my stomach.

"Hey," Alexis says instantly, his voice smooth on the other line.

I feel heat pinch my cheeks. "Uh, hey."

"It's Thursday," he says matter-of-factly. "I'm out of classes early if you want to stop by. Maybe we could get dinner."

I feel my mouth hang open.

Was it just this easy?

Was he just gonna forget the whole thing?

"Oh, I—"

He cuts me off. "The next train leaves in fifteen minutes."

I rush back into class and tell Ali I'll be leaving early. Before he can offer me a ride, I snatch my backpack from my desk and sling it over my shoulders. Ms. Barrera's eyes follow me as I breeze through the door. I think I hear her call out to me, but I can't be sure. The sound of her voice is warped by the memory of Leti's departure: without saying goodbye, and with the doors slamming behind me.

TWENTY

THE NEXT DAY, I HELP LETI ORGANIZE THE GUEST LIST FOR HER PAR-ents' annual Posada. Besides all their hypocrisy, it's the most Catholic thing the Barragóns do.

Every year, rain or shine, they pull the hand-sewn costumes from their storage closet and reenact María and José's journey to the manger to birth Jesús. Each year thus far, Leti has dressed up as the Virgin Mary. I point out the irony in it this year, but she says I'm being offensive.

Leti is sitting across from me at my kitchen table, peering at the names on the guest list. We're responsible for double-checking the list and sending the mail-in invites. Nobody really mails invitations anymore, but Señora Barragón says it's a sign of tradition. Whatever. We would usually be at her house so that she could approve the list and criticize us for sticking the stamps on crookedly, but since I was there for the news about the baby, her parents don't really want to see me.

"Are you sure it's okay that I come?" I ask Leti.

"You have to come, Belén. Your family is always invited. If you guys don't come, it'll look bad."

I want to tell her she sounds exactly like her ma, but I glance at the guest list. "Why does Señora Hernández hyphenate her last name? If your last name is already Hernández, why make it Hernández twice?"

"Because it's traditional, Belén. Cross her name out, anyway. She's in México for the holidays."

I cross Señora Hernández-Hernández and her family off the list, feeling satisfied. "I don't think I'd ever hyphenate my last name, it's already so long. Like, imagínate. Belén Dolores Itzel del Toro-Juarez?"

Leti doesn't look up from her list. "Where'd the Juarez come from?"

"That's Alexis's last name."

Leti holds her bulging stomach, gripping at it like she's about to be sick. "Stop, Belén."

"What?" I ask. "I can't be excited?"

"Excited for what? You're not his girlfriend, let alone his wife."

"I know, but—"

Her eyes dart to mine, squinted beneath the mass of her brows. She lowers her voice to a whisper. "You gave him a *blow job*. I know. Please, let's get through the list."

"Nobody's here, Leti." I laugh. "You can say it louder."

She shakes her head and presses her short nails against the temples of her forehead, wrinkles springing to her skin.

After it happened, Leti was the first person I told. I pressed my phone to my cheek in the back seat of my Uber and told her I didn't care how stressed or upset she was, that I needed to tell someone about it.

Everything happened so quickly. On the way to Alexis's apartment, I leaned my head against the window of my BART train. I gazed at the passing Coliseum, at the slate of stations, at the gray of the sky. I watched Oakland blur beneath my body, feeling like I was flying.

Nothing else but that feeling mattered.

Even if Alexis immediately pulled me into his room, even if the thought of Alexis maybe having a girlfriend kept seeping into my brain, even if something deep in my stomach told me something was wrong. I pushed it all away.

Once we lay on his bed, the rush of everything was so intense.

The mattress didn't feel as small, and we touched everywhere we hadn't before.

I'd never touched a penis before, but it felt warmer than I expected it to, and hairier too. Were guys not expected to shave? I thought back to all the porn I'd watched, and I couldn't remember if the guys had pubes or not. All the women had their hair waxed bare or manicured into stars or strips.

I don't know what I expected a penis to smell like, but that definitely was *not* it. The potent smell of sweat and oil filled my nostrils, making me want to gag.

It tasted even worse.

I stopped breathing through my nose and breathed through my

mouth as much as I could, my jaw aching. I mimicked what I'd seen people do in porn, realizing those people were really professionals. I tried to pretend I knew what I was doing, but no amount of porn could have prepared me for this.

All those videos made it look easy. Made it look fun.

I felt like puking.

But the feeling afterward was nothing like the feeling during. All the weight accumulated on my chest from looking at the personal statement began uncoiling from my body. I lay there, euphoric, waiting for Alexis to reciprocate, wondering how much better I'd feel after. But Alexis didn't move. Instead, once he was finished, he turned away from me, grabbed his phone, and called for an Uber.

I look at Leti. "Can I invite him?"

"Who?"

"Alexis."

Leti sighs, looking down at her list again. "I mean, I guess. I don't think he'll come, but you can invite him."

"What do you mean you don't think he'll come?"

She shrugs. "Like, why would he come, you know? You're not together or anything."

I wave her off. "Yeah, whatever."

"Can you go get the songbooks from your ma's room now?"

My ma was always responsible for the Posada songbooks. She had made them ages ago, with blurry lyrics printed atop festive construction paper, distorted images of Jesús and manger animals stretching between the verses.

Leti had been bugging me about them for days. But I'd been

avoiding my ma's room since it turned into just my ma's room. Back when she shared it with my pa, I never really thought about it. But now when I pass her door, I always hold my breath.

I sigh and get up, standing in front of my ma's door, peering through the slit, watching the gray of the sky spill onto her bedsheets. I push the door open, breath held, and crouch beside her mattress. I dig below her bed for her storage containers, pulling the closest one toward my chest. I snap off the plastic lid and fish my hand inside, reaching for the songbooks. But instead, I pull out a stack of photos.

All of them with my pa in them.

During my ma's annual spring-cleaning routine in April, she removed all the photos of my pa from the house. She didn't even replace the photos with anything either. Instead, the living room walls displayed frames of nothing. By May, Ava had put the frames in the storage closet. The walls have been bare since.

I never knew what my ma did with the pictures. I guess this is it.

I shove my hand back into the box and pull a pile of T-shirts that have been folded my ma's signature way, with creases sharp enough to draw blood. All of them are my pa's size, extralarge, and smell faintly of the cologne we'd buy him every Christmas. The scent makes me nauseated—my nostrils overwhelmed with the smell of musk and memory.

I push everything back into the box, then pause at a photo of me as a child. I pull it up and see my pa is seated beside me in the picture, the two of us at the Mormon Temple in the Oakland Hills.

Though we're not Mormon, my ma would drag us there every winter to see the Christmas display. I used to mistake the temple for

Disneyland because of its similarity to a castle—towering over Oakland, glowing warmly at night. My ma would guide us through the Christmas lights and force us to take pictures in front of the life-sized nativity scene. The figures were made of hollowed plastic and lit from inside, manger animals illuminating the pathway of palm trees.

My ma positioned my pa and me near a camel, holding her camera at eye level. I remember not wanting to smile, my cheeks sagging off my face. Still, she pushed us closer together, singing a parodied version of that Juan Gabriel song she sang every time my pa and I shared a similarity—which, apparently, was always.

"Se parece tanto a ti," she sang, her breath clouding white in the winter air. She gestured to my pa with a sweeping arm as she sang, and I could feel him stiffen beside me, his expression stoic. He also hated smiling for pictures. I sat rigidly on his lap, his arms awkwardly draped around my waist, our mouths twin scowls.

I pinch the photo between my fingers, beginning to hear everyone's voice winding in my mind—the same wide cheeks, the same curly hair, the same dark eyes. I shove the pictures back into the box and push it deep under the bed, as far into the corner as it can go.

I hand Leti the songbooks. I found them after painstakingly rummaging through five other boxes full of my pa's things. When I finally got them, it felt impossible to move. I lay on the floor for a while, watching the afternoon strain through the window and swell onto my body.

Leti stands up to grab them, triggering the motion-detected Santa my ma bought from the Coliseum Pulga years ago. It's so old that the robotic choreography is contorted and sad, the lyrics to "Jingle Bell Rock" muffled in the speaker. It's our only decoration up this year and looking at it makes me want to die.

Leti studies the songbooks in her palms for a moment. Then, she blurts, "If you're going to do it with him, you need to be careful."

I blink at her.

"You should get on the pill or something, make sure you bring condoms."

I slump beside her in my chair. Her tone is panicked, urgency sharp in her voice, as if I'm about to make the biggest mistake of my life. I look at her. Even with her stomach stretching, it's hard to imagine her doing anything like that. "Did it hurt?"

"Come on, Belén," she said, putting her list down. "I don't want to talk about this."

"You brought it up!"

"For *you*." Her eyes widen.

I give her a look. We've talked about it before, in her alarmed state after she realized her period was late.

She sighs. "No, it didn't hurt. It just felt kind of like stretching something out a little. Tight."

I nod. "I shouldn't worry?"

She shrugs. "I don't know. Everybody's different. I don't know how stretched out you are."

I smack my lips, smiling a little bit. "And he had condoms?" I ask, imagining the humiliation of going to a drugstore to buy condoms myself.

"Yeah, but you never know. That's why I'm saying to be extra careful—don't be tonta like me."

I look at her. She doesn't look embarrassed today, more matter of fact. It's hard to tell with her sometimes. Some days, she's settled with her circumstance. Other days, her throat is too enclosed with guilt to speak.

Leti lowers her head, looking back at the guest list, signaling the end of the conversation.

I look toward Ava's door, my shoulders deflated. Even if she were home, I know she'd never have this talk with me. Her hands would glue to her hips, her voice would rise, and I'd immediately get lectured. Then I look at my ma's door, promising emptiness in more ways than one.

"How come you did it?" I ask Leti earnestly.

It feels embarrassing and backwards asking her about sex, but I don't know who else to ask. Leti exhales sharply through her nose, clearly annoyed, then looks at me. My gaze, stained with sincerity, makes her eyes soften. "Because I was never allowed to do anything fun," she says. "And because I wanted to. You want to?"

"Duh," I say, and we laugh. Everything between us feels lighter hearing the other laugh.

"You're nervous, huh?" she asks me.

I shrug. "Kinda."

"You shouldn't be after Friday."

Leti smiles, the creases around her eyes folding tightly together, telling me about the sound of the car rattling as she and Quentin moved in the back seat when they first had sex.

The laughter is quick to cease, the memory of Quentin drifting between us. I haven't seen him in a few days, and he won't respond to my messages. I don't have to ask to know he wasn't invited to the Posada, and I hope he's okay. But sometimes, it feels nice just being with Leti.

It reminds me of how things used to be, before Quentin was around, before the baby nestled in her stomach, before my pa left, before everything felt so tangled.

TWENTY-ONE

I KEEP STARING AT MY PHONE. I INVITED ALEXIS TO THE POSADA, but he never responded. Between sitting at Leti's dining room table and preparing aguinaldos in cellophane bags, I've been checking my phone to see if he's texted. It's rhythmic at this point: Duvalín, mazapán, orange, phone. Duvalín, mazapán, orange, phone. Duvalín, mazapán, orange, phone.

My ma is behind me, helping Señora Barragón with the ponche. She trims and peels sticks of sugarcane, their green skin flying against jars of guayabas lined along the counter. Ava usually helps her with that, but she didn't come with us this year. She said she had plans with Matías, but I think she just doesn't want to be around me more than she has to be. So, my ma and I came alone.

It was the most uncomfortable car ride of my life.

Maybe even worse than Thanksgiving.

I sat stiffly beside my ma, worried that with any wrong move I might make her cry. As we drove down Foothill, I felt weight scrape against my stomach. I was hoping Alexis would reply to offset the feeling, but every time I looked at my phone and saw nothing, I felt worse.

I usually complained about the burned Posada CD my ma played in the car every year, but tonight, I was silent. I let all the Spanish Christmas songs that felt insensitively optimistic color the gaps of quiet. We drove around potholes, listening to the "El Burrito Sabanero" stutter on the CD that had scratched from its annual years of use. Then, to make things worse, my ma started talking to me.

"Your pa named you after this song," she said.

"'El Burrito Sabanero'?"

She smiled, which made me soften. "No, this one."

I listened to "Campanas de Belén" sound through the speakers. When we were younger, Veronica and Valeria used to mock me while they sang it, imitating the high-pitched tone of the choir, rhythmically pulling at my hair with the sound of each bell.

My ma continues. "He said that when you were born, it was like bells ringing."

I nodded and slumped back, feeling weight crawl from my stomach and fill the hollow spaces of my ribs. I'd always liked that my ma's name was my middle name. It made me like I was finally sharing a similarity with her—even if it was just in print, in calling.

But, I never knew that my pa had picked my first name. How was something that was mine still something that was his?

I glanced at her from the rearview mirror. In the blue glow of the car stereo, my ma looked younger. Her makeup made her look less sad. Maybe that was the point. And somehow it also looked like she wanted to keep talking. Like maybe we were having a moment. But when I opened my mouth to respond, she pulled the car into a parking spot and turned off the ignition.

"Let's go," she said.

And, like that, the moment ended.

Leti helps with the last of the aguinaldos, fluffing the cellophane until they're perfect. After we're finished, I follow her to her room to change into our costumes.

No matter how many times I'm in Leti's room, I'm always a little nauseated by its smell. Everything in here reeks of Zote laundry soap—it clings to her bedsheets, her clothes, and even the carpet beneath us. I look around at the Precious Moments trinkets collected from baby showers, Quinceañeras, and First Communions lining her vanity—the eyes of the figurines that are soft and sloped and sad. I glance at the flea-market animal blanket sprawled at the foot of the bed, distorting the bodies of two cranes dipping into a lake, finding my angel costume folded neatly beside it.

The costume was made years ago out of an old bedsheet, sewn together with gilded thread. I used to drown in the fabric, but now it tugs uncomfortably at the fullness of my chest, making the heaviness feel worse. I'm pulling on my pair of angel wings when I glance at Leti. If I thought my costume didn't fit, she's nearly popping out of hers.

"Damn," I tell her. "You're *hella* big."

She rolls her eyes at me. Her costume was always sack-like and shapeless, but this year she needs help pulling it over her stomach. I kneel onto the carpet and tug at the hem of the dress until it unravels freely at her knees. I stand up and examine her at an arm's length. The dress itself has always been ugly—it's a humble, shit-colored brown with a white stripe down its center. But this year, it looks especially unflattering. It clings to Leti's stomach, the indentation of her belly button pressing against the cotton. Leti looks at herself in the mirror, her shoulders falling with a deep exhale.

"At least you don't have to put the pillow beneath the gown this year," I say. I'm trying to lighten the mood—for her, but really, for both of us. This is the first Posada we've gone to without my pa or Ava. I'm beginning to worry that their absence was somehow my fault, which made the scraping in my chest pull deeper and deeper.

"I look like a cow," Leti says.

I smile, cuz it's kind of true.

I pick up the blue, star-patterned veil and drape it over her head, pinning it in place with a few bobby pins.

"You look fine," I say.

Truthfully, in my head, I'm hoping everyone diverts their eyes to her cousin, Manny, who plays José every year. We used to paint a fake beard onto his cheeks with brown eyeshadow, but he's old enough now that he has that wiry stubble growing out of his pimples. Maybe they'll look at all the craters on his face instead of wondering how Leti's stomach looks so much more realistic this year.

I tell Leti this, but she doesn't buy it.

Instead, she turns in the mirror, her hand circling over her stomach. "My parents are going to announce it tonight to everyone."

"Oh, yeah?"

"They're saying it's the new light of immaculate conception."

I squint, thinking about how the Barragón family would rather lie about their own religion before admitting their daughter was having sex.

"Damn," I say. "It's kinda crazy that your parents are Catholic and have, like, premiere seating in hell."

She shoots me a look. Then we both laugh.

The Posada attendees divide themselves into two groups: indoor singers and outdoor singers. The outdoor singers are the actors in the nativity scene, so Leti and I walk outside and into the cold, dragging our props behind us.

Every year, we stand on the corner of Foothill and East 17th, waiting for Señora Barragón to give us the signal to start. And every year, I still feel exposed here. Even with Leti dressed as the Virgin Mary, cars honk at us, rolling their windows down to whistle. But still, we stand and wait, our backs hazy with the light of the liquor store marquee, our faces bright with the glow of candles.

When it's time to begin, Leti's tía distributes the songbooks. We turn to the Canto de Posadas and begin walking down the streets of Oakland, candles flickering in the wind as Leti and Manny guide us back toward the house. The crowd carries the props my ma made with extra school supplies—canes made from yardsticks, manger animals made from milk crates and papier-mâché.

By the time we're at the door, the hem of my angel costume is black from dragging across the sidewalk. We begin singing into the door, humiliatingly begging for shelter. It feels embarrassing every year, but Leti and I have learned how to make it fun.

When we were younger, we used to sing off-key to throw everybody off, getting scolded by my ma when we were allowed inside. My ma stays inside every year, and though we're usually apart, the door between us feels different this time. Almost right.

When we finish the song, Señora Barragón opens the door and starts chanting about santos peregrinos. We sit around the living room and pray to bless the house. You'd think it'd be short and sweet after forcing all of Fruitvale to watch us literally reenact the trek to Bethlehem, but Catholics can pray for fucking ever.

Leti sits across from me, reciting prayers by memory, her parents on either side of her. Looking at the three of them sitting so closely together makes me realize how far apart my ma and I are. I'm on the couch, and she's by the door. I'm staring at her, and she's staring at the floor.

I'm grateful when the prayers end so that I don't have to keep looking at her. So that I can distract myself from the ache sticking to my skin.

I rush into the kitchen for food, trying to gorge myself to drown the feeling. I pile my plate with bolillos and frijoles, inhaling everything as quickly as I can. I peer at the ponche and wince at its boiled fruit, then pour a cup of champurrado instead. I'm grabbing a concha for dessert when Señora Barragón starts calling everyone into the living room.

I brush concha crumbs from my costume, looking for my ma amid the crowd. I don't see her. In her place are the Barragóns' church friends, gathering around as they would at Mass. Señora Barragón walks to the front of the room, where she begins telling the story of the Posadas. How each one is supposed to mark María and José's travels from Nazareth as they searched for refuge and finally found it in Belén and blah blah blah.

I watch Leti's face fixate in composure, a practiced poise to her smile. But just as Señora Barragón begins announcing Leti's pregnancy, I feel my phone buzzing in the pocket of my jeans, the glow of the screen illuminating through my angel costume. It's Alexis.

I look up at Leti, who is staring directly at me. I hold my phone up to her, smiling widely, but all she does is blink at me.

I shove my food into the garbage and duck into her room to pick up the call.

"Hey," Alexis says. "Are you busy?"

"No," I blurt.

"I'm home for winter break. You wanna come through?"

I've never taken off the angel costume so fast in my life.

I leave the wings and halo on Leti's dresser, the gown folded sloppily at the foot of the bed. By the time I'm back in the hallway, I peer into the living room. The mouths of attendees agape, faces coated in confusion.

I look at Leti, who looks like she's dissociating into another dimension.

I can't deal with that right now.

I turn around and try to exit through the kitchen door that leads to the small, concrete backyard. But I see my ma there, sitting on a bench between Señora Barragón's tomato plants. Her shoulders are slouched and frail with sadness, her body blurred in the blue of the night.

Not dealing with that either.

So, I leave the way Leti taught me.

Through her window, down the fire escape, and crossing the street to the bus stop. In my hurry, I jump onto the first bus that arrives. As it pulls away, I watch the liquor store marquee muddle into disks of light. I consider texting my ma to tell her I left. But I don't.

I know she won't even notice that I'm gone.

TWENTY-TWO

THERE ARE NO BUSES THAT LEAD TO ALEXIS'S HOUSE.

I learned that after getting on the wrong bus, then getting on another wrong bus, then calling him to embarrassingly admit that I didn't know the bus route to his house. He ordered me an Uber, and I waited for it at the same stop Leti and I use to get to school every morning. In the dark, I stared at Liam and Lauren's real estate ad, their faces obscured by new graffiti.

When my Uber arrived, I got into the back seat and leaned my head forward, my forehead pushing against the back of a headrest. I felt like all the burden in my body accumulated from the Posada was dwindling, like I was floating.

But after being dropped off, I stand across the street from Alexis's house and feel an itch at my chest.

There are no bus stops near his house, because no buses run up here.

There are no billboards.

There are no liquor stores.

There are no sagging telephone wires.

Just rows and rows of houses among hills and hills and hills.

Oakland is so large that it has the power to still make me feel lost. I've lived here my whole life and I've never even been on this side. Here, in the Montclair district, everything is tucked away protectively—behind tall pillars and iron gates and money. When Alexis told me he was from Oakland, I thought he meant *my* Oakland. But being here reminds me of the length of my arm, the limit of my own reach.

I turn around and see the rest of the city from the inclination. I'm so far from home that everything looks like a remnant of its shape, reduced to an orb of light in the horizon. I wonder where everything is amid the city's constellation—where my house is and where Leti's house is and where my ma is and where my pa is. I think about all the buses driving past them, weaving in and out of lanes, never once crossing to come up this steep hill.

I look at Alexis's house. I squint at it, my eyes zooming in and out of its magnitude. Had I known this is where I would be going, I wouldn't have even jumped on the bus at all.

I feel so embarrassed that I assumed Alexis was from Fruitvale, so embarrassed that I got lost, so embarrassed that I called asking for his help. So embarrassed.

I stare at the door, surprised by its nakedness. There's no metal security door in front of the real door, like at my house. My fist hovers between the door and the doorbell, unsure of how to announce my arrival, when the door swings open.

Alexis appears, wearing a pair of gray sweatpants and a loose T-shirt.

"Hey," he says, then cocks his head to the side, "my room is this way."

I follow him inside, trying not to stare at the staged appearance of the house: folded blankets, fresh flowers, framed family photos. In one photo, I see Alexis pressed beside two people who, I guess, are his parents. Looking at the three of them so close to each other, so comfortable in each other's presence, makes me remember the photo of my pa and me at the Mormon Temple. It makes me feel heavier.

I unpeel my eyes from the picture, looking at the medical diplomas that are displayed atop a marble fireplace, demanding attention.

"Your parents are doctors?" I ask, squinting at the degrees.

"Huh?" he calls. He's walking down a hallway. When he realizes I'm not following him, he turns on his heels, socks gliding against the polished floors.

I gesture to the diplomas.

"Oh," he says. "My dad is. That other one is my mom's Juris Doctor."

I nod, pretending to know what that means, staring at the certificates. I remember all the arguments my pa and ma had about my ma having gone to college. I bet Alexis's parents never argued about that at all. Based on the photos, I bet they never argued about anything.

In my lingering, Alexis lets out a long sigh.

"Do you wanna go to my room?" he asks.

I follow him as he leads us past the kitchen. It's painted deep shades of red and orange, with shining stainless-steel appliances that distort my reflection. He guides me into his bedroom, which mirrors his apartment: The blinds are half-drawn. The lights are dim. The laundry is on the floor. The most interesting thing in here is the windowsill, lined with books pressing against the pane, family photos used as bookends.

I sit on his bed, feeling the mattress springs bounce beneath me. It springs harder when Alexis plops down beside me. In the dim light, I study his face. His hair is longer, the tips of his curls tangling into the swoop of his eyelashes, the stubble on his jaw trickling to the corners of his mouth. He leans over to touch my waist, and I'm reminded of why I rushed over here.

We start kissing.

He inches over me slowly, and despite him pressing his entire body weight onto mine, this is the lightest I've felt since entering the house. All the thoughts about his neighborhood and his parents begin dissipating, replaced by the feeling of his hand against my skin. Because I was anticipating this would happen soon, I'm not nervous when he begins unbuttoning my jeans. I've been wearing cool underwear all week just in case he called. It was itchy and uncomfortable and I often wondered if wearing it was even worth it.

But everything feels worth it when he slides my jeans off, the denim pooling at the end of the bed. I lie there in my T-shirt and underwear, and when he moves to touch my bra, I begin unclasping it myself. When we're both undressed, Alexis asks if I want to do it.

222

I try to nod as casually as possible.

All the weight in my body feels like it has evaporated, leaving a quick drum in its place.

He reaches his arm between the narrow space of his mattress and the wall, fumbling around for a condom. When he can't find one, he goes to the bathroom down the hall, a towel draped around his waist.

I look down at my toes, thinking of all the times I've thought about the day I would finally have sex. And now here I am, naked for the first time on some boy's bed, grateful to whatever God exists that this is finally happening. I squirm along the mattress in excitement, almost squealing, then try to relax. I can't look too eager. I look ahead at Alexis's window, reading the book titles to calm down, until I see one of the photos along the sill.

I spring out of bed.

There, framed and all, is a photo of Alexis by Sather Gate, near the streetlight where he'd told me I looked beautiful just a few months ago. But instead of me there with him, he's with a girl with bright blond hair. They're both wearing matching Cal sweatshirts, fingers laced between their laps, lips pressed together in a kiss.

I hear Alexis's footsteps down the hall.

I dart back into bed, positioning my body to lie exactly as I had been. I stare at the blankness of the ceiling, wondering what to do.

Alexis sits on the edge of the mattress, rolling a condom over his penis. It's neon green, which I think is kind of dumb. In the rare instances I watch porn where people wear condoms, it's for sure never *green*. I wonder if it's flavored—like sour apple or something.

I breathe.

I'm trying to focus on anything that isn't that photo.

But when Alexis climbs on top of me, it's all I can think about. He sets both of his hands on either side of me, and I peer past the hair on his arms toward the frame. He leans down, pressing his legs between mine to spread them open.

I stare at the ceiling. The pendulum in my chest swings from heavy to light, aching with indecision. I wonder if I should say anything at all. The last time I did, Alexis ignored me for weeks. Maybe I should just be quiet.

But I feel a scraping in my throat, heat rising to my tongue. I try to swallow the feeling, watching as Alexis moves closer to me, presses his chest onto mine, but it unravels in my mouth. "Do you have a girlfriend?" I blurt.

Alexis pulls his face away from mine. "Huh?" he asks.

I tilt the tip of my chin toward the photo, and Alexis's eyes widen a centimeter. His eyes flicker in shock, pupils dilated. He's quiet for a moment, frozen in place. I can feel my heart beating in my ears, its thuds the only thing measuring time.

"Yeah," he finally says through an exhale, his chest deflating. "Do you want to stop?"

I feel it beginning.

The pendulum is at a pause, moving decisively toward heaviness. The feeling creeps from the tips of my toenails to the joints in my knees, snaking through my stomach and pounding against my ribs. The feeling that had started in the car with my ma, now center to my body, pinning me to the mattress.

It is the only thing consistent in my life.

More than my ma, more than Leti, and especially more than my pa. I close my eyes and try to imagine the feeling disintegrating, seeping through the pores of my skin. But when I open my eyes, Alexis's face squarely on top of mine, the feeling is still there—echoing through my chest.

This is the only thing I have left to make it go away.

Even if I know it's wrong.

It's the only thing I have tonight that is exciting—the only thing in my life that doesn't remind me of the gravity keeping me here.

I kiss Alexis.

When our tongues dance, the feeling numbs. Between pants, he asks if I'm sure, and I close my eyes and nod. As he kisses me, the memory of the heaviness is buried, replaced by the excitement blooming between my legs.

And then I feel him slip inside of me.

It doesn't feel bad.

It doesn't feel good.

It doesn't really feel like anything.

It almost feels tight, like an elastic that stretches as Alexis moves back and forth, in and out. I'm grateful that it doesn't hurt, but I'm not sure what to do. When Alexis starts grunting and moaning like it feels good, I start grunting and moaning like it feels good. Is this what people do? Just moan because the other person moaned?

He keeps going.

I still don't really feel anything.

I keep moaning, imitating what I hear in porn, then look around the room. I look at the ceiling fan that has dust on it. I look at a spiderweb by the window. I look at a garbage bin in the corner. When my eyes wander to the windowsill, the white photo frame stark in the blue of the bedroom, I turn my eyes toward the curtains.

Even with Alexis's girlfriend's face positioned away from mine, I feel her eyes burning through the glossy paper, through the glass panel, through Alexis's body, and into my skin. And just when I tell myself to forget about her, to pay attention to whatever is happening, Alexis lets out one long, low grunt, and pulls out of me.

He rolls over and lies beside me for a moment, catching his breath. Then he sits up near the edge of his bed, spreads his legs, and pinches the condom from his penis. He flings it into the trash can. I lie there, looking at the bright green latex spilling over the rim, unaware of what to do next.

I guess it's over.

There's no aftermath in porn.

At least I wouldn't know about one.

After I finish, I usually throw my phone away from me, feeling disgusted by whatever I was watching. Feeling ashamed for the orgasm I'd had. But here, there was no orgasm. No opportunity for me to feel euphoric and then ashamed. No opportunity for me to feel anything.

This is all offbeat, crooked.

I look at my phone—less than five minutes have passed since this all started.

Alexis grabs the towel that he used around his waist. From here, I can smell that it's stale and mildewy. He wipes the sweat from his forehead, then passes it to me as if there's something I need to wipe myself. I've sweat more walking the mile during gym class. I look at the towel, look at him, and set the towel down.

"How was that for you?" he asks. His back is to me, shielding me from the photo. I wonder if he's looking at it, but then he reaches down to pull his boxers on.

"Uh . . ." I start.

I don't know what to say.

Was that really it?

I can't ask him that.

Would it be rude to ask?

Maybe.

It would definitely make shit awkward, like that other time. So, I tug on my bra and T-shirt and say, "Uh, good."

"Good," he says.

He goes to get a glass of water. I slip on my underwear, then walk across the room to grab my jeans, which are tangled in a heap by Alexis's closet. I struggle into them, feeling like a sausage while I jump to pull them over my hips, adjusting the waistband in the mirror. When I'm dressed, I look at my reflection. I expected to look different, but I don't. Still the same big hair and big chest and big hips.

The only thing that is different in the pang in my stomach, a blossoming pain that feels familiar, reminiscent of all the nights I'd watch my ma in the living room. With the darkening gradient of the evening marking the hour, she would wait for my pa. On the nights he came home, reeking of other women, my ma would just get up and follow him to their room. Sometimes she'd be so tired of all the arguing that she would just feel grateful my pa came home at all. Feeling grateful to have some relief to offset her sadness.

I tug at the ends of my hair, the coils of curls that are the proof I am my father's daughter, dark and visible around my shoulders. Nothing like the feeling in my stomach, which grows with every look in the mirror, a pain that comes with believing this is the most I have ever reminded myself of my ma.

SPRING

TWENTY-THREE

SPRINGTIME IN OAKLAND IS SOMETHING DIFFERENT. ALL THE CAR exhaust still fogs up the same, but the air smells cleaner. Almost sweet. I'm reminded of how beautiful it is.

News reports are always giving Oakland a bad reputation, calling it the most dangerous city in the Bay Area, posting homicide rates, going on about gang violence and sex trafficking. All that can be true, but what's also true is that when me and Leti walk onto Foothill after school, the sun hits the Mac Dre mural just right. Cars swerve to make themselves seen. It makes me feel important, and it almost makes me forget for a second how bad Leti wants to leave.

And she'll be on her way soon.

While we continue down Foothill, Leti stops walking. She grips my arm—her long, pregnancy-strong nails piercing into my skin. I'm about to whip around and yell from pain when Leti starts screaming and sobbing. She unclenches her hand from my arm and holds her phone tightly, jumping up and down.

In her fit of movement, I see bits of her phone screen, where her acceptance from Berkeley is bright and bold. It was the one she'd been waiting for all week, even after all the acceptances everywhere else— UCLA, Stanford, USC.

It was the only one she wanted.

We hug right away, but our arms can't wrap around each other. We're separated by the bulge of her stomach. Regardless, when I feel her tears dampen the fabric of my T-shirt, I feel my own tears trickle down my face. They come from happiness, but they also come from comfort. It's the first time I've felt relieved in months.

I've been *praying* for Leti to get into Berkeley.

Not only because it's what she's always wanted, but because everything has felt impossible lately. I spent most of my winter break in bed. Between Ava spending her days off at home, completely ignoring me, and my ma crying about how my pa didn't call at Christmas, I felt like I was tied to my mattress.

The only time I got up was when Alexis would invite me to his place. When that happened, I went to see him in hopes of finding some physical relief.

But that didn't come either.

We'd been having sex for months, but I never had an orgasm. I never really felt anything, apart from guilt. Every time we do it, I feel terrible about myself afterward, but I don't know what else to do to try to get this feeling off my body.

I was beginning to worry that seeing Alexis wasn't enough. That if things with him fell apart and Leti didn't get into Berkeley, I would have no one to help distract me from his heaviness.

But seeing Leti's acceptance washes me with relief. Next year, she'll only be twenty minutes away, just like we've always planned.

I grip her tighter.

When we unpeel from each other's embrace, Leti wipes her tears with the back of her palm. We continue down the street, Leti speaking through thick blubbers about how she actually did it—she actually got into Berkeley.

She walks differently after reading her email, lighter somehow, and I'm grateful I don't have to keep hearing about her waiting for the results. I feel like my ears have nearly swollen shut from listening to her this year, especially lately. Over break, Leti constantly called me. If she wasn't going on and on about college acceptances, she was going on and on about her family.

I learned that she and Quentin made up right before Christmas. She was quick to tell me, glossing over the details to talk about the baby shower that Najia and her mom were planning. I immediately wondered if Leti's parents would be invited, but I didn't ask. Despite Leti and Quentin making up, Leti still seemed to be on edge all the time. I thought it made sense with her moving into the later stages of her pregnancy right during college acceptance season, but sometimes it felt like she was mad at me. She always had this tone, like she was waiting for me to read her mind or something. Fucking Virgo.

We walk to the frutero. When he sees us in the distance, he immediately begins preparing bags of pepino and sandía. While he cuts the watermelon into symmetrical spears, he glances at Leti's stomach. It looks like his eyes are making sense of Leti's meltdown a few months ago, but he doesn't say anything. I can tell Leti is grateful for that.

People stop and stare all the time now that she's big-big. Her feet don't fit her chanclas and she has to sew these black elastic bands along the waistband of her jeans. Nobody in school has really made a big deal about it, except for Leti's snotty AP classmates. They're supposed to be smart, but they act so fucking stupid—looking at Leti like she's some kind of zoo animal.

But the rest of the school thinks it's old news.

There's like three pregnant girls every school year. They usually disappear when they're big like Leti, going to some continuation school or doing packets at home. But because Leti is so close to graduating, she's gotta tough it out and finish like normal.

I pay for Leti's fruit to celebrate her acceptance, giving the frutero my last five until I make up with Ava. He smiles at us, his brown skin Technicolor beneath the shade of the umbrella on his cart. He throws in an extra bag of mango, and gestures to Leti's stomach.

"Cuídate, mija," he says, and turns back to his cutting board.

We sit in the same plaza, near the Oscar Grant mural by Fruitvale Station, eating our fruta. There, Leti's lightness is anchored instantly.

"I hope Quentin got in," she says, looking down at her phone. "He says he hasn't gotten an email yet."

"He will," I tell her. "And if you have questions about the campus, I can ask Alexis to show you guys around."

She keeps her eyes glued to her phone. "You're still talking to him?"

"Yeah."

"You're being safe, right?"

"Yes, Ma." I nudge her, trying to get her to smile. "We only do it a few times a week."

She doesn't smile. She just nods. "Just be careful."

She always gets like this when I bring up Alexis. Her nose bunches up like she's smelled something bad, and I don't even know why I lied when she asked about us having sex—I told her it was great. Even though it hasn't been, I've been hoping that one day it will be. I invited him over to my house for the first time today, hoping that maybe doing it in my own bed would make it better.

And I *especially* didn't tell her about Alexis having a girlfriend. I knew she would judge me, and I was trying really hard not to judge myself.

Plus, I've been careful. I went to the same clinic I took Leti to and got on the pill. It makes my boobs hurt and my skin break out, but it's better than being pregnant.

When we're finished eating, I throw my Ziploc bag into a trash can and say goodbye to Leti.

She bites a spear of pepino. "You're going to see Alexis?"

I nod and walk toward the sidewalk. She doesn't say anything.

With every step I take forward, I imagine Leti becoming smaller and smaller. I picture her with the bag of mango balanced along the curve of her stomach, taking in the sunshine while she sits on the bench.

I approach the bus stop, then turn to look at her. But when I look, that version of her is nowhere to be found.

Leti is gone, not even there at all.

TWENTY-FOUR

I REALLY MISS GOING TO GÜERA'S.

Not because I miss sweeping hair, but because I miss getting a part of Ava's tips to go to Wendy's. Without them, I'm back to eating microwavable vegetables. When I get home, my stomach desperately growls for fries, but I ransack our freezer and dump a bunch of Tajín onto a bag of peas. A real pobrecita meal.

When I'm finished eating, I walk to Ava's room to steal some of her perfume before Alexis arrives. I stand in the center of her room, looking at the light slanting through the blinds, Ava's bedsheets painted in diagonal stripes.

Her tocador is chaotic, lined edge to edge with hair products, but I find a few perfume bottles on a display tray. I grab one and puff it against the nape of my neck. When I go to return it, I see that it was covering two pharmacy bottles, both obnoxiously orange. I pick one up and turn it around to read the label: ZOLOFT.

The first time I saw a birth control packet, it was in one of Ava's makeup bags. I fished out the purple pack and tried to make out what was printed along the foil, trying to read the words her nails hadn't yet punctured. I wonder if this is the same thing, only repackaged. But something unsettling pulls at my stomach. I'm grateful Alexis texts me that he's outside before it can pull any deeper.

I return the bottles, spritz another puff of perfume between my thighs, and shut Ava's door behind me.

I peer at Alexis through the crisscross wiring of the security door. He's wearing a blue T-shirt beneath his backpack, his hands gripping its straps. I prop open the door.

"Hey," he says, slipping by me to get inside.

We stand in the living room, where I'm suddenly aware of how different my house looks compared to his. I don't really want him looking at any of it—the blank walls and the empty kitchen and scuffed floor. Just the thought of it makes me embarrassed. I grab his hand and pull him toward my room, trying to outrun my embarrassment, and lock the door.

Then I kiss him. His lips feel rough against mine, chapped and peeled, but I slip my tongue through them anyway. I lead him to my bed, where he climbs on top of me. We begin undressing. Hope swells in my chest, and I pray that this time will finally be it. Finally the time it feels good.

I reach for the condoms I now keep in my nightstand, fumbling beneath Alexis's chest to get one open. I feel the same excitement between my legs, the sensation widening when Alexis touches me. It's followed by the same pressure between my thighs, elastic that stretches as he moves within me.

But the only other thing I feel is dampness along my face.

Alexis's hair dangles an inch above my nose, his sweat spiraling through his curls and landing on my cheeks.

My eyes move to my window. Pigeons press their weight onto the phone wires, the sneakers tied to them dipping lower, their shoelaces flying in gusts of wind. I thought doing it at my house would somehow make this better, but all I can think about is the weight of the wire getting heavier. It matches the feeling creeping up from my toes, snaking its way to my chest.

This is the first time this has happened.

Every other time we've had sex, I've been so focused on trying to finally have an orgasm, that I couldn't feel anything but hope strain inside of me. But today, I can't focus. I try to—I begin to moan like it feels good, even close my eyes to see if it helps. But behind my lids all I can see is the photo on Alexis's windowsill. The pills on Ava's vanity. The pigeons pressing, wide wings spread when the wire snaps.

Alexis finishes.

It's theatrical, like watching a dog take its last breaths. He pants and rolls onto his back and wipes his sweat with whatever is nearby. This time, it's my bedsheets.

I stare at the ceiling. I remember lying here months ago, wondering if I would ever be having sex here, if I would be looking at this exact ceiling, if I would feel any lighter afterward. But now that I have, nothing is different.

The heaviness has followed me here.

I watch as Alexis stands up, but I feel like I'm not really looking at him. I feel like I'm not really here.

"How was that for you?" he asks.

I give my routine "fine" and stand slowly to get dressed. Alexis does the same. While he zips up his pants, he tells me he'll be free again on Saturday.

"Abigail, my, uh—has this thing, and then, uh," he stammers, tugging on his shirt. For the first time, I watch his cheeks grow pink. His eyes dart around, avoiding mine in every corner of my room. "I'll be free at three."

It's the first time he's ever told me her name.

I never wanted to know it.

I try to push it away before I can remember it, but my mind breaks her name into syllables, pressing each letter into the flesh of my brain. I wish I could tell him that I never wanted to know her name. That I just wanted to be with him. That I just wanted to feel better.

But instead, I say, "Yeah."

Alexis has to go to class, so I walk him out. In the few steps from my room to the door, I feel like my body is filling with lead, every step threatening to break the floorboards beneath me, threatening to have the ground swallow me whole.

We stand in the threshold, where I see the neighborhood kids in symmetrical lines, forming teams for a soccer game in the street. Alexis slings his backpack over his shoulder, and I glance at the clock on the stovetop. I calculate in my mind, then shake my head. "You just missed the bus to BART. Next one comes in fifteen minutes. You can wait here if you want."

He cocks his head back in surprise. "I didn't take the bus."

"Oh, how'd you get here then?"

He laughs a little. "I took an Uber. I wouldn't take a bus around here. It's kinda dangerous."

Outside, a whistle blows.

Alexis looks toward the street, where the soccer game is beginning. When his Uber arrives, he approaches the sidewalk. A soccer ball rolls his way, but he doesn't kick it back to the kids. Instead, he climbs into the back seat of the car, disappearing into the horizon of concrete.

TWENTY-FIVE

MS. BARRERA HAS WRITTEN "CONGRATULATIONS, ALI" ON THE board. Ali got into Howard yesterday. As soon as he got the news, he rushed to her class in tears. Today, she's organized a celebration to honor him. She walked down to a liquor store and got those individual bottles of Martinelli's cider, the kind that are shaped like fat apples, and a platter of Chinese food. Though she's sitting behind her desk, grading or whatever, she looks up on occasion to smile at both of us while we eat.

"I've never seen you cry like that. Or, at all, I guess," I tell Ali.

He laughs. "I don't think I've ever cried that hard."

"How'd your mom react?"

"She cried harder than I did. At first, they were happy tears. Then they were sad ones."

I scrape rice around my plate. "Cuz you're leaving?"

He shrugs. "I guess that was it, at first. Then she started crying because she felt bad. She was saying how my dad should've been there for big moments like this."

"Yeah," I say, looking down at my plate. "My ma was on that for Christmas."

"I didn't really know what to say. I was half celebrating, half trying to console her."

He gets quiet after that.

"You good?" I ask.

He nods. "Yeah. It's just, like, even though I haven't ever met him, he's still robbing me of my moments, you know?"

"Yeah," I say. "I know."

When we've finished eating, we clean up and stack our chairs onto our desks. Ms. Barrera congratulates Ali again and looks at me a beat longer than she should. She hasn't mentioned anything about community college since our last talk, and though I'm grateful for that, her look suggests otherwise.

Ali and I walk to the parking lot. The hallway is plastered with flyers reminding us to order our caps and gowns for graduation in a few weeks, lifting up as we breeze past them. When we walk through the quad, I'm reminded of when I used to think the stretch from its grass to the parking lot was long. Now, everything feels smaller. Kind of suffocating. Maybe that's how things feel when you're ready to leave them. Maybe that's how my pa felt about me.

Ali gives me a ride home. On the way, he plays Prince, who sings about doves crying. Ali tells me about when the song was written and how it was produced and when it was released. He does this every time he drives me anywhere, carefully curving his car around the potholes lining the street. I glance outside, where people are bustling on the sidewalk, enjoying the incoming promise of summertime.

But even with so many people outside, I begin to feel lonely. I know that nobody will be there when I get home. And, in a few months, I won't even have car rides with Ali to buffer that blow.

I try to push down the thought.

I know it brings on the heaviness.

But lately, I can't get the heaviness away.

No matter how much sunlight beams outside. No matter how many times I have sex with Alexis. No matter the faith of the future. It gets so heavy that it feels inescapable. The only time I'm hopeful is when I think of helping Leti with the baby when it's born. It's the only thing keeping my head above water, keeping me from drowning.

Ali pulls into my neighborhood, flicking on his emergency lights and double-parking near the driveway.

"Thanks for not messing it up for me," he says.

I kind of laugh. "You don't need to thank me. You would've gotten in anyway. All I did was turn in my homework, for once."

"I go to this place on International to get tacos when I wanna celebrate something. You wanna come with me?"

I nod. "That sounds good."

I hear noise coming from my porch. My heart almost soars, thinking my ma might be home. But when I look, I see Leti sitting on the porch steps. I say bye to Ali and go to greet her. She uses one hand to grip onto the handrail, the other holding the curve of her stomach as she hoists herself up. Her shadow is wide against the cracked concrete of the driveway.

"Hey," I tell her. "I didn't know you were coming over."

"Yeah," she says softly. "I need to talk to you."

Ali waves at Leti as he pulls away, and I gesture to the front door. "You wanna come in?"

She shakes her head and sits on the steps. I settle beside her, watching as she moves into her Sunday-school posture, straightening her back and tucking her knees together tightly. The sunshine hits us face-on, illuminating pieces of her braid into fiery shades of brown. She looks ahead at my neighbor's house, and then up at the pigeons on the phone wires. They fly in flocks.

In the stillness, I feel my hands begin to sweat, panic pressing into my palms. The last time she was this still we were sitting in her living room, explaining her pregnancy to her pa. It must be really bad.

"What is it?" I ask.

"Quentin got into Berkeley," she says.

I let out a breath of relief. "Jesus, Leti. You scared me. That's great."

She's silent.

She stares up at the cloudless sky, her brown eyes wide against its blue. She closes them, the skin around her lids tightening into folds. She inhales sharply, then blurts, "I'm going to USC."

I blink, trying to process what she has just said. Leti goes on.

"Quentin got into USC too, so we're both going. I'm not staying here. We can't stay here."

Whatever panic I felt in my palms plummets to my stomach, settling at its base.

"B-but you both got into Berkeley. *You* got into Berkeley," I stammer.

"Belén, I can't stay here," she says again, exasperation weaving in her voice. "You don't know what it's been like at home. I can't take it anymore."

I'm trying to listen, trying to understand. But I can't get past the fact that she's leaving.

"But you won't even be living with them," I say. "Didn't you look up family housing or whatever at Berkeley? Don't you get an apartment on campus or something?"

"I *can't* stay here," she repeats. "Even if I'm twenty minutes away, it's too close. I know my ma. She'll call and want me to come home on the weekends because she'll need help taking care of my pa. I'd never get anything done—even without the baby. At least if I go far, I have the excuse of distance."

"But if you leave, they'll be so angry. They'll, like, disown you." I immediately regret saying this.

I know Leti is right, I know her parents will never change, I know it would never work with them involved. But I'm hiding behind the Barragóns, because I feel my brain forming limbs, reaching for anything to remove the realization that is writhing in my chest: the awareness that USC is seven hours away, that there will be no escape next year if Leti is gone, that I will be alone.

She laughs a little. "So what? Would that be worse than how they are now?" I don't have to look at her to tell her eyes are watering. Every time she's about to cry, her voice gets wavy and crooked.

"I've *tried* with them." She sniffs. "Since we told my pa, I have tried having the conversations. I've read all these long articles about how to talk to parents about racism, I've read all the teen mom books, I've read all the theory, I have *tried*. They don't want to hear it. They're so deeply ashamed." She pauses. "I don't want my child to have grandparents who hate them. Who wish they were lighter or not Black or whatever they choose to traumatize them about. They already did that to me."

She sets her arms down, resting them along the bend of her stomach. "My ma is wrong about so many things. But she came to this country when she was pregnant, hoping to give me a better life than the one she had. I think I can sacrifice something as small as Berkeley to give my baby something better—even if that means not seeing my parents." She inhales sharply, "And I knew Quentin was right, but I just didn't know what to do. It was so hard to make this choice because—"

She pauses for a moment. Tears tease at the corner of her eyes, then quickly roll down her cheeks. "Because, you know what? I know it doesn't make any sense. I know it's probably stupid. But I love my parents. And I wish I didn't, and I wished they loved me the way I love them. Enough to try with me. But I can't be here anymore, I can't see them anymore. After the summer, I have to go."

I take a breath. Something in my chest releases, a blossoming admission I'd been burying so deep inside myself: despite it all, I still love my pa. Even though he chose to leave me. And I've never been able to say it because I know how it sounds—it sounds like my ma talking. How can I love someone who left me? How pathetic can I be?

It's the first time I feel Leti is braver than me, to admit that, despite it all. It's the first time I feel connected to Leti in the context of her family, even through the thick of differences. It's the first time I feel entwined to her so intimately.

And it's the first time I feel like I can't care.

Because she's leaving.

I am trying to listen to her, but it's hard. It is physically hard. Her words are muffled by the pulsing of my heartbeat in my ears. My breath hiccups in my lungs, the width of my chest feeling like it's beginning to enclose. "But can't you go somewhere closer? Like Davis or whatever?"

As soon as I say this, her eyes soften with disappointment. She clears a sob from her throat. "I didn't apply there. USC gave me a really good scholarship—I wouldn't have to pay for anything. Quentin has family in LA, and they've already offered to help. It solves a lot of our problems."

"How long have you had this planned?" I ask. It's what I've been wondering for almost a year about my pa. How long had he known he would be leaving me before he left?

Leti breathes in deeply. "Since winter break. Quentin and I talked it over."

I blink at her, remembering her theatrics a few days ago when she got into Berkeley. "You knew you weren't going to go when you got in?"

She doesn't look at me. She only nods. "I was just proud of myself. That I did it."

I know it makes sense. I repeat this to myself, hoping that will make it easier: I know it makes sense, I know it makes sense, I know it makes sense.

But all I can feel is the coldness in my stomach.

I feel like I'm sitting in the car with my ma on the afternoon she pulled me out of class.

I close my eyes and remember her hands on the steering wheel, the radio on, the house empty. And now it's all going to happen again. Everything, not just my house, will be empty.

I swallow my own heartbeat. "But you haven't even been on a good tour at Berkeley. Maybe I can get Alexis to show you and Quentin around and—"

She snorts, her sadness twisting into annoyance. "Oh my God, Belén." She spits. "Are you seriously bringing up Alexis right now? I'm telling you that I need to move across the state to get away from my racist family and you want your fake boyfriend to show me around a school you know I truly *want* to go to?"

I sit up, shocked at her quick change in tone. Leti has never talked to me this way. We've bickered before and gotten into small fights, but she's never raised her voice like this. I take a deep breath. "All I'm saying is—"

"You guys aren't even dating!" she shouts, "You're so obsessed with this guy who you aren't even *dating*."

"I am not obsessed with him," I cut in. "I know that we're not together or anything—we're just having fun."

"*Do* you know that?" She scoffs. "You're at his beck and call like a dog. He's, like, twenty, having sex with some girl in high school. He's disgusting."

"That's not true, he—"

She rolls her eyes at me. "He has a girlfriend, Belén. I tried to tell

248

you that after the party. They were all over each other inside the house, and then I saw him with you."

I look at her. There's a crease wedged between her brows, a crescent similar to a moon, only appearing in the height of darkness. I glance down at my sneakers, feeling the palpable jab of air punching between my ribs. I don't want to tell her, but I feel the prickling of admission crawling up my throat.

"I know," I say.

The small tone of my voice is surprising, even to myself.

"You know?" The wedge grows deeper. "You know?" she repeats.

I turn away from her, toward the earthquake cracks in the pavement.

"You've been ditching me to go be with some guy who *you* knew was just using you?" she shouts.

I roll my eyes. "Leti, I have *not* been ditching you."

"You left me alone in a room full of people with my parents lying through their teeth about the miracle of immaculate conception!"

Leti flings her braid over her shoulder, its tail almost whipping against my face. I imagine heat waves suspended near her lips, her anger warping the air I'm breathing. "I can't believe you're *that* girl. ¿No tienes vergüenza?"

This is the same question Ava asked me that night, after Thanksgiving dinner.

The symmetry sends a sting into my chest.

I turn to face her, my eyes squinted. "What girl?"

She scoffs again. "You know what I mean, Belén. It's disgusting."

I do know what she means. I hear it in her tone, the one that mimics her ma's. She means what her pa said when he shouted at me in her living room, what men say when they whistle at me while I walk, what most people think when they look at my chest, unaware of the weight it holds beneath its surface: loose.

I know what I'm doing with Alexis is wrong.

But Leti doesn't even know *why* I'm doing it. She's never even asked me.

And hearing her reduce me to a label, when I've never done that to her, sends fire into my lungs. In all the times that Ava told me that my temper was like my pa's, I imagined her words shapeshifting to form a scapegoat. But now, that cooling in my stomach rises into heat, anger bubbling into my chest. I feel exactly like my father's daughter.

"You're gonna judge *me*?" I ask her.

She looks at me. "Belén, it's wrong—"

"Leti, you're seventeen and you're fucking pregnant. *You're* gonna judge me?"

She stands up, hoisting the weight of her body against her chest, her back arching as she supports herself. She spins toward me, her hand holding her stomach. "You don't know what you're talking about, Belén. You're always focused on what you have going on, so wrapped up in yourself."

Her eyes beam down at mine, and I squint at her.

"*I'm* so wrapped up in myself? I was there for your pregnancy test, your panic attacks, your first ultrasound, and I'm wrapped up in *myself*? I have other things to worry about, Leti."

She shakes her head and turns around, her back shielding me from the sun. "Like what? School? You don't *do* school, Belén. You make it clear."

"School is not life. I have my own shit going on that I try to put on pause to be there for your pregnancy."

She whips around and turns to me, the tail of her braid snake-like, wrapping around her neck. "Of course I know that!" she shouts. "You're *always* talking about it. Alexis this and that and he's so smart and you give him a blow job and he reads theory and he has long eyelashes and you're having sex four times a week. I hear about it all the time." She turns away from me. "I'm so tired of hearing about it."

"You're too smart to say shit like this," I tell her. I shake my head furiously, the coils of my curls obscuring my vision. "Put some of that AP track into your fucking head. If you really think my whole life revolves around him, you're really fucking stupid, Leti."

"What else do you have to worry about, Belén? Your family isn't at your throat all the time. You don't have pressure about school." She shakes her head. "You don't know how good you have it."

"Fuck you," I tell her. "My family isn't at my throat because I don't know where my family even is. You think I'm so wrapped up in my shit, but I've tried to be there for you. When's the last time you asked me about what I was going through?"

"Your pa just left," Leti says evenly, like that's the end of the story. Like I hadn't wished for months that everything associated with him disappeared. Like I didn't find him hidden everywhere: in boxes, in conversations, in reflections.

Her simplification of it, when I've tried to be there for her in her most complicated moments, makes me feel so small.

She starts saying something else, but I'm already standing up and going inside. I slam the door behind me. A minute later, I hear her footsteps walk off the driveway. I glance through the blinds and watch her wide, round stomach vanish completely into the distance. I sit on the couch, staring at the dust outlines where pictures of my family used to be. The emptiness of the house matching the same one I feel inside.

TWENTY-SIX

I HAVE TO GET DRESSED TO SEE ALEXIS.

It feels hard to breathe, and even harder to get up. But this is the only thing I have left to try to make myself feel better. The only thing that can get me out of bed.

I squint at the sunlight angling through the telephone wires, its rays invading my eyes and making my head ache. I'm lying on my bed, replaying the argument with Leti over and over in a loop.

I haven't seen her since it happened.

It's been nearly two weeks, but with a school as big as ours, it's easy to avoid each other. I've bumped into Quentin a few times in the hallway. He'll always start by talking to me like everything is normal, but after a while he'll encourage me to talk to Leti. Any time that happens, I'm quick to say I have to go.

The loop of her shouting winds tightly in my head. I move into a cycle: think of a better comeback, feel sad, think of something sharper to say, feel sadder. After an hour of this, I finally get the energy to put on a pound of lip gloss and run mousse through my hair, only to feel worse when I get dressed.

All my lying down and feeling weight has finally caught up to me, so most of my skirts are too tight. I ransack the hampers in our coat closet—they're always vomiting up my ma and Ava's wardrobe. They're both a little bigger than me, so I figure I can find something wearable. I fish my hand through the plastic, finding every possible bra in our house smeared with deodorant, before pulling on something black. It's a polo shirt I've never seen before.

I turn it my way, studying the red-and-yellow checkered bottom fraying along the hem. I flip the shirt inside out, realizing it's a uniform shirt. My ma's name is unmistakably embroidered on its left side: DOLORES.

It looks like the type of polos workers wear at fast-food restaurants, the fabric thick with the smell of salt and frying oil. I dig my hands deeper through the hamper, where I find two identical shirts twisted between black Dickies pants.

I hold the clothes to my chest and sit there, on the floor, wondering if I am just in some bizarre egg hunt with the saddest items my ma could think of hiding around the house. Or maybe they'd been in plain sight, and I had just never noticed them. That thought makes me even sadder.

I look at the shirts, pulling against the seams of the fabric that has become tough with dried sweat, making sense of everything. My ma gone until the sky was black, working after work. The past due notices that came, but the water that never stopped flowing. The smell of food tangled in her hair, though she never touched the stove.

I imagine my pa, with her emergency savings he stole from the freezer. All the security that could have rescued her from the embarrassment of deprivation being spent on the deposit for his new apartment.

My ma had been working so much. At school, after school, to protect me as much as she could from the humiliation of my pa's absence. Meanwhile my pa could not be bothered.

My brain begins ping-ponging, bouncing from my ma to my pa. I feel guilty then grateful then relieved then revolted. In the exchange, Leti's comment about my pa whispers in my mind, the sound like cotton being pulled against my eardrum.

If only he had really left. If only we were all not stuck trying to fix everything he left behind.

I feel sweat at the webs of my fingers. I pull at my palms, hoping that will make it go away, but when I touch my skin, I begin to feel like it's not mine. Like someone else is in my body.

I stand up and shake my head, trying to get the thoughts out of my mind, the sound out of my ears. I shove the clothes back into the hamper, struggling to shut the closet until I push the weight of my body against the door. I rush into my room and put on whatever skirt constricts my circulation the least, and sprint to the bus stop, trying to outrun the feeling crawling through my body.

I stand on the platform at Fruitvale Station. The heaviness in my chest has transformed into tightness, my heart pounding in my throat. I feel like I might unravel at any moment, like I might burst through the seams of this skirt.

I wish I wasn't by myself.

I wish Leti were here.

I feel the gaze of a group of men sitting behind me, eyes sharp like glass against my back. Men are inescapable, no matter where I go.

My BART train rushes to a stop in front of me, its breeze sending my curls tangling into my hoops. The train is packed with the Saturday rush of people headed for the city, which means no seats are empty. I hold on to a rail with one hand and keep the other tight on my skirt, watching Oakland pass beneath me. It's the first time I'm on my way to Alexis's place and don't feel like I'm flying. Instead, I feel like I'm bound to the floor of this train, rooted in this reality.

I look up at Alexis's apartment, shielding my eyes with the palm of my hand, the sunlight heavy on my skin. When Alexis opens the door, he stares straight at my thighs, eyes softening. I try to mirror his expression, but instead of feeling excited, I just think about how he's wearing the ugliest pair of cargo shorts I've seen in my entire life.

We don't say hi to each other. I push past him and head to his room, where I kick off my shoes and unpeel my shirt. He closes the door and begins undressing. The quickness of it all doesn't feel passionate or spontaneous like it did the first few times. It feels expected. Robotic.

We climb into his bed, and I close my eyes. It's hard to imagine a God above me, through the ceiling of Alexis's room, but I pray this just makes the feeling in my chest go away, that this settles the racing in my heart.

The tightness turns to stretching. The same one as always. I imagine an elastic band pulling within my body, stretching in its extremity, until it snaps, releasing a weight that pounds against my ribs.

I am so heavy.

Maybe the heaviest I've ever been in my life.

Every thought is magnetized to my chest. I can't stop thinking about Leti, or my mom serving food after work, or my pa's face. I can't even moan to fill the silence, because my lungs are pressing together, struggling for breath.

I listen to Alexis's grunts and stare out the window, at the concrete that leads to campus, thinking about how Leti was supposed to be there in August. And how, naturally, I would be beside her. When she leaves, moves hours away from me, I won't have anybody anymore.

Even now, with Alexis on top me, I don't have anybody.

He finishes.

Dull disappointment settles in my chest.

He rolls onto his back and wipes his sweat with his palm, the wetness flicking against my forehead.

He sits up, balancing his weight on his elbows. "Are you okay?" he asks.

"Huh?"

"Are you okay?" he repeats. "I've been talking and you haven't said anything."

I look up at the ceiling. I've never told Alexis about any of it—I've made it a point not to. But I feel like I'm dying. I don't have anything else left to try to feel better. "My best friend and I got into this fight. It's just on my mind." As soon as the words fly out of my mouth, relief spreads through my skin, something similar to a salve.

My lips move before my brain has time to settle them, my body chasing after any alleviation. "She got into Berkeley, but she decided to go to USC. I just wasn't prepared for her to want to leave."

He snorts. "Why would she do that? Berkeley is a better school."

I blink, amazed that's the part he's focused on. "USC gave her a better financial aid package. But she's pregnant, and the baby is due soon. Her family isn't supporting her, but her boyfriend has family in LA that could help them out." I know I'm rambling—the tone of my voice is reminiscent of when I heard Leti explain it all to Ms. Barrera. But I can't stop. The heaviness lightens rhythmically with every word that is let out. "But I don't know what to do without her here. She's been the only person I've had since I was—"

"She's *pregnant*?" He cuts me off, his tone true in its awe. If Alexis hadn't interrupted me, the words may have never stopped tumbling out of my mouth. But now, I clamp it shut.

I'm surprised that he's surprised.

Maybe nobody on his side of the hill had ever heard of a real-life teen pregnancy. Or maybe had the money to deal with it in other ways.

"Yeah."

"And she wants to go to *college*?"

I look over at him. His face is a mixture of disbelief and disgust. "Uh, yeah."

"How?"

"I just said how."

"But that will never work."

258

My brows pinch together. "Why not?"

"It's *college*. And at USC? It's going to be a full load."

"Yeah, but she's smart," I say. "It'll be hard, but I don't know anybody who works harder than Leti."

"It won't be hard, it will be impossible." He scoffs. "You have classes in the morning, sometimes at night, then there's reading in between sections and study groups. She just shouldn't have gotten pregnant if she wanted to go to college."

I squint at him. "Okay, but she already *is* pregnant. And she got *into* a school like that. Why would they admit her if they didn't want her to do well?"

He snorts. "Diversity points? Everyone wants to say they admitted a pregnant girl. They'll put it on the pamphlets and on their success stories page, but she won't succeed." He says this with finality in his tone, like he's punctuating the conversation.

"She won't succeed?" I repeat.

From my periphery, I see him roll his eyes. "It's amazing she even got in. I'm sure she's smart, but they probably only let her in because of her story."

I don't say anything. The relief I felt dissipates, leaving anger in its place. I sit up taller and shake my head.

"So, if you're telling me that she got in because of her story, how did you get in?"

"I had the grades," he says matter-of-factly.

"She has the grades."

"Yeah, but that pregnancy story for sure gave her a boost."

"And you don't think you had any fucking boosts?"

He cocks his head back. "Jesus, calm down."

I climb off the bed, my feet firm against the carpeted floor. I bend down and pick my clothes up piece by piece, catching the reflection of my naked body in his mirror.

"There's a difference," Alexis says, peering over at me from his bed. "I had good grades. Your friend probably has good grades too, but that pregnancy story definitely set her over the top to all the admissions offices." I hate how he refers to Leti as "my friend." I hate how he knows nothing about her, nothing about me, at all.

"And you don't think living in the hills set you over the top? Having doctors for parents?"

"My mom is a lawyer."

I look at him.

He shrugs and waves a hand at me dismissively. "I worked hard to get here."

"If that's true, then it's a fucking shame. All that work to get into this school for you to be a fucking idiot." I shove my legs into my skirt, zipping it up behind me.

He raises his eyebrows at me, as if I'm the one here with audacity. His face is illuminated by the light of day, sweat beading against his forehead, eyes squinted with ferocity. I've never seen him look like this before, but his gaze is recognizable. The same one shared by men who shouted at me on the street, who reached for my body, who followed me home.

I think about what Leti said, and I feel embarrassed. She had known without ever meeting him. And even though I was still upset with her, I couldn't let anybody, especially not someone like Alexis, talk down on all she had done to get to where she was going.

Alexis sits up and begins fumbling around for his boxers. He starts to talk, but I'm louder.

"Who the fuck do you think you are to talk that way? As if you're better than anyone because you go to this school," I shout, pinning on my hoops.

He keeps shaking his head, his curls bouncing in the sunlight. "I knew this was a mistake. I knew you were too immature."

"I'm too immature?" I ask. "You're cheating on your girlfriend with me, and *I'm* immature?"

"You knew about it. Don't act so innocent." He scoffs.

"I'm not saying I'm innocent, but I'm at least smarter than you are."

"How can you say that? Look at where you are." He points to the window, gesturing to the campus only a few blocks away. "I knew taking your virginity would make you like this. Girls always say it's not a big deal, but it always turns into something like this."

"*Take?* What did you take?" I ask. "You're so concerned about yourself that I've never, ever finished with you. You just go at it. You go to this big-deal school but you're too stupid to know if someone cums?" He flings the sheets away from his body, rolling out of bed. He stands in front of me while I clasp on my bra, looking shorter than I remembered him.

"Every time we have sex I ask if it was good for you," he spits out, an accusatory finger pointed at my chest. "You always say yes."

I scoff. "How was I supposed to feel comfortable telling you that you're bad at sex? I couldn't even tell you I thought we were moving too fast. You act so bothered by *everything*."

"Just because you don't finish doesn't mean—"

I tug on my jacket and roll my eyes. "God, forgive me for thinking that being good at sex is about two fucking people, that it means you please your partner. Are you this bad with your girlfriend? Or am I just a body to you?"

He shakes his head, eyes rolled to the ceiling. He steps around me and extends an arm, gesturing toward the door. I feel the limit of his intelligence wedging between us. Is he too arrogant to notice where life has given him the leg up? Too egotistical to be empathetic?

The words hang between us, and he blinks at me, confused at why any of what I said matters. And that's when I realize, that's exactly what I was to him. Just a body.

I lace up my sneakers, the last thing I need to get out of here, and stand and look at my reflection in the mirror, my body disfigured in the waves of the cheap glass.

I leave, not bothering to look at Alexis before I go. He slams the door behind me.

I board a bus, watching as Berkeley's campus smears behind me, a palette of blue and yellow and pain and promise. I try to imagine Leti somewhere in its muddled colors, but when my imagination can't make those ends meet, I stare at the headrest in front of me. This is the only thing I can lean on now, the only thing holding me up as the heaviness begins building in my body.

TWENTY-SEVEN

I WAIT FOR ALI ON THE STEPS OF MY HOUSE. I TAKE DEEP BREATHS, trying to get out of this sour mood. I feel like anything might set me off again. I've deleted Alexis's number, but I still feel heat layering the weight in my chest.

I don't want to ruin Ali's celebration, so when his car pulls up, I plaster on a smile that I pray he thinks is normal.

"Hey," he mumbles, turning onto the road.

"Hey," I say, trying my best to sound cheery. "Where are we going again?"

"That taco spot I told you about." His tone is curt.

I look over at him. His grip is so tight on his steering wheel, it looks like the bones of his knuckles are threatening to rupture his skin.

"Is something wrong?" I ask.

"Yup," he says, "but I'll tell you when we get there."

He doesn't say anything else. He puts his music on shuffle, which he never does. I wait for him to go into the spiel about the song playing, like always. Instead, he's silent. I listen to the thick bass of a D'Angelo song course through the car, lyrics that wonder when he'll see someone again.

Ali parks off International, and we climb out of his car. Outside, it smells like summertime. Like hot pavement and gasoline and sunshine. The sun is beginning to set, and our shadows cling and stretch against the pavement. We approach a restaurant called El Farolito, its white walls contrasted by the yellow booths lining its sides.

The menu glows overhead, photos of tacos and quesadillas illuminated by a buzzing, dim bulb. I wish I had enough money to treat Ali to a celebratory meal, but I've resorted to paying for everything with the emergency stacks of quarters I keep in my closet. Maybe, once Ava and I make up, he and I can celebrate again.

Ali orders, his gaze fixed to the floor, and I follow behind him. We move to sit at a booth closest to the door, a waiter delivering a platter of chips and salsa between us.

"What's wrong?" I ask him. I've never seen him like this, not even when we were talking about our personal statements at Oakland Grill. His hands are clasped together along the table, and I notice his eyes are red and swollen, like he's been crying.

He shakes his head. "I can't go to Howard."

I stop the chip I'm holding midair, then toss it back into the basket. "What do you mean?"

"I can't afford it," he says. This is followed by a long pause, where Ali stares at the table, as if thinking of what to say.

"I called the financial aid office to review my package," he continues. "I thought I was going to get a scholarship, but I didn't get it. It's a private school. And there's out-of-state fees. I can't afford it," he repeats.

He looks so deflated saying it aloud, then buries his face into his hands.

I take a sharp breath. "But what about—"

"No." He shakes his head. "That's it. I talked to my mama. She can't take a parent loan, she'd never be approved for one. She says I may qualify for private loans, but that they usually cost double when you have to pay them back. She keeps telling me that it's been so hard for her to get on her feet, she doesn't want me to take any shortcuts that might backfire later." He blinks, his eyes glassy with tears. "So I can't go."

The waiter brings out our food.

Neither of us touch it.

I stare at my plate, then glimpse at Ali, who is doing the same. I don't know what to say. A selfish part of me thinks that maybe this is good news, maybe I won't be all alone after Leti leaves. But that doesn't feel right. My chest hurts. I never thought it was possible to experience heartbreak that had nothing to do with me.

"I'm so sorry," I say. "I'm *so* sorry."

It's the only thing I can say.

I reach out for his hand and hold it, and he softens a little. I see tears run down his cheeks. I grab a napkin from a dispenser and hand it to him.

Ali sobs for a little while. I don't know what to do, so I keep grabbing napkins and piling them into the center of the table until there is a mountain of paper snow between us.

"Take a deep breath," I tell him.

I watch his shoulders rise and fall. "I worked so hard."

"I know," I say.

He shakes his head again. "I worked *so* hard. I went to summer workshops, after-school sessions, I milked all I've been through in an essay to get people to care." He pauses for a while, his voice slanting upward and breaking between a sob. "And I got *in*. But the only thing in the way is money. Like always."

He grabs one of the napkins from the center of the table and wipes down his face. "It gets worse when I start wondering," he says. "I wonder what it would've been like if I didn't grow up like this. If my ma hadn't been with someone who was so bad with money, would that, like, I don't know, make our life with money easier? Or if my pa was still around and was just different, you know? Would it work out for me then?"

I nod, because I do know. Not in the same circumstance, but I know.

I don't know what else to tell Ali, because it's not like I can tell him it will get better. I don't know if that's true, not even for myself. Every day I wonder if my chest wouldn't feel so heavy if my pa had stuck around.

But there are no answers, because he's gone.

It's just me and my face, my body, and my weight.

"I don't know if we'll ever get those answers," I tell him, handing him another napkin. "And I can't tell you there's some miracle that's going to happen. It is what it is. We are where we are."

"That's the hard part. Sometimes there isn't a solution."

"Yeah, but you have one. Have you talked to Ms. Barrera about a gap year? Or community college?"

He nods. "She told me to defer and try for next year. But a year is a long time," he says, exhaling. "Lots can change."

"Definitely," I say, thinking of this time last year. Me and Leti. Without the baby to worry about, without college to worry about—just the two of us. Now, I haven't seen her in weeks.

"But," I tell him, "for you, I know it's going to work out."

He sighs. "I hope so. This whole thing almost feels like I didn't deserve to get in."

I shake my head, hard. Just the thought of Alexis makes my body itch with anger. "That's not true. Stupid people get into good schools all the time."

He nods again, slowly. "Yeah. I know. I just wish it were easier. I wish I'd just gotten the scholarship."

I wonder about the scholarship and wonder about Leti. I never knew money was such a big part of going to college—that you couldn't go if you couldn't pay. It seems so blatantly unfair. I wonder if she'd been worrying about paying for school like this—but with her anxiety about the baby clouding everything else, I'd never even asked her.

Ali begins to eat his tacos, meat falling at either side of the tortilla and dribbling grease onto the table. I try to offer more napkins, but the dispenser is out.

I stand up to grab the dispenser from the table in front of us. But when I glance up, it feels like all the air has been vacuumed out of the room and funneled into my throat.

I freeze.

There, in front of me, is my pa.

His back is to me, but I know it's him. I recognize the guayabera that Ava gave him for Father's Day, the cologne my ma got him for Christmas clinging to the cotton. He looks the exact same as the last time I saw him, before that morning my ma picked me up from class.

He looks like my pa.

He looks like me.

There's a young woman beside him, her black hair streaked in thick, yellow highlights. Her jeans are tight. Her heels are tall. Her face is smooth. She looks about Ava's age, if not a little older. But she looks too young. She turns toward me, studying my face closely, peering at it with recognition. Like everyone else, she must see my father.

I am frozen in place, but my thoughts are racing. I can hear them over the thrumming of my heart, reaching for any hope buried in my body: She may just think I'm staring. She may just turn around. She may just ignore it.

I should leave.

I should leave.

I should leave.

She tugs on my pa's shirtsleeve and points her chin toward me.

My pa looks at me.

I don't know what I expected, but his eyes remain flat.

Lifeless.

Like he is looking at a stranger.

My lips part, but I don't have anything to say. I don't even know what to call him. Not knowing whether to call my own father by "Pa" or by his first name makes the thudding in my chest pound harder.

Then, his eyes flicker. Like he also finally understands what's happening. Like he has finally pinned down the face of someone he used to know, once so familiar, whose name he can no longer remember.

I look back at the woman and I panic. Because I see myself in her, too. Accompanying a man with other obligations. Comforted by someone who chooses not to care about what takes precedence.

When I look at my pa again, I realize that I don't need to worry about what to call him. Because he has turned toward his date, shrugging.

And then I realize that here I am, carrying my pa in his hair, in his face. All this weight forced onto my body. He wasn't carrying it today because he had never been carrying it at all.

All the days Ava attempted his job, the hours my ma spent working, the nights I spent anchored to my bed, he spent enjoying the relief we had all been chasing. The joy that felt so out of reach. Responsibility lifted from his shoulders, forcing it onto the three of us. Forcing us into scrutiny, into loss, into work.

I see Ali from the corner of my eye. His eyes are wide, flicking back and forth between me and my pa. He looks at us the way this woman had looked at us. Like watching a pair of mirrors face each other. Like watching a snake eat its own tail.

Ali's eyes dart between me and my pa. Me and my pa, me and my pa.

My pa turns his back to me.

I run.

I weave past the fruteros and paleteros on the sidewalk, trampling through shadows along the concrete. I elbow people out of my way, bustling through the crowds on International. I bolt across traffic and through parking lots, feeling my heels ache from the force of my body hammering against the concrete. My heart pulses in my ears. The sun is menacing in the sky, accusatory as it points right at me.

I pause for a moment, looking to my left and my right. Ava's salon is a block away, but I can't go there. Leti's house is a few blocks up, but I can't go there either. I feel dizzy. Overwhelmed by former choices that have disintegrated to nothing. Each divot in the concrete is the open palm of an intersection, and I still have nowhere to go.

My heart begins beating faster.

I keep running, slicing through the people in Fruitvale Village. I duck into the BART station, my heels slamming against the turnstile when I hop over it. I climb the stairs two at a time, a train approaching right when I get to the platform. I don't read the overhead sign to see where it's going, I just jump through its open doors. I tumble into the train car, my knees landing against the floor with a smack.

I sit with my back against the bike rail. The BART conductor muffles our next stop in the speaker, but I can't understand him. I'm too busy holding my knees. Holding myself.

The train whirrs and begins pulling out of Fruitvale Station. I look down at my sneakers. I can't bring myself to look up at the platform. I know I'll just be disappointed that I am alone on this train. That it was my turn to leave. That my pa never even considered following me.

TWENTY-EIGHT

BART LINES ARE THICK VEINS THAT CROSS THROUGH THE BAY AREA, their platforms bleeding into unrecognizable suburbs. I peer at each neighborhood while I train hop, the sun gradually descending while I find a new line to ride. So far, I've taken the red line, then the orange line, then the yellow line.

I look out the plastic windows at the cities passing below me. When Leti and I were younger, we'd train hop because we had nothing else to do. We would imagine the types of people who lived in the houses that were so unfamiliar to ours—trying to glimpse through the windows that stared back at us.

But tonight, it's just me looking.

I try to imagine like I had with Leti, but my pa is crammed into every corner of my thoughts. Any time I see a house, I wonder if he'd been living there, across all these arteries of train lines, apart from me.

I feel my palms sweat.

I stop at MacArthur Station to transfer to the next line. The outdoor platform is almost empty, but it feels narrow. It's crowded with metal gates, sandwiched between two freeways. I sit on a circular bench at the end of the platform, feeling the warmth of the breeze, and stare at the ads nailed into the fence. Liam and Lauren are selling a home somewhere in Oakland. Their eyes follow me with every move, like they've followed Leti and me every morning at our bus stop.

Every thought of Leti is a stone in my stomach.

I wonder what she's doing. If the baby has grown even bigger in the days we haven't seen one another.

I wish I could talk to her.

I think the worst feeling, after seeing my pa, was racing around Fruitvale and gazing toward the direction of her house, realizing I couldn't go there anymore.

I look down at my legs, feeling the breeze of the traffic whip against them. The cars on the freeways turn on their headlights as the sun dips behind the Downtown Oakland skyline. I look up at the overpasses that are near me. The fragments of sky behind their concrete are orange and deep blue, like old Warriors uniforms. But the color is interrupted by the phone wires that stretch between poles, the cranes in the distance, the gray that always seems to hover over my head.

My palms won't stop sweating. I spread my fingers and shake my hands, feeling air thrash between the webs of my skin, but they remain damp. I'm trying to steady my heart, but it won't stop pounding. It beats quickly, like it had when I saw my pa just standing there. Turning his back toward me.

I try to calm down.

I take deep breaths, but every time I inhale, car exhaust fills my lungs. I cough and wheeze, the taste of gasoline stark on my tongue, making my eyes water. My breath gets shallow. My vision blurs. I see strangers pouring in and out of BART trains. So many of them, cramming together like sardines, while I'm alone.

Instead of feeling heavy, I just feel anxious.

Like the yellow headlights of the cars are eyes striking into my body.

Like the phone wires over my head are pressing onto my chest.

I look ahead, at the Port of Oakland in the distance, the same view Ali and I had looked at when we talked about our fathers.

A train zooms in front of me, obscuring my vision. It's southbound, so I know it'll stop through Fruitvale Station. But I can't bring myself to get into it. I know I'll just have to walk home, where I'll probably be alone. But there's nowhere else for me to go. Not Güera's, or Leti's house, or Alexis's apartment. Home, and its emptiness, is unavoidable.

The thought of needing to return makes my heart beat even faster. I feel like I'm back on Mamá Tere's couch on Thanksgiving. Like my body is unpeeling from itself. Like my heart is like a drum in my ears.

I close my eyes and try to shake the sound out of my head, my curls flying all around me. When I open them, my vision is striped by locks of hair that have fallen in front of my face. Looking at them makes me think of my pa's hair. I shut my eyes again, but the pounding won't stop.

My legs start shaking.

The southbound train pulls out of the station, but I know another will come in seven minutes, then another, and another, its cyclical promise making me nervous.

I pull my legs in tightly, trying to get them to stop trembling. I wrap my arms around them and bury my face into my knees.

My heart won't stop racing.

I don't know what's happening.

I feel so stupid for not having just told my pa everything, right then and there. I should have embarrassed him, forced him to try to feel the anger he left me to feel. But I know he was probably relieved that I ran out and left, so that he wouldn't have to do it again.

Thoughts wind tightly through my brain, wondering who that woman was and how they met and what they are doing. But the one that sticks out most in my head, the one I've been wondering since last spring, since Leti told me she was moving, is the loudest: What about me made me so easy to abandon?

And if my pa can leave me, if I'm supposed to be just like him: How have I already abandoned myself?

I pull my knees in tighter, but it doesn't help. It's warm out, but my whole body is trembling like I'm freezing. My teeth start chattering. It isn't until I look up again, at another southbound train pulling out of the station, that I feel the dampness of tears on my cheeks.

The light poles overhead buzz and flicker on, washing everything deep yellow, illuminating my tear-stained thighs.

I try to steady my breathing, but a sob exits my throat. Its intensity makes my abs ache, my back hunch, my shoulders heave. I try to stifle it, but more come. They are loud enough to cut through the sound of traffic, loud enough to make heads turn. People exit a train behind me, glancing at me when they board the escalator to the exit turnstiles. They look at me with concern, with worry, with pity. They look at me the way my pa hadn't.

And then, just like he did, they leave.

TWENTY-NINE

I'M NOT SURE HOW THIS HAPPENED.

My ma is beside me, her hair damp from the shower, legs tightly crossed, hands clasped around a Styrofoam cup of coffee.

We're in an office that looks too strategically designed, like the waiting room at Leti's clinic. An oil diffuser sputters out a stream. Tissues bloom out of cardboard boxes. Worldly art is on the walls.

The quiet of the office is interrupted by the sound of nails clicking against a keyboard. A woman with deep skin and black hair is sitting across from me and my ma, her "mmhmms" are almost rhythmic to my ma's answers about my general health. Questions I'm surprised she even knows the answer to. I stare at the nameplate on the desk: Dra. Zocorro.

Her name is funny. How do you become a therapist with a name that means help?

"Belén?" Dra. Zocorro asks.

"Huh?"

She smiles, the folds around her mouth wide and deep. "Can you answer the question, please?"

I blink at her.

"I asked how you've been doing in school."

"Oh." I pause. Then, I lie. "Fine, I guess."

She nods. "Did you apply to colleges?"

"No."

My ma fidgets beside me.

"Okay," she says, "and what about friends, do you have a best friend?"

I let out a breath. "No."

"Leti." My ma interjects, as if she's correcting me. As if she knows anything.

I look at her. Then I shake my head.

My ma's eyes widen. "Since when?"

I look up at the ceiling. There's a brown water stain that sweeps across the tiles like a birthmark. I squint at it, trying to remember when Leti and I argued. I'm so tired that time stretches in my brain, elastic and wide without any definite end. "Maybe two weeks ago. I don't know."

Dra. Zocorro continues to type, her nails clacking against the plastic keys. She does this without glancing at the keyboard or her screen, and instead looks at me head-on. She looks kind enough. She has a round face. She has freckles. She wears a cardigan. But I've never seen someone type so maniacally.

"Okay," she says, "what about any other friends?"

"Yeah." I shrug.

"What is the name of your friend?" my ma asks. "The one who was at the house last night?"

I glance at her. Her eyes are swollen with wonder. "Ali."

My ma nods seriously, like she is mentally savoring the name, turning it over in her memory.

Dra. Zocorro gives a single nod, then asks, "And what about your family?"

My ma and I both stiffen.

Dra. Zocorro stops typing.

She looks at us both, her gaze expectant. After a moment, she lifts her hands from her keyboard and picks up a clipboard on her desk. She does that adult thing of licking her index finger while flipping through the forms my ma filled out in the waiting room.

"Ms. Itzel—"

"Del Toro," my ma corrects.

I glance at my ma, but she looks straight ahead. Dra. Zocorro nods and moves a pen swiftly over the documents. "Ms. Del Toro, you say here that Belén ran into her father and arrived at home having a panic attack?"

My ma shifts in her seat.

I'm still unsure of how that all unraveled. The last thing I really remember is crying at the BART station. Everything else is smudged in my memory. Blurs of riding the bus home, the blue light of the AC Transit beaming overhead. Visions of sitting on my porch steps, looking at the earthquake cracks where my pa would park his truck.

Flickers of lying in my living room, where Ali and Ava sat across from me.

But, at the front of my mind is my ma's face—so wide and close to mine, it was like looking through a fishbowl. Instead of worry or anger, she looked protective. The sound of my pa's name did not make her shrink, but instead made her expression blaze.

The last thing I fully remember is hearing Ali's car pull out of the driveway. Then I slept.

I woke up on the couch this morning, the sound of Ava shutting the front door startling me awake. When I sat up, my ma came out of the kitchen and brought me a plate of eggs. They were drizzled with Tapatío, how I'd eaten it since I was a kid. The fact that she remembered made me feel terrible. But then she hugged me tightly, told me she loved me, then told me to take a shower and get dressed. I thought that I was dreaming.

We didn't talk the entire car ride here. I didn't know where we were going, and I didn't have the energy to ask. I've never been hungover, but I imagined this is how it would feel. Like all my limbs were full of sand.

My ma turned on the radio to fill the silence, setting the dial to 102.9 KBLX. Despite Tower of Power being on, she didn't sing along like usual. Tower of Power turned to Maxwell, Maxwell turned to Anita Baker, Anita Baker turned to Tony! Toni! Toné! They sang about thinking of someone, and I thought of Ali, when he played Tony! Toni! Toné! in his car and explained that they, like Tower of Power, like us, were from Oakland.

When we pulled into the pediatric center of the hospital, I didn't

279

really feel anything either. My brain, my heart, my chest, all felt so exhausted after yesterday. No matter how hard I tried to feel anything, I just felt numb.

And now we're here, with Dra. Zocorro staring at both of us, waiting for an answer. I turn the phrase "panic attack" over in my head. It sounds so dramatic, so accusatory.

As if she's read my mind, Dra. Zocorro pulls out a pale green pamphlet and hands it to me. I unfold it and read a bullet-point list about panic attack symptoms: sweating, heart palpitations, intrusive thoughts, constant worrying.

It reminds me of the pamphlets by the counselors' office, equally as condescending and diagnostic. Because none of these symptoms bring up the context. Like, on paper, I guess it makes sense. But the phrase seems so excessive.

How was I *supposed* to react to seeing someone I never thought I'd see again? Who I never thought would *want* to see me again? Maybe I would've prepared more, but it was like my pa vanished into nothing. Maybe I did cry so hard that when I looked at my reflection this morning, my eyelids were raw and pink, but what else was I supposed to do? See my pa and run into the arms he never bothered to open?

Was my reaction wrong? Was my reaction worthy of something that would require me to sit here with two people just staring at me?

I don't say anything, I just fold the pamphlet into a tight square and shove it into the pocket of my jeans, prepared to throw it away on my way out.

"Yes," my ma finally says, breaking the silence between the three of us, "Belén's father left our family about a year ago. She hadn't seen him since, and she ran into him when she was with her friend."

Dra. Zocorro's eyebrows slope together in concern. "How did you feel seeing him, Belén?"

"Uh," I say, my lips parting. The irritation settles, and it feels like all my words are stuck in my throat, clogged behind embarrassment. "I don't know."

Dra. Zocorro looks at me for a long time. I think her eyes might bore a hole into my skull. "Well, Belén, I want to see you once a week for a few months to discuss how you're feeling. How does that sound to you?"

I don't say anything.

After a long beat of silence, my ma cuts in. "Mija," she says, "it will be good for you."

My brain begins ping-ponging again. How come *I* have to meet with Dra. Zocorro once a week? I didn't ask to be born, and now I have to deal with being burdened by the aftermath of my parents' bad decisions?

Maybe, if my pa had just been a better father, I wouldn't have to do all this. Maybe, if my ma had just taken his departure better and checked in on me every once in a while, we'd be at the laundromat washing clothes like we used to do every Saturday. Really, shouldn't my parents be here? In some coaching program?

But it's all on me.

The weight only gets heavier.

"Belén?" Dra. Zocorro asks. "What do you think?"

I'm about to open my mouth to say no. I remember all the red flags in my student file, vibrant reminders of my truancy. I'm sure I can figure out a way to skip sessions here.

But then I catch my ma's reflection in the window. New wrinkles that have sprouted along her skin, wedged firmly between her brows. I look at her hands, her nails short and chipped, and wonder where they have been. Probably the same place Ali's ma's hands had been—pressed in prayer, wrung with work. I meet her gaze and realize, for the first time, that I have her eyes. Deep brown, full of expression. Her pupils dilate with worry when she sees me.

I glance at the clock nailed above the door. It's almost noon. I wonder what the last Saturday I spent with my ma was. When I can't remember, sadness swells in my chest.

I look at the floor. The deep blue, stain-resistant carpet lined from a fresh vacuum. Dra. Zocorro's leather Clarks. My summer sandals. And my ma's shoes, a pair of black sneakers with a thick, curved sole along the bottoms. Sensible shoes, like Ava's. The kind you wear when you work.

When you're stuck trying to do someone else's job.

I sigh.

"Yeah," I tell Dra. Zocorro, "that sounds good."

THIRTY

THE RECEPTIONIST ASKS MY MA IF SHE SHOULD PRINT EXTRA COPIES for my pa. We're by the front desk, finishing intake forms. I pretend I'm not listening, wandering toward the hallway instead. "No," my ma says, turning around to make sure I'm out of earshot, "it's just me."

I move toward the end of the hall, by a window so wide it encompasses almost the entire wall. I look below at the 580 beneath me, cars zooming in bright strokes of color: black on gray, white on gray, red on gray, gray on gray. I wonder where they're all going when I feel so stuck.

My ma brushes past my shoulder when she's finished, and we take the elevator down together. In its steel-paneled walls, I can see both of our bodies, infinitely reflecting until we are nothing but shapes.

In the parking lot, I see Ava's car parked beside Ma's. When I get closer, Ava gets out. She slams the door behind her, and rushes to give me a hug so tight I think my ribs are breaking beneath the squeeze.

"Are you okay?" she asks me. She still hasn't let me go. I take a deep breath, inhaling the familiar scent of expensive shampoo and burnt hair. She just came from work. "I'm sorry, I could only take a half day. You know what the lady who owns my shop is like."

I blink at her. I don't know why, but I feel like crying. "It's okay."

My ma waits behind us, gazing out of the parking structure, at the pockets of sky behind the slate.

"Why don't we go to the lake?" she asks.

While my ma drives, I think of the last time we went to Lake Merritt as a family. It must have been years ago. My ma would wrap burritos in aluminum foil, cut sandía into triangles, and bring it with her in one of my pa's large construction lunch boxes. We'd eat on the peeling, green picnic tables by the bird observatory that I always mistook for a huge soccer post. Ava and I would kick around the sand in the play structure, and my ma would hover, yelling at us to not get so dirty. I try to think of what my pa did while the three of us were busy, but I can't remember at all. It was like he was never there, even then.

We park and stake out a spot near the pergola, its columns wrapped with tree branches, its roof streaming in the light in a crosshatch. We spread an animal-print blanket across the grass, sitting on the distorted image of a tiger. Ava eventually joins us, and for a moment the three of us just sit there, gazing at the lake. The people on the other side are small dots in the distance, similar to the memory of my pa.

My ma turns around, peering at the food trucks lining the parking

284

meters behind us. "I'll go get us some lunch."

She walks toward the trucks, leaving Ava and me beside each other.

"Was she nice?" Ava asks.

"Was who nice?"

"The therapist."

I look at her, but she's still looking ahead. "She was fine, I guess."

"You know you can ask for another one if you don't like her. They never tell you that you can do that, but you can."

I blink.

"My first one was not very good. I got a new one last month, she's better for me."

I'm not sure what to say.

So I don't say anything.

I look at Ava's profile instead. I can usually tell when she's going to cry—her nose gets pink and her eyebrows twitch, but when tears float down her cheeks today, they are unexpected, even to me.

"I'm sorry," she says, "I should have been there for you more. I could tell you weren't doing well, but I wasn't doing well either. I only recently started talking to someone, and they put me on these pills. They made me feel like I was sleepwalking, but I think they're beginning to work. I kept telling myself to ask you more, I just didn't know how."

"The pills in your room?" I blurt out.

Ava can cry, but she can keep it real too. She's still my sister. She glowers at me. "You went into my room?"

"Sorry," I tell her. I don't tell her the truth, that I went in to get perfume, but that I felt like a string pulled me inside, wandering through her things like I used to do when I was younger. When I missed her.

She shakes her head, but I can see a trace of a smile. "Yes, the ones in my room."

"But how come? You had one of these too?"

She wipes her eyes with the back of her palm. "No," she says, "I just, I don't know, felt different. I was always sad, always angry."

"You were always angry," I agree.

She nudges me a little bit. "Stop it." She sighs, the reflection of the lake glimmering against her deep eyes. "But it made me worry. Because I felt like I was always reminding myself of someone, like I was always behaving like someone. I couldn't put my finger on it, until that night on Thanksgiving, and it felt like something inside of me snapped. I had this, like, strange déjà vu in the kitchen and I finally realized I reminded myself of Pa."

I'd always wanted to hear her admit it, that she was just as much like Pa as I was. I always imagined it'd bring me some kind of satisfaction. But hearing it doesn't make me feel any better. It just makes me feel like we are both on the same level, tethered together to the ground.

She picks fistfuls of grass from the dirt, their blades falling between her manicured nails. "It made me freak out a little bit. I felt so bad afterward, for all the things I said to you. But I didn't know how to apologize." She pauses. "No one had ever apologized to us."

Ava inhales, her breath rattling in her throat. "And I was just so tired. I was trying to go to work and take care of Ma and keep up with you and keep up with me. It was a lot to carry."

I knew exactly how she felt. Even if it was a little bit different. No matter the make of the weight, it all weighed equally.

"Yeah," I tell her, "I just always felt heavy. And then it was like all the weight came off at once, but it felt awful."

She nods, her blond highlights glittering in the sunlight. "Like that, yeah. I was trying really hard to set a good example for you. But it got hard for me too. And then, Matías . . ."

The thought of Matías makes me want to roll my eyes out of my head. "What about Matías?"

"I dumped him," she says, laughing. When I laugh too, I think our laughs sound similar. Hers is a little lower, but together they harmonize. I wonder which of our parents they came from, but maybe this was something for only the two of us, only for us to share.

She pushes her hair behind her ears. "He was such a loser. I saw myself taking care of him for the rest of my life. Sort of like Ma with Pa, and I didn't wanna do that to myself. Things have to end at some point."

Her words echo in my head: things have to end. But where do things begin? That always leaves me confused. Being my pa's daughter, I feel like I'm in an infinite cycle without anyone specific at its starting place. I know I can blame him all I want, but circles always come back around. I know one day I'll have to pick a new starting point. I know one day I'll have to be in charge of being different.

Ava sniffles a little bit and wipes her nose with the edge of the blanket.

"I'm proud of you," she says.

I'm stunned. My head cocks back, and I immediately scoff. "For what? Crying?"

I'm only kidding, but she nods. "Yeah. Cuz I didn't for a long time. And you didn't for a long time."

"So?"

"Can you imagine if we didn't for the rest of our lives?"

I look back at the lake. A frutero pushes a cart past, ringing his bell. It makes me think of Leti, and an emptiness in my stomach pangs. I shrug. "I didn't want to cry, it just happened."

"How come?"

"I didn't wanna be like Ma." I breathe deep, the damp smell of the lake mixing with the grass beneath me. I knew that if my pa could whirl in me like circles, so could my ma. I tried to always escape the feeling of heaviness because I saw how it affected her. She'd cried so often, tears lapping against her body until she was almost eroded, almost gone. "All she does is cry. Like, what if I started and it never stopped?"

Ava nods. "I used to be so upset about that. I kind of thought it was pathetic. But there's something important about feeling it. Have you noticed she's better lately?"

"No," I tell her. "I never see her."

Ava pauses, but then she takes a deep breath. "She's working, you know? She doesn't want to worry you with the bills, but it was hard for a little bit. We both were scraping together what we had left."

"I could've helped," I say. "I still can."

Ava smiles. "Maybe you can now. But you couldn't then. You looked like a zombie, desvelada. Didn't even ask me to cut your hair." She picks up one of my curls, which is admittedly fried on the ends from all the straightening. "But she's better."

I turn around to see my ma handing a taquero some cash. She makes small talk, her Spanish fluttering out of her lips, like she used to.

"It's better to say it," Ava says. "To admit what happened. How else are we supposed to let it go?"

I shake my head. "It's fucked up, though. That we have something to let go of. I never asked to have anything at all."

"But now we do." Ava sighs. "It's not fair. He left, and nothing is going to change that, not even being angry about it. And I'm not saying you shouldn't be angry. I still am. He makes the mess, but we clean it up. But I don't want to have so much of the mess on me anymore, you know?"

She shakes her head. "I know our family makes it hard. I was at Mamá Tere's the other week—she was going on and on about Pa. He says it's our fault, that we pushed him out." She lets out a deep breath. "I got into this huge argument with her because it was so clear to me that he wanted to leave. Nobody who wants to make something work behaves that way. But the only thing we can control is what we do after."

I think of the Sor Juana poem buried somewhere in the depths of my backpack. The line about men misting a mirror, then complaining it wasn't clean. I remember thinking it was about men who complained about harm they caused but never repaired. But today, it reminds me of all the mirrors I have avoided in my life, fearing the reflection inside of it would show me my pa's face. At least I was learning to look at myself. Maybe he would never do that.

I want to say something else, something smart like her. But Ava wraps her arms around my shoulders.

"I love you," she says. "I'm sorry we have to clean it up."

The embrace catches me off guard, my joints stiff beneath the embrace. But eventually, I soften. I hug her back.

My ma approaches us, expertly cradling paper plates covered in tinfoil in her arms. The three of us eat our tacos along the blanket. We tell time by watching shadows replace the sun, their gray stretching over us, a darkness that is almost welcome.

On the rare occasions the three of us would ever be together, something always felt missing, a pain blooming in its place like a phantom limb. But today, I feel we are steady, sharp like the edges of a triangle. And today, for the first time in months, when I glance over to look at my ma, she is already looking back at me.

THIRTY-ONE

ALI HAS FLOWERS FOR ME. THE STEMS ARE CROOKED AND BENT, THE yellow petals of the daisies slightly brown. Ms. Barrera has a sub today, so instead of going to her classroom after sixth period, we're sitting in the school parking lot. He extends them over to me from the driver's seat.

"My mama says yellow is for hoping someone gets well soon," he says. "I didn't really know how to classify what happened, so this is the best I could do. I got them yesterday and carried them in my backpack all day, so I'm sorry if they're a little bit dead."

I look at them and smile a little. "You think I'm sick?" I joke.

"No offense," he says, starting his car, "but you didn't see your face that day."

"That's fair," I say, palming the head of a daisy. "Thank you."

"How are you feeling?" he asks, veering away from the school and onto the road.

"Better. Yesterday kind of felt like a dream, but today is okay."

"Did he call?"

"No," I say. "But I didn't expect him to."

Ali nods, and begins turning away from International, toward my house. Then I realize that today is Monday, the first day I'm scheduled to see Dra. Zocorro after school.

"Wait," I tell him. "Would you mind dropping me off at the clinic downtown?"

"Sure," he says, switching lanes. He doesn't ask anything else, which makes me feel safe to tell him.

"I went to a therapist on Saturday."

"That's cool." He smiles. "How was it?"

I shrug. "I've only talked to her once."

"My ma took me to one once. But I didn't like her—she was this old white lady. Didn't understand a thing I was saying. I was hoping to find a Black therapist when I went to Howard, but . . ."

"Yeah," I say, matching his soft tone, "I'm sorry. If you want, I can get you some information from inside."

He smiles a bit. "Keep the pamphlets coming."

The buildings of Downtown Oakland are pillars around us, shading us from the spring sunshine. After a while of silence, I look over at him. "Thanks for coming to my house to make sure I was okay."

"Oh," he says, like he hadn't even considered it a big deal, "of course. I didn't want to follow you right after you left. Really, I didn't know what to do. But also, I figured you probably needed time to yourself."

"I did," I told him. "I just cried for a while."

"My mama says salt water can purify wounds, so it should also purify our hearts. You know, Mom shit."

"She sounds wise."

"Your mama is wise too, though. She was straight up in defense mode. When I came to the door and mentioned your name, she gave me a *look*. But as soon as I explained what happened, she was like a lioness. Your sister too. I never wanna be on their bad side." He pauses for a second. "It reminded me of you. How they talk, how they look."

My eyes widen. I look over at him, but his eyes are glued to the road. "Really? Everybody says I look like my pa."

"Him?" he jokes. "No, honestly. You really do. Like, *really* do—it's kinda scary. But you're not like him."

I cock my head back. "How would you know that?"

"You're not a coward," he says matter-of-factly. "I don't know about you or your pa like that, but I watched that whole thing go down. You could see that man shrink when he saw you."

"Shrink?" I repeat.

He nods. "Absolutely. That woman he was with looked at you more than he did. It looked like he only opened his mouth when he knew you were going to leave." He shakes his head. "What he did after you left was even worse."

I turn to Ali, whose eyes are fixed on the road. "What happened?"

"That man sat down with his date and ate his food. He sat facing me, too. And I just stared at him. He was avoiding my gaze, but when he finally looked at me, he looked so scared. Deer in the headlights shit. It was like it was the first time someone had ever really seen him. And then, I got up and left. I didn't know where you went, but I felt like it was the right thing to do to see if you were okay. It's what I would've wanted if it were me."

I'm relieved to know. To know I hadn't been imagining it all—my pa was as I pictured him. As selfish as I suspected.

"You don't think your pa is a coward?" Ali asks, pulling off the freeway.

"I just thought he was selfish."

"You can be two things at once," he says, "but to see you and turn his back like that? He's definitely a coward."

"I could've said something, too," I respond.

Ali shakes his head, the sun flaring behind his profile, making his earrings glitter. "It's different. You're the kid, he's the parent. He owes *you*."

Ali double-parks in front of the clinic. I zip the flowers into my empty backpack, saddened by the fact that they'll probably be totally dead by the time I get home.

"Thanks," I tell him. "I've never really talked to anyone else about this before."

He gestures to the building. "Well, you're about to."

I smile and say goodbye, then step toward the hospital. The sensor on the glass doors of the entrance teases me, sending the doors to open and closed, open and closed. In a moment of them shutting, I am confronted by my reflection. It's not the first time I see my pa in all of my features, his hair tied to my head, his eyes burrowed into my skull, his mouth angled on my face. But it's the first time I also see myself.

I sit across from Dra. Zocorro, on the same couch my ma and I sat on a few days ago. The emptiness beside me makes me nervous, suddenly aware that I am here alone.

Dra. Zocorro flicks on a desk lamp. I notice a pile of coloring books on an end table, stacked beneath a collection of nested bowls. They look how I feel—each holding more of the same, and each still holding nothing.

"How are you today, Belén?" she asks, sitting on her pale green computer chair. She smiles, her dark red lipstick contrasting against her teeth. They're so white and proportionate, they look like the Chiclets kids sell in México.

"Fine."

"You nervous?"

I shrug.

"I know this probably feels strange and new. But tell me about yourself. What do you like to do?"

God, I hate talking to adults about what I like to do.

As soon as I say I like to read, they talk to me like I'm a genius, only to be disappointed when they realize I'm failing. But there's no choice here. It's just me and her. I shift in my seat. "I like to read."

She nods, but she doesn't take notes, which makes me feel better. Something about not hearing her nails click against the keyboard calms me down a little bit. "What do you read? You must read a lot in school, I'm sure."

"Yeah," I say, because it's not a lie. I *do* read a lot in school. Just not the things Ms. Foley tells me to read.

"What attracts you to reading?"

"I don't know. It helps me forget what I'm feeling, I guess."

She nods again, very quickly this time. "Yeah, it can be helpful for that. But why would you want to forget a feeling?"

I freeze along the couch, squinting at her. I feel like I fell right into her "Aha moment" trap. "I don't know, sometimes I just don't wanna feel them right away."

"Sure," she says, "just as long as they don't come spilling out all at once."

I pause. Is this a jab? I look at her, and her mouth is formed into a smirk. I kind of respect her for it. "I guess so," I say.

"Do you think you can walk me through that evening, when that happened with your dad? It's okay if it's too soon."

I almost don't want to talk about it. After talking with Ava and Ali, I feel like I've regurgitated the same story a million times. It makes my heart feel worn. But I glance at the clock nailed above the door. We have a little under an hour left. What's the point of therapy if you don't "talk about it"?

"It's fine."

She shifts in her chair. "What do you think seeing your father provoked in you?"

I shrug. "It was scary, I guess."

"Was he threatening?"

"No," I say, "he was just there. I almost forgot what he looked like. For such a long time I would close my eyes and try to picture his face, and nothing would come up. But then I'd look in the mirror and feel okay."

"What about the mirror was helpful?"

"I'd look in the mirror and, I don't know." I glance out the window. Trees bloom in the park below us, petals of cherry blossoms like pink confetti along the grass. "Everyone says we're the spitting image of each other. So when I'd see myself, I'd see him."

She blinks. "Is that challenging for you? People saying you look like someone you sometimes don't remember? Someone you can't see?"

"Yeah," I say. "It's fucked up."

"How so?"

I shrug again. "Everybody says we're the same. And the person I'm supposed to be like abandons me? It makes me wonder if I'll ever do that to myself."

"Abandon yourself?" she asks.

"I guess. I don't know."

Dra. Zocorro pauses for a long while. In the lull, I can hear the oil diffuser sputter. A stream of vapor funneling through a small opening, then dispersing into the air.

"You know that's not true, right?" she asks. "You're not your father."

I feel sweat seep into the creases of my arms. "I know," I lie.

"Your parents are a big part of who you are, but you are not them. There are some parts we can't change, but you can control who you become. It isn't always symbiotic."

My eyebrows furrow. "What's that mean?"

"It means that it's not always give and take. In our culture, it seems that way. Your family is supposed to be your priority. But it doesn't have to be—it seems like your father doesn't believe that. You can take the good from him, but you don't have to take the bad."

I sigh. "Is that even a choice? Like, isn't it just in my DNA?"

"Some of that is true," she says while nodding. "Some of it, like your appearance, is genetic. Some of your behavioral patterns are genetic as well, and we can talk about that more. But the interesting part about behavior is that a lot of it can be shaped. I know you all hate when adults say this, but you're so young. There's so much time to become who you are and make your own choices." She pauses, peering at me with a stillness in her eyes. Her gaze isn't judgmental or expectant. It feels nice being looked at without anyone having any comparisons to make.

She smiles a little bit. "People talk a lot about the circle of life. You are not alive, then you're alive, then you're not alive. But your actual life is not bound to circles. Just because your parents move in one, doesn't mean you have to move in the same one. Your life can be angled, much more different."

I blink at her. I don't know what to say. With everyone telling me that me and my pa were so alike, I thought these circles were inevitable. Sometimes they didn't even feel like circles—they felt like spirals.

"Can you explain what you meant by abandoning yourself?"

I breathe in, air tickling the base of my throat. "I don't know. Like, I know I'm physically here. But sometimes I feel like I betrayed myself."

"Yourself, like your values?"

"Yeah." I pause. "I don't think I've made great choices." I look at the floor. I know what I did with Alexis was wrong. The shame of letting him use me that way, of letting myself be used that way, has been itching at me for weeks. Leti's words, tainted with her ma's tone, with her pious judgment, had been snaking around in my head. But some of that judgment came from me, too. I knew better. I should've done better.

"What were you hoping to gain from making those choices?"

I shrug. "I was hoping to forget everything that was going on. But I kind of fucked up through it."

She tilts her head. "You're allowed to make mistakes, Belén. You especially. When you are reacting to a circumstance you didn't ask to be in, you may not make the best choices. You can observe your behavior without judging yourself for it."

I blink at her.

She recrosses her legs. "What were you hoping to gain in forgetting what was happening with your dad?"

"I don't know. Like, why would I want to feel that, you know?"

"Feel what?"

"Feel sad."

"What happened with your dad made you sad?"

It's the first time someone has asked me that.

The straightforwardness of the sentence makes me feel ridiculous. Because it's so short, so small, so simple. So easy for Dra. Zocorro to describe. And somehow, for a year, it felt like the most complicated thing of my life. But that was it: I was sad.

"Yeah."

"What did that sadness feel like?"

"I just felt heavy. Physically heavy. Like there was something over my head or on my chest or in my body. It felt awful. So, why would I want to feel that on purpose, you know?"

"So, you distracted yourself?"

"I guess so."

She nods. "And you feel you betrayed yourself in the process?"

"Yeah."

Dra. Zocorro tilts her head again. "Well, Belén, what did you fear would happen if you allowed yourself to just feel sad? To feel that heaviness?"

I look at her. "I've never felt like that was an option."

"Why?"

I glance at the ceiling, at that stretching stain. "I worried that I'd be like my ma. Just, like, crying all the time."

"What would be so bad about crying?"

I think back to the conversation Ava and I had. "Cuz what if I never stopped?"

"You think you would cry indefinitely?"

I squint. "Well, no. But I feel like it would change me."

"Change you how?"

"Like I'd be a different person. A sad person."

Dra. Zocorro nods again. "And what kind of person do you think you are now?"

I blink at her. "I don't know."

"Well, Belén, it sounds like you're thinking of this as a dichotomy: either you feel the sadness and you become it, or you distract yourself from it. Is that right?"

"Yeah."

"How do you think distracting yourself worked for you?"

300

I stare at her. When I feel my eyes get glassy, I look at my sneakers. I wish I could say that it worked.

But I failed.

I read so many books and went to so many appointments and had so much terrible sex and avoided so many mirrors and made so many mistakes, and I still failed.

And it's so embarrassing—to feel failure.

Because if all of that had worked, I wouldn't be here, feeling the wetness streaming down my cheeks, the tears twisting into my hair.

When I tell Dra. Zocorro this, she plucks a tissue from a box on her desk and hands it to me, shaking her head gently. "You did not fail. Trust me when I say that this was going to happen eventually. Distracting yourself from pain doesn't always work the way we think it might. You cannot meander around your feelings." She smiles at me, watching as I wipe my face. "But there is a healthy medium there. You can feel sad without becoming sadness."

I grab another tissue and rub my eyes, trying not to think about how corny everything she's saying is. I look at her through the tangle of my wet lashes. She leans her chin against the heel of her hand, studying me.

"Are you okay to keep going?" she asks.

I nod.

"I want to ask a little more about your dad. How would you describe him?"

A cold rush floods to the pit of my stomach, thinking of the conversation Ali and I had in the car. "Selfish. Cowardly."

"What makes him that way to you?"

"He left," I say quickly. "Parents get divorced all the time—that's normal. But he just left."

"How was it different?"

"Cuz he had me," I say. I don't mean to say it loudly, but I do. The magnitude of my voice makes my throat close up a bit, like I'm ready to cry again. "You can break up or whatever. But he had responsibilities—he *has* responsibilities." I think of what Ali said in the car. "Like, I'm the kid. He's supposed to at least be a father. But he can't even do that."

Dra. Zocorro nods very firmly. "You're right, Belén. You deserve a lot better."

It makes me feel better that she agrees with me. I had only ever heard people say they deserved better when they were romantic with someone. My ma deserved a better husband. Ava deserved a better boyfriend. But I had never heard someone say it about a parent. But it's true. I did deserve better. So did Ava. So did Ali. So did Leti.

But knowing I deserved more didn't make not having it any easier.

"It's not fair," I tell Dra. Zocorro, peering at the light slanting from beneath her door.

"What's not fair?"

"Why can't I just have that, you know?"

Dra. Zocorro nods again, thoughtfully. "I know it must be hard to think about your father leaving as a loss. But you have gained so much."

I snort. "Like what? Anger?"

"Yes, like anger. But maybe also perspective, reflection."

I glance behind her. Just like Ms. Barrera, she has her diplomas displayed on the wall. I stare at them. Isn't she supposed to be smart? I know she's a doctor and everything, but it seems like such a stupid thing to say. How can a loss be a place for gain?

When I ask her this, she smiles.

"I am not saying what he did was right, and I'm not challenging you to be optimistic. I just want you to turn this experience onto its head and see it from a different angle."

We go back and forth for a while, because it's the most confusing concept I've been presented with. After some time, she glances at the clock on the wall. "We are out of time for today, Belén. But we can continue this conversation in our next session. Okay?"

"Sure," I say through a sigh.

Dra. Zocorro walks me out, sending me off with a smile and a sweeping arm gesturing to the elevator. I stand at the end of the hall, in front of the same large window I'd looked at while my ma was filling out paperwork. My bus won't be here for another fifteen minutes, so I gaze at the view, feeling my tangled insides ache. If therapy is supposed to make people feel better, why does it feel like my chest is in knots?

I peer beneath the overpass, at the cars inching into Downtown Oakland, and see a familiar truck parked by a meter. It's a red as familiar to me as my own blood. But to be sure, I walk toward the other end of the window to see the back of the car. And there, along the bumper, is a large "Hecho en México" sticker. It's Señor Barragón's truck.

I wonder for a moment what he's doing here. He spends most of his days at work, painting houses on the opposite side of Oakland. Then

I look across the street, where I see Quentin's car parked beneath the overpass. My heart leaps into my throat, thrumming with realization. Leti made her birth plan at this clinic, but the baby isn't supposed to be due for another few weeks. But there's no other reason her pa and Quentin would be here today.

I whip my head around to the clinic's directory, following the maze of a map with a shaky finger until it lands on the Labor and Delivery section of the hospital. I rush into the elevator, repeatedly pressing the button for the fourth floor, the tip of my nail bending in my urgency. I close my eyes with the doors of the elevator, praying I haven't missed it. Praying I haven't missed the birth of Leti's baby.

THIRTY-TWO

NO ONE IS IN THE WAITING ROOM.

I run to the next waiting lounge, but it's just as empty as the first one. I rush up to the help desk to ask the receptionist if anyone named Leticia has checked in, but she says she isn't authorized to share that type of information. What kind of fucking help is that?

I sprint to the next check-in desk, but instead of finding a receptionist in the waiting area, I see Ms. Barrera sitting on one of the armchairs.

She peers up from the book she's reading, eyes widening in surprise. "Belén, I didn't know you'd be coming."

"Did she have the baby?" I'm nearly shouting between pants. I hunch over, grip my thighs, and try to catch my breath.

Ms. Barrera shakes her head. "No. Quentin called me early this morning and said that her water broke. I took the day off to be here in case she needed help."

I exhale a sigh of relief so hard that my backpack slips off my shoulder and thuds onto the floor.

"But her parents are here, right?" I ask.

Ms. Barrera shoots me a look. "Yeah, they're being, um"—she rolls her eyes upward, as if the right words are painted along the ceiling—"they're being her parents."

I slump into the chair beside her, nodding. "You mean 'useless.' How long has she been in labor?"

"Since about seven this morning," she explains. "I've been here since then, popping in and out to see if she needs anything."

"Seven a.m.? That's *hella* long," I say, wondering if Leti took that painkiller she'd been worrying about. She'd forced me to watch so many videos about its side effects and listen to her pro-and-con list to decide whether or not she should take it.

"Is that normal?" I ask.

"It's not out of the ordinary," Ms. Barrera says, "But it's not great. The baby is a few weeks early, but it shouldn't complicate anything too badly. At least that's what the doctor said."

Leave it to the baby to be early—just like its damn mother. "So, she's just been lying there in pain for, like, nine hours?"

"Yes," Ms. Barrera says, sighing, "it's been hard on her. And on him."

She gestures across the way, where Quentin is exiting the elevator. He carries a sandwich covered in plastic wrap in one hand, a cup of Jell-O in the other. He looks pale, like he's just seen a ghost. But when he sees me, relief washes over him.

"Thank *God* you're here," he says, dropping the food and lifting me up for a tight hug.

"Why aren't you in *there*?" I ask, feeling an overwhelming urge to strangle him. How is he getting lunch when Leti is in labor?

Ms. Barrera cuts in. "He's been in there all day. I've been telling him for a few hours that he needs to eat."

"I feel like I'm going to throw up," he says, sitting beside me and putting his head between his knees. "And I know, I know. *I'm* not the one in labor. This isn't about me. But I feel awful."

I pat him on the back. "You'll be okay. Did she take that painkiller?"

"The epidural?" he asks, pressing his knees tighter against his head.

"Yeah, that I guess."

"No," he says, releasing a deep breath. "She wants to have a natural childbirth."

I shake my head. "Damn. Leti is so smart but so dumb sometimes."

"It's a complicated choice," Ms. Barrera interjects.

"You should go in," Quentin tells me, his voice muffled between his thighs.

"Me?" I ask.

He nods.

"She's mad at me," I say. A pang of pain presses against my stomach. "She didn't even tell me her water broke."

"She didn't have time to," Quentin says. "I called everybody. I called you too, but you didn't pick up."

I check my phone and see that he'd called me during my session

307

with Dra. Zocorro. I also see a text from my ma, asking if I'm feeling okay after therapy. It's strange seeing her name on my phone like this. I hesitate on what to respond, my thumbs hovering over the keyboard, but I tell her about Leti instead. Her response is quick, saying that she'll be here after her staff meeting.

"You think she'd want me in there?" I ask Quentin.

He lifts his head up. "Her parents are in there, just sitting around. My parents are there too, but it's not the same. She *needs* you there. I can go with you."

"Don't you need to eat?"

He shakes his head. "There's no way I'm keeping anything down right now." He picks up his food, hands it to Ms. Barrera, then stands, letting out a deep breath. We start for the door together, and I hear Leti shriek. It's high-pitched and painful. I wonder if she's having contractions or if her ma is speaking.

Ms. Barrera says she'll stay here to wait for the rest of Quentin's family. Quentin and I walk to the threshold between the waiting area and the hall of examination rooms. He opens the door, revealing Leti's room. She lies in a hospital bed, drenched in sweat, her hair loose and stuck to her cheeks. Señor Barragón is sitting, watching a soccer game on his phone. Señora Barragón is beside him, sewing, holding her needle eye level as she runs thread through it.

When Leti sees me, her mouth drops. She immediately lifts her arms, wiggling her hands toward me.

"Belén!" she shouts.

I'm ready to walk toward her when a nurse approaches me and Quentin. She hands him a set of scrubs, then looks over at me. "I'm sorry," she says, "but only family is allowed into the room."

I look over at Leti, who glances at the nurse. "She's my sister!" she shrieks. "She's my sister!"

Then we both burst into tears.

THIRTY-THREE

LETI HAS A DAUGHTER.

She names her Alma Belén Barragón-Anderson. She is the most beautiful thing I've seen in my life.

So beautiful I don't even have time to think about how ridiculous Quentin's last name sounds hyphenated with her own. Especially because Leti gave her daughter my name. Mine.

Her labor kicked into full-gear an hour after I sat with her in the delivery room. Quentin and I were both laser-focused, dressed in blue scrubs. My hat didn't fit over my head because of my hair, but it didn't matter.

When the doctor came in and instructed Leti to open her legs, Señor Barragón left. He shook his head with disgust and said, "That's what got her in this mess to begin with."

Señora Barragón watched her husband leave the room. For the first time since I came inside, she looked at me.

In my near six years of knowing her, it was the first time she looked at me without the sharpness of her criticism, without the roll of an eye. She looked at me with the sincerity of someone seeking advice.

I nodded at her, urging her to help. But quickly, she returned her gaze to her cross-stitch, pulling the thread through the embroidery hoop. She moved her head from left to right, shaking it with dissuasion.

Quentin stood by Leti's side, wiping the sweat from her face. I held her hand, offering whatever encouragement I could. It was like all the pep talks in the six years of our friendship were preparation for this moment. Quentin's parents prayed, hands clasped together, but I knew Leti wasn't connecting with it. She only ever prayed in Spanish.

Which is why when she slipped her fingers between my palms in lieu of a rosary, I just let her. She prayed in between sobs, the words thick between her teeth. I don't really know prayers like that, so I just kept nodding and saying, "Uh-huh, amen."

When it was time for Leti to push, it didn't take long. It seemed earned after her almost ten-hour labor. Quentin swapped out rag after rag, mopping the sweat trailing down her forehead. The doctor and Quentin's parents loudly kept yelling to push and push and push.

And then, over all of Leti's praying, I heard a piercing cry.

I glanced up and saw a baby in the arms of the doctor, who announced proudly that the sex was female.

I'm not gonna lie, the baby looked pretty fucking gross. Her hair was matted and her eyes bulged and it looked like she was drenched in blood and vomit. And still, with that, I was amazed she existed.

Quentin's surgical mask dampened with tears as his father helped him cut the umbilical cord, and Leti's face was overcome with relief when she had her first moment of skin-to-skin contact. And then we all cried. A chorus of clumsy sobs climbing from our throats, interrupted by jagged gasps for air.

After the nurse cleaned Alma up and swaddled her, Leti handed her to Quentin's parents. They fawned and wept, and then they offered her to Señora Barragón, who peeked up at me. I nodded again, itching with hope. But instead, she wrapped a piece of thread around her fingers until the tips were purple. I could feel that she wanted to do something or say something, but she sat still. Quentin handed Alma back to Leti, and looked toward the door, waiting for her pa. Señor Barragón never returned.

Then Leti let me hold her.

I sat down on a hospital chair and stiffened my grip. I asked the nurse to hover behind me the entire time to correct my form, because I was terrified I'd drop her.

With Alma cradled against my arms, I saw how much she looked like Leti. Her skin was deep and her hair was black, her lips were curved and pinched, her chin soft. I couldn't believe she was real. That the afternoon of helping Leti take pregnancy test after pregnancy test, and the months of watching her almost unravel in front of me, all led to this. To me shaking my head at Dra. Zocorro's advice— marveling at the family I had gained in my father leaving.

As I looked at Alma, I couldn't understand how the Barragóns were choosing this loss.

And then my stomach sank, because I understood.

I understood why Leti had to leave.

She had to.

I knew it as soon as Quentin brought it up that night in his car, as soon as Leti had said it on my steps, but the truth cemented into my body when I saw Señora Barragón glance at Alma, then glance at the floor. No matter how hard I knew Leti would try, her parents were comfortable in their cycle, repeating it until they spiraled into solitude.

After some time, I left Leti's room to give her time to rest. In the waiting room now, I see my ma sitting beside a tall window, her dark hair almost blending seamlessly with the sky behind her. She hands me a change of clothes and a combo from the Wendy's drive-thru. I look at them, amazed at what she remembers about me—my favorite order, my most comfortable pair of sweatpants.

I change in the bathroom and nearly bump into Señor and Señora Barragón on my way back to the waiting room. They both move toward the elevators, avoiding my gaze in their departure.

I sit beside Quentin in the waiting room, trying to get comfortable on the overstuffed love seat. His extended family has arrived, Najia among them, toting blooming bouquets and balloons. A nurse escorts them to the NICU to meet Alma, while my ma and Ms. Barrera unravel into a conversation about teaching, Styrofoam cups of vending machine coffee steaming between them.

Quentin tips his head back onto the hospital wall, sighing deeply. "Damn."

"What?"

He shrugs. "I'm wondering who to pick as godfather. It was so easy for her to pick you, but it's gonna take me a while."

"She said that?"

"Said what?"

"That I was going to be the godmother?"

He snorts. "Of course. For someone so smart, you can be so dumb sometimes."

I let out a breath. "I thought she hated me."

"She thought you hated her."

"I could never hate her," I say. "She said hurtful things, but I could never hate her."

"She could never hate you," he says. "You act like it was easy for her to choose to leave. When she would talk about things working with her family, she meant you, too. She loves you."

We sit together for a while, letting words suspend between us. Quentin's family eventually joins us, wiping away tears. As we wait together, Ms. Barrera pulls out a deck of cards. Quentin's dad teaches me how to shuffle a deck, and his mom teaches me how to play Kings in the Corner. The sun and moon shift in cycle behind us, and by the morning, sunlight slopes through the blinds, painting us all in stripes of yellow.

Most of the adults have fallen asleep, but Quentin and I are on high alert. A nurse sweeps past us, delivering a platter covered in a beige plastic dome to Leti's room. We follow her, watching as Leti holds Alma close to her chest.

Quentin helps arrange the breakfast platter over Leti's thighs while the nurse motions to take Alma back to the NICU. When it's just the three of us again, Quentin gives me a pointed look. "I'm gonna leave now, give you two some time."

Leti uncovers her food, revealing a sad assortment of soggy hash browns, rubbery eggs, and strawberry yogurt.

"Ew," I say.

She's looks at me.

Then we both laugh.

I run to the waiting room and bring the leftovers from my Wendy's meal, feeling so grateful for my ma, who even opted for the extralarge fries. I shake the bag in my hand, looking at Leti.

"You want some fries?" I ask.

"No." She shakes her head. "I shouldn't."

"You shouldn't? You just pushed a baby out of your vagina and you're not gonna let yourself enjoy fries?"

"Okay, come here."

I rush to her side and dump my food onto her tray. I wish we had fruta, for celebration's sake, but this will have to do.

Leti shoves handfuls of fries into her mouth with the urgency of someone who has never eaten before. Even though they're stale, she seems overwhelmed by relief. The grease and salt line her lips, and she wipes her glossy fingers onto a napkin. When she's finished eating, she looks at me. Her eyes immediately swell with tears, fat droplets falling onto her cheeks.

"I'm so sorry, Belén," she says, "I'm sorry I said all those things about you. I was so petty, and so pregnant, I wasn't thinking right."

"Leti, it's fine. There are bigger things to worry about right now."

"No, it's not fine. You've been there through the whole thing, and

I was just so upset you were leaving all the time to see Alexis. I was so jealous."

I snort. "Of me and Alexis?"

She glares at me from beneath her brows. "No offense, Belén, but few people could be jealous of someone being with Alexis."

I smile at her. "I know. That's over."

She picks up another fry and crosses herself. "Thank God. What happened?"

"Just didn't work out," I tell her. I don't want her to hear about every terrible thing Alexis said about her. Enough people have filled her head with doubts.

She nods. "It was jealousy about Berkeley. All my life I've dreamed about going there. And there you were, going all the time and having so much fun. Every time you went, I just knew in my gut I wouldn't ever get to experience that. I knew that I couldn't go there—even if I did get in."

She pauses, wiping her face with the neckline of her hospital gown. "Sometimes, I would pray that the admissions office would deny me. I thought it would be easier that way, so I wouldn't have to make a decision. But when I got in, I cried because I knew I had done it, but then I cried because I knew I had to make a choice to leave."

I couldn't imagine Leti praying she would be denied. All I'd ever heard was her praying to be admitted. But the day she told me she was going to USC, I realized there was so much of her thought process I never got to hear. So much of her that I didn't know.

She goes on. "Then I said all that stuff about your family. I'm so sorry. Your ma has always been nice to me. Did you know she got me my first pack of prenatals?"

My eyebrows raise. I'd told my ma Leti was pregnant once, in passing, but all she did was nod. I didn't think she'd even heard me—nothing could lift her head above water. "No."

She nods. "Yeah. I ran into her once at the pharmacy section of Mi Tierra. I was running an errand for my ma and I was freaking out, trying to pick the right ones. I didn't even know if she knew, if you'd told her yet. But I told her, and she didn't look at me any different. She just bought me the prenatals and told me to call if I needed money for more."

I couldn't imagine my ma doing something as normal as running an errand. Up until I found her work uniform, she didn't exist to me outside of the rare moments I saw her at home. She was like my pa in that way, unimaginable in her absence. I blink at Leti. "Did you?"

"No." She breathes. "I was so embarrassed that she was being so kind to me, while my ma thought I was so disgusting. I know your ma hasn't been the same since your pa left, but I felt so guilty."

"*You* felt guilty?"

"I knew that you were going through a hard time with your pa leaving, and I knew it was wrong, but—" Leti inhales sharply, trying to steady her breath, but the sobs come anyway. Her shoulders rattle with intensity, her breath whistling through her throat. "But all I could do was wish my pa would disappear." I start crying, reaching to hold her hand. She reaches for the wad of napkins, wiping her tears with the embossed Wendy's logo.

"And I felt awful because I saw how it was affecting you, but I just didn't know what to do. I know it's so much more complicated and

I know I should've asked about it more—I *should* ask about it more, because that must be hurting you so badly."

"I saw my pa just over the weekend," I say. "I ran into him at this restaurant when I was with Ali."

Leti's eyes widen, the soft of her sadness replaced with firm concern. "Really? What happened?"

I shrug. "He didn't really do anything. I ran out of there and train hopped until I had this, like, panic attack, I guess. That's what my therapist says it was."

She coughs. "Therapist?"

I nod. "Yeah, I came home freaking out and my ma took me to one. I met with her upstairs. It was nice talking to her—I know I haven't been dealing with things right."

She looks at me. "What do you mean?"

"I was running away from everything. Trying to be with Alexis and be there for you. And some of that was genuine, but a lot of it wasn't." I pause, the honesty stinging throughout my body. "That's how I knew you were having the baby. I was leaving her office, and I saw your pa's truck and Quentin's car outside."

"Divine timing," she says, her lips teasing a smile. "You know I would've told you if I could have. And you know you could have called me when you saw him."

I shake my head. "I didn't know that."

She sniffs. "Yeah. I guess not. But I would've answered." She grips at my hand. "It was so hard for me to tell you I chose USC because we've never been apart like that. I didn't want to leave you. I knew you'd be so upset."

"But you're not leaving me, Leti," I tell her, that truth rapturing and repairing. "And I'm not upset. I'm proud of you."

She cocks her head back. "Stop, Belén. This is serious."

"I am being serious," I tell her, humbled and annoyed that Dra. Zocorro is already turning out to be right. "It was wrong of him, but my pa leaving made so much room for things he can't ruin by being around. Like I have a goddaughter now, a whole different member of my family. I'm not sure what your parents will gain, hopefully decency, no offense, but *you're* going to gain so much more. Your daughter is going to gain so much more. If being a good parent to your daughter means being a bad daughter to your parents, it's worth you moving."

She shakes her head, her hair flying around her face. It's so odd to see her hair down like this. "I thought you'd be so angry. I thought you'd think I was a coward or something."

"Leti, this is the bravest thing you've ever done."

I let out a breath. All of my life I've been used to Leti being so quiet and fragile. Sometimes I thought my body was wider just to shield hers, my mouth bigger just to speak for her. But when it mattered, she always outdid me. Ran laps around me, like the first day I met her.

"I think I've been underestimating you," I tell her. "I can't imagine being pregnant, telling my parents about it, and then choosing to give birth without any painkillers." She laughs, but I continue. "The bravery it takes to put your daughter before your dreams is unimaginable to me. Especially since so many people, so many parents, don't do that."

She squeezes my hand. "Thank you, Belén. You were brave when I couldn't be."

We talk for a while, catching each other up on everything we'd missed while we were gone. While Leti speaks, I notice the blue bags beneath her eyes, heavy marks of exhaustion. She's in the middle of telling me about how Alma came before the baby shower Najia had planned could even happen, when she dozes off completely and falls asleep.

I finish the rest of the stale fries and stand up to meet my ma in the waiting room. I pick up before I go, moving Leti's breakfast trays to a tabletop and throwing away the greasy Wendy's bag. I'm preparing to leave when I look over at Leti, her face striped by dark locks of her hair.

I move to her and collect her hair, pushing it gently to one side. Carefully, I run my fingers through it and divide it into two sections, fishtail braiding the way Ava taught me to when we were younger.

But I look at it, and it doesn't feel right.

I let the hair go and start over, splitting the hair into three even sections, my hands double-Dutching as I weave the hair over itself. I make a standard, three-sectioned braid, secure it with an elastic band, and nestle it over Leti's shoulder. I take a step back to look at her. Even after having the baby, she looks like I remember her, with the boring braid snaking down her chest, the same one that made her so brave.

THIRTY-FOUR

DOWNTOWN OAKLAND IS BRIGHT AROUND US. MY MA DRIVES home, setting the radio to 102.9 KBLX, keeping the volume low. I can hardly hear Sade over the rumble of the car. We wait at a long, red light near Lake Merritt, beside Fairyland. The water moves in ripples beside us, but inside the car I feel still. Safe.

"Leti told me you got her prenatal vitamins," I say, my eyes still fixed on the water.

She tilts her head, remembering. "Oh, yes. At Mi Tierra."

"Yeah." I pause. "That was really nice of you."

"It was nothing." She inhales sharply, the sound jagged between us. "I know what it's like to feel ostracized from your family, when you can't ask them for help."

I look at her, but she's looking straight ahead. She tucks a stray hair behind her ear. "You know, I'm happy she had a girl. It's a very special thing to be a mother to a daughter."

I look outside the window, at the traffic light suspended above us. It turns green.

"I'm so sorry I haven't been a good mother to you," she blurts.

I whip my head quickly to look at my ma, who is crying. For the first time in over a year, her tears don't bother me. Maybe because they aren't about my pa, but about me, instead. I sit up straight, feeling a lump rise in my throat. "Ma, it's okay. Don't cry."

"I talked to your teacher, who isn't even your teacher, and she said all these kind things about you—how you are so smart, always reading. She said you wrote your college essay about your pa and that it moved her to tears. But how your grades have dropped since your pa left." She sniffs. "And I knew, but I didn't know what to do. I felt like I was paralyzed by sadness."

"Ma—"

"When he left, I felt like I had nobody." She stares at the cars zooming around us. "Your pa was the first person I met when I came to this country. I couldn't even speak English yet. I met him in a hallway full of kids who didn't know what language I was speaking, and he helped me find a classroom. His English was so good—I thought he was like a compass. When he left, I felt like I had no direction. I felt so alone."

"Ma, that's not true," I say, thinking of my tía Myrna, who is always around when I never want her to be.

"I know it's not true. I had you. I had your sister." She wipes her face, the tips of her fingers grazing her face. "But I felt so alone that I let *you* feel alone."

My ma had always told me that she and my pa met in school, but never about this. She's never told me how lonely she was. Or how much my pa meant to her. By the time I was born, all they did was argue. It was difficult to imagine anything before that.

"Your pa was my best friend," she says, "but he had so many problems, so much resentment. He's been trying to distract himself from it for so long—which is why I think he betrayed me so many times. When he finally left, I was almost relieved. But I was so sad, I hadn't felt that alone since I came to this country. I forgot I was anything but lonely. I forgot I was your ma."

"But, ma—"

She shakes her head. "I neglected you. And with your pa gone, you deserve to have one good parent. But I am always stuck wishing you could have both, like if I didn't make the mistake of being with him, you wouldn't be hurting so badly."

"It wasn't a mistake," I tell her. "We all thought he was different."

"Mija, it's not that simple. I am responsible for you."

"Okay, but so is he. But he doesn't take responsibility. *You* are doing the best you can." The lump in my throat melts, replaced by tears dripping from my lashes onto my sweatpants. "You are working two jobs to keep things afloat. What is he doing?"

She whips her head to me, her cheeks wet. "Who told you? I told Ava not to say anything."

"I found your uniform in the laundry."

She sighs. "You weren't supposed to know about that."

"But maybe I should have. I was so mad at you. I thought you were avoiding me."

Her brows slope together. "Belén, I love you." Tears stream faster down her face, a mudslide of emotion. "That's why I was gone all the time, to work to help you. But still, I should have done better. I am trying to do everything by myself, but—"

"How can you do everything?" I ask her. "Ma, *he* was supposed to do something. You're trying your best."

"But mija, you are capable of so much more. Your teacher says you weren't even in the right classes to apply for school. I am supposed to guide you, but I was so stuck. I feel so embarrassed I've been behaving this way toward you."

"*You're* embarrassed? Ma, *he* should be embarrassed."

I look ahead at the headlights blurring along the freeway, warping in my tears. "It's nobody's fault he left except his. All year I felt so heavy, like something was living on my chest. But when I saw pa at the restaurant, I realized he didn't feel any of that. He was out there, enjoying his life."

I see anger flicker across her face, but I continue. "But Ma, maybe we can learn from that. He is selfish. He is cowardly. But blaming ourselves for what he did isn't going to do anything. When are we going to enjoy our lives? When are we going to let him hold that weight?"

A pause settles between us. Sade turns to Bobby Caldwell. Bobby Caldwell turns to the Gap Band. By the time the Gap Band turns to Earth, Wind & Fire, my ma is lowering the volume and pulling into the driveway.

She turns off the ignition. We sit in the car for a moment, our kitchen light glowing yellow inside. Ava's shadow passes by the sink. I glance at my ma, at her hands, which grip the steering wheel tightly. Her knuckles are white.

I try to think about what I did when she picked me up from school that afternoon. When DeBarge was in the background while she cried and sobbed and breathed like she was drowning. All I can remember is just sitting there—unaware that this would be the first time of many she would sob in front of me, and I wouldn't know what to do.

So, I did nothing.

Now, I look at the knuckles of her hands, the bones that look like they're ready to rip through her skin, and I reach out my hand to touch them. The first time I've really touched her in almost a year. My ma's face warps in confusion, until she uncurls her palm from the steering wheel and holds my fingers. Her expression softens and she lets out a long breath.

"But what if he never carries the weight?" she asks.

"Then he doesn't," I say. "But we can't do that for him."

My ma takes a deep breath, looking ahead at the house. Then she squeezes my hand.

Inside, Ava is in the kitchen pouring coffee into mugs. When she sees me, she looks excited. She hands me a mug and I move over to the Coffee-Mate, ready for the comments about my pa to start. But they never do. Instead, Ava opens a panadería box, sliding it over to me.

My ma and I take a piece of pan and sit at the table. Ava joins us and sits where my pa used to sit, on the chair closest to the door.

The three of us begin talking. I tell Ava about Leti's baby, and she smiles when she hears that she had a daughter. We talk while we reach over each other's arms for more pan, trying to stretch the conversation.

Ava and I reach for the last concha, something we would always fight about when we were younger, but she looks at me and breaks it into three, handing the last piece to our ma.

And I realize this is how it will be.

The three of us, empty hands reaching over each other only to end up sharing. I look at my ma, crumbs pooling onto the place mat beneath her. I look at her fingers and wonder how often she has felt she has come up shorthanded, only to make it work every time.

I glance at my ma and my sister, shocked that the house feels so full with a desolate chair beside me. Then I look at the empty, grease-stained panadería box. I am overwhelmed by how sad I am that there is nothing tethering us to the table anymore. But my ma stands up and wipes her palms along her jeans.

"¿Más café?" she asks, and Ava and I smile.

THIRTY-FIVE

I HELP LETI SLIP ON HER GRADUATION ROBE. THE POLYESTER FABRIC sends static to her skin, strands of her hair standing straight like pins. She helps me bobby pin my cap onto my head, and then we both look at each other in my bathroom mirror.

I never imagined us graduating like this.

I at least thought we'd look older.

But the only thing that's changed is the faja beneath Leti's dress, stuffed with pads I put in her bra in case she starts leaking during the principal's speech. The gowns cost forty dollars just to rent for the afternoon, and I don't know if they'd charge her more if she ruined hers with breast milk.

Outside, I hear my ma bouncing Alma on her knee.

Leti turns to me and adjusts my collar.

"Are you ready?" she asks.

I let out a breath, then nod.

We meet Quentin in the living room. He's sitting on the couch amid all the blankets on my makeshift bed since Leti and Alma have been in my room for a few weeks. In other circumstances, my ma would probably yell at me for leaving a mess in front of the company. But Quentin is family.

After Leti had been discharged from the hospital, she and Alma went home. I stopped by every day for about a week, helping Leti do loads of laundry, and familiarizing my nostrils to the smell of baby shit while I changed diapers. I had to do it because Quentin couldn't. And because her parents wouldn't.

Between Tecates and WWE, Señor Barragón reminded Leti that Quentin was never allowed into his home again. And between Alma's piercing cries, Señora Barragón seemed to shrink. I expected her to at least say what she'd said when Leti was pregnant—that she had never had help with Leti, so she wouldn't be helping her now. But she didn't even look at Leti, or at Alma. She only ever looked at the floor.

After a few weeks, I gave Leti the nudge she'd been waiting for.

Because Leti had already been packing for USC, packing to leave her parents was easy. She left all the trinkets on her counters and packed only what mattered—a Bible, her books, and the clothes she prayed would fit her again soon.

Quentin and my ma waited for us, their cars idling near the driveway of the duplex. My ma attempted to talk to the Barragóns about Leti's departure, but they said nothing. After that, she helped Leti pack.

Quentin held Alma while we made trip after trip up and down the duplex's stairs. Señora Barragón was mopping the kitchen floor, Joan Sebastian sounding through her radio. Señor Barragón was drinking beer, his eyes aimless on the television. To them, it seemed to be any other day. Even when Leti made it obvious she wanted to say goodbye, lingering by the door with her bag slumped at her feet, they never even looked up.

Leti left her house keys atop the television and turned on her heels quickly, stepping down the duplex's stairs two at a time. I couldn't stand being around Señor and Señora Barragón, but something inside of me wrung tightly, wishing they could be better for Alma. So, I waited longer, standing in the threshold for a moment, hoping for one of them to stop Leti on her way out. Señora Barragón eventually looked at me. I cocked my head to the side, urging her to at least say goodbye, but she looked at the floor again.

I closed the door behind me.

Quentin didn't play any music on the drive to my house. I rode in the back, Alma in the baby seat beside me, watching as Quentin reached over to squeeze Leti's knee. Leti kept her gaze fixed on the window, liquor stores passing in its reflection. I thought of all of the circles and angles of life, imagining Leti with a pencil in her hand, drawing the shapes of her choosing.

I looked at the duplex become smaller as we drove away, watching the red roof eventually melt into the horizon, realizing parents don't have to be the ones to leave to be the people who let go.

So now we stand here, with Quentin, my ma, Alma, and Ava in my new makeshift bedroom, gawking at me and Leti with wide eyes. The six of us head to the front yard, where Leti and I balance our heels against the earthquake cracks on the driveway to take pictures.

Ava did me and Leti's hair, the three of us cramped in the bathroom with the air reeking of hairspray. She braided Leti's hair with intricacy, and my ma helped decorate Leti's cap with red and gold glitter to celebrate her acceptance to USC.

My ma takes Alma while Ava begins positioning me and Leti in the warm sunlight, asking us to turn this way and that way for photos. Quentin sandwiches between us, smiling widely, his AP medals refracting in the sunshine.

We take two cars and drive to the back of the school, where there are chairs set up along the football field. I see Ali up ahead and want to call him over, but he's busy talking to someone near the gate. My ma and Ava take Alma and have a seat along the bleachers, while Leti and I find seats up front on the fold-out chairs. Quentin goes to greet his family, and I set a pamphlet between the two of us to reserve his seat, watching as Ms. Barrera sits in the staff section, holding a program overhead to shield her from the sun.

I look around at all the graduation caps that are decorated with names of schools I don't recognize. At all the AP kids with their golden tassels and honor roll cords looped around their necks. It makes me kind of embarrassed—I feel like it's a miracle I'm even graduating.

I know I passed my personal statement assignment and earned my place, but if I ever want to go to college, Ms. Barrera explained to me that I'd have to take community college classes to make up for what I missed these last two years. For a while, that made me feel terrible.

Like I allowed myself a proximity to my pa that was so shameful. Still, I signed up last week, grateful enough to have at least made it here.

Seeing Dra. Zocorro every week has been useful, even if I don't always want to say so. She keeps reminding me that I am reacting to a circumstance, but I am not responsible for it. I'm still trying to figure out what she really means, but for now, it helps.

Quentin returns and joins us, staring at the seat reserved for him between Leti and me. He picks up the pamphlet and asks Leti to switch spots with him so that Leti and I can sit next to each other.

"Are you sure?" I ask him.

He smiles. "Of course."

The ceremony starts, and we stand and rise with the call of the principal. Our school is too overcrowded for theatrics, so we spend most of the ceremony sitting beneath the foggy Bay Area sunlight, listening as BART trains pass above us.

I turn around to see the bleachers behind us. In the distance, there are faces dotted along the seats, helium balloons suspended midair. I see my ma and Ava, my ma clapping Alma's small hands together when they begin announcing the graduating class. They sit beside Quentin's family, who have made posters out of bright neon cardboard. It almost makes me forget that Leti's parents aren't here. That my pa isn't here. With them together this way, there is no room for empty spaces.

THIRTY-SIX

I FIND ALI TOWARD THE END OF THE CEREMONY. HE'S TAKING PHO-
tos with a small group of people who I can tell are his family. They all
have the same width between their eyes, the same type of infectious
smile. The only outlier is Gerardo, from Oakland Grill, who blesses
Ali the same way he did the morning we worked on our statements.

I'm rocking Alma in the shade of a frutero's umbrella while Leti
takes a photo with Quentin's mom. I hand Alma over to her, and Leti
carries her expertly, bringing her up close to smell her hair. I look
at Leti, her graduation robe bustling behind her, her USC cap, her
honor roll cords tangled beneath her AP medals, holding her daughter in her arms. My eyes begin to water.

From the corner of my eye, I see Ali's family dispersing, joining
the slow trek of people heading to the parking lot. I tell my ma I'll
meet her at the car and snake through throngs of students, elbowing

my way through bouquets of flowers and balloon arrangements. Ali turns around and sees me, beaming brightly.

We embrace warmly, the candy leis around his neck crinkling against my weight. He introduces me to his ma, a short woman who takes me in with the thick of her arms.

"Thank you for keeping my son company after school," she tells me. "I worried with all the studying that he wouldn't make any friends."

"C'mon, Ma," Ali says, blushing. "You don't have to embarrass me."

I smile at her. "Thank you for all the OfficeMax paper."

Her laughter bounces through the crowd, her smile matching Ali's.

I look at Ali, who is shaking his head at his mother. "I'll meet you at the car."

Ali's ma waves him away and stays behind, talking with the rest of his family, her pride palpable. Ali and I walk slowly toward the bleachers. They're vacant now, littered with empty bottles of Hennessy.

We sit on the lowest row, the metal hot beneath our gowns, staring at our school ahead. The football field stretches widely across campus. From here, Ms. Foley's portable looks so far away, so insignificant.

"I have something to show you," Ali says. He takes off his graduation cap and turns it over, revealing a painted image of a bison, "HOWARD" written in bold letters atop.

My eyes widen. "What? Since when?"

Ali's smile is so wide that I see his cheeks curve inward, dimples modest along his skin. "Last week."

"Congratulations!" I shout so loudly a few heads almost turn. I give Ali a hug, squeezing him as tightly as I can. "What happened?

Did you get a scholarship?"

He teeters his head from side to side. "Kind of." He sighs. "My mama scraped up all she had left and decided to dip into a big part of her savings account. I told her not to."

He shakes his head and sets his graduation cap on his knee, the breeze rocking his tassel gently. "She said I shouldn't have to worry about her all the time, that kids aren't supposed to be parents. But with my pa as proof . . ." His voice trails off. "Anyway, she said she felt she was coming up short as a ma."

I still couldn't understand how our mothers, who were consistently surrendering everything, always felt like they weren't doing enough. Meanwhile, our fathers were nowhere to be found, nowhere to be bothered.

"I've heard that before," I say.

"Yeah." He looks up at the families leaving the field, all huddling together, magnetized by joy. "I told her she does more than she needs to, but she said she couldn't live with herself seeing me struggle and knowing I could've been getting ahead, even if things were tighter for her. You know, real Mom shit. Always on some sacrifice.

"So, she was able to front a quarter of my tuition. Ms. Barrera helped me call the financial aid office and they said that I could get a scholarship if I went to one of those summer bridge programs for underserved youth or whatever. The title upset me, but I don't have time to be picky right now. It starts in a few weeks. *And* my mama got me a job at OfficeMax in the meantime, so I'll get all my college binders for free. I can probably get you a discount on that fancy paper."

"Oh, I can't get it for free?"

"Nah." He laughs. "I'm not risking my tuition payment for you."

"I might need it, though."

He raises his eyebrows. "Oh for real?"

I nod. "Yeah. I talked to Ms. Barrera and she helped me enroll at Laney. I'm gonna be there for a few years to make up some credits, and then transfer. Hopefully."

"You'll transfer fine," he says, his smile wide. "It's gonna be a breeze for you."

Ali and I look ahead. Most of the families have gone by now, the desolate remnants of celebration strewn across the field. Limp streamers, deflated balloons, pools of confetti all blowing away, making room for whatever comes next.

I glance at him, and for the first time in a long time, I see similarities in someone who is not my pa. I used to pray privately that my pa would turn out all right—even if I never saw him again. Like his own success would make it possible for me to fulfill my own. Like his shadow was strung to my body.

But I see Ali and his Howard graduation cap, and his budding scholarship, and his OfficeMax job, and I feel lighter. I know that despite our similarities, there are stark differences. But he makes me feel like it's possible for me too.

It's silent, spare a booming laughter so distinct I know it belongs to my ma. I look toward the entrance of the parking lot, where I see my ma talking to Ali's ma, somehow immersed in conversation, wading in the depths of laughter. I wonder what they could possibly be talking about, two strangers who just met at a high school graduation. But then I feel Ali shift beside me and know. The two of them, like the two of us, are bound by loss, and buoyed by resilience.

SUMMER

THIRTY-SEVEN

I'VE ONLY EVER BEEN TO ONE BAPTISM IN MY LIFE. IT WAS FOR ONE of those relatives who isn't a relative but you call them a relative, and my ma was the madrina. All I remember was hurting my knees from kneeling on the church pews and eating cold rice and beans in some-body's backyard. I was young and unaware of all of the meticulous work and sacrifice stitched into the creation of a christening.

Leti spent weeks preparing me for this. Explaining the rituals, the prayers, the outfits, the weird oils rubbed onto the baby's head.

She tried her best to be patient with me but occasionally she'd stop and ask, "Didn't you learn this in Sunday school? Or did you cut class then, too?"

My ma spent days sewing beads onto Alma's christening dress. Ava helped her measure lace patterns, and I told them not to make one of those bonnets that make babies look like shepherds, but my ma made one anyway.

It now sits lopsided on top of Alma's head, fastened below her chin in a satin bow. On any other baby it would probably look really ugly, but somehow seeing Alma in the whole getup makes me want to cry. I cradle her in my arms, blinking away tears.

Malcolm, Quentin's older brother and Alma's soon-to-be god-father, is beside me on the plush, red carpeting of the church stage. He tugs at my dress sleeve and gestures for me to pass Alma to Padre José, whose arms are outstretched.

The priest then pours holy water over Alma's head three times, and Alma, true to her mother's nature, doesn't shift once despite looking notably uncomfortable. Afterward, we all pray to close the ceremony, and when the priest hands Alma to Leti, Leti's sniffles echo through-out the nave of St. Jarlath's.

We step outside and huddle on the steps, the Sunday morning sunlight refracted in the church's stained-glass windows, painting us in squares of orange and red. Ali curves around us to take the oblig-atory family photos Alma will grow to be embarrassed by, probably wondering why I hadn't advocated more fiercely for the removal of the bonnet.

Leti and Quentin balance Alma between the two of them, Quen-tin dressed in the same navy-blue suit he wore the day he went to the Barragón home, Leti in a knee-length señora skirt set. I stand beside Leti in my Ross Sunday best, and Ali arranges my ma, Ava, and Ms. Barrera behind me. Quentin's family aligns themselves behind Quen-tin, and we all squint and smile into the sunlight.

Leti's parents are not here. I joked with Leti privately a week before the ceremony, saying, "It's because the point of the baptism is to ward bad spirits away."

But Leti's face fell when I said that, and she showed me a box that had been set on the front porch earlier that morning.

"My ma dropped these off," she said, pulling out a pair of white baby socks, a needle-pointed rose on each heel, the tops trimmed with lace.

"How do you know it was her?" I asked. I didn't tell her what I knew: that the roses on the heels of the socks matched the pattern Señora Barragón had been working on while Leti was in delivery.

"I don't know," she said. "It's hard to explain. I guess it's just a feeling."

But I did know.

Earlier that same week, Ava and I both received cards in the mail. Both were packaged in bright yellow envelopes and held cards with watercolor sunflowers along the front. The inside was blank, save for three crisp hundred-dollar bills.

While Leti and my ma were fitting Alma for her dress, I knocked quietly on Ava's door. She sat at her vanity, the air in her room reeking of the flat iron. I gently held up the card, and she looked at it in the reflection of the mirror.

"I know," she said.

"You think it's him?"

"Absolutely."

I leaned against the door. "How do you know?"

She shrugged. "I guess I don't know. I just feel it."

I looked down at my card, at the money that felt like it was burning my palms, singeing my skin.

"Should we tell Ma?" I asked Ava.

Ava turned around and looked at the floor. Then, she took a deep breath. "No. She seems to be doing better lately, especially with Alma around."

That was true. Ever since Leti and Alma took my room, it was like my ma was possessed by happiness. She had quit her second job, but still enrolled to teach summer school. The bills were being paid on time, with my help managing the accounts. She listened to 102.9 KBLX while blow-drying her hair, singing lyrics off-key. She smiled.

The house felt full again, and though I knew Leti and Alma had something to do with it, I also knew the feeling would remain after August, when they both moved to Los Angeles.

I looked back at the money in my palms. I knew I should use it for my books for school, but spending it felt wrong. I felt like it didn't belong to me. Like if I bought something for myself, it would be like everything my pa did, or didn't do, was okay. Like this one-time payment made up for his year-long absence.

He hadn't called since we saw each other at El Farolito, but he'd stopped by the house one evening while we were out. He took the rest of his clothes my ma stored beneath her bed, leaving the remaining family photos in the hatbox beside it.

I half expected Ma to lose her mind when we came home. The iron security door was left open, a bad habit of my pa's that my ma always despised, and when we went inside, we could almost feel his presence around. Her room was clouded by the smell of his cologne and hair gel, and he'd left the storage boxes that held his clothes strewn along the floor. It almost felt like a respectful robbery.

I looked to my ma, waiting for her to erratically burst into tears or call my tía Myrna to console her. But when she realized he'd been around, she didn't do anything but drive to Home Depot to replace the locks.

Though holding his money made me feel gross, not spending it felt wasteful. I knew I couldn't offer it to my ma without explaining where I miraculously conjured three hundred dollars, so I decided to split it between Alma's baptism gift and Ali's going-away present. And if my pa decided to continuously send money but never call, I'd have to reconcile a way to tell my ma. But somewhere deep within me I knew this would be the only attempt at closure he would make, and that almost felt better than having to deal with him any longer.

I give Alma her gift in the middle of the photo session. A dainty, nameplate bracelet—a Mexican child rite of passage that I knew Leti wouldn't be able to afford for a while. Leti's eyes widen at the gesture as I clasp the bracelet around Alma's thick wrist, watching the gold catch the sunlight. Across the way, Ali gestures for us to huddle together for one last photo. Cars pass behind him on Fruitvale Avenue, tamaleros set up shop by the Foothill Vacuum Cleaner Center, and the eleven a.m. Mass begins congregating impatiently near the church steps.

Leti pulls me in tightly, she and I balancing Alma's weight between our arms. Above us, the church bells ring to mark the hour, the same ones my pa heard when I was born, like they, too, are grateful the three of us finally made it here.

After Mass, we all go back to the house to celebrate. The party is half a baptism celebration and half the baby shower Leti never got to have since Alma came early. We all sit in the backyard, among the pale-yellow tablecloths and decorations tacked to the fence. There are posters of the knockoff Winnie the Pooh they have at the pulga. His eyebrows are too slanted and thick and make him look sort of evil, but we did our best with our budget.

Quentin's family came over last night to help prepare the food, and Ali set up a modest DJ booth, equipped with one Bluetooth speaker and a long queue of music.

He sits beside me now, thumbing through the playlist about parenthood, Stevie Wonder sounding between us while Ali digs into his food. His ma is inside with Ms. Barrera, helping my ma prepare the flan. His bulky camera weighs down his neck and he sets it along the fold-out table, right beside the Precious Moments recuerdos Leti picked for party favors.

I pick up the camera and examine it.

"This is really nice," I tell him, feeling the camera's weight anchor my hand down.

"Yup, a professional-grade rental from OfficeMax for the occasion," he says, smiling. "I'll try to send you all the photos before I go."

"Next week, right?"

He nods. "Next week. It's amazing—I've never even been on an airplane, and now I'm going on this, like, twelve-hour flight. I have a long layover in Phoenix, and I know people say that layovers are terrible, but I'm kind of excited."

"You're weird," I tell him. "You can be excited for the flight, but for the layover? Calm down."

He laughs, the skin around his eyes crinkling. "All right, all right."

"These may help, though," I tell him, reaching over to the gift table. I hand him a pale pink bag printed with tiny storks. "It's not baby clothes, I promise."

He smiles and digs through the bag, pushing the tissue paper aside and revealing a pair of headphones. His eyebrows rise, his eyes widen.

"Your ma got me a good OfficeMax-approved discount," I explain, hoping he doesn't ask where the money for the gesture came from. "The sales associate there said these are the ones you'd been looking at for a while."

"Yeah, the same ones I'd never be able to afford. Wow, even the box feels nice." He runs his fingers over the soft-matte cardboard and flips the box, reading the details along the back.

"I thought they might help you study, or on your layover, I guess."

He smiles at me, and I notice his eyes watering.

"Please don't cry," I blurt.

He laughs and stands to hug me, the headphones tight in his grip. "This is one of the nicest things anyone has given me. Thank you, Belén." He pauses. "I'm sorry, I didn't get you anything. I didn't think—"

"Don't apologize," I urge. "I got these as a going-away gift, but I also really owe you a thank-you."

He cocks his head back. "For what?"

We sit again, and Ali leans forward, pressing his elbows on the edge of his knees, still studying the packaging. Ava starts milling around us, picking up stray paper plates and empty soda cans, preparing for dessert.

I shrug. "I don't know. I've never met anybody who understands it all like you do. I read your essay and I felt really seen. It made me feel hopeful. At the start of the school year, I didn't have anything figured out—and I really don't have it all figured out yet, but I have something going for me. I just want to say thank you. You helped a lot."

He shakes his head. "Nah, that wasn't cuz of me. I mean, maybe I forced you to do your homework for once, but the rest is all you." He pauses. "But I hear you. It's hard to meet someone who's gone through what we've gone through and still has a good head on their shoulders."

I scoff and roll my eyes a little bit. "I wouldn't say all that."

"I would," he says. "Look, there are so many people you can become in your life. It's a miracle we aren't becoming the outline somebody left for us."

I pause, letting his words hang between us, turning them over in my head. Maybe a month ago, I would've answered that with "yet." We aren't those outlines, yet. But after a few sessions with Dra. Zocorro, I leave the sentence at a standstill.

I look up. Summer swells around us, smearing the sky pink and white. I imagine its magnitude cloaking over every part of Oakland, and if we are so grateful, cloaking over every version of us that has yet to come.

The cold starts to settle in with the sunset, and we go inside for dessert. Ava distributes proportionate squares of flan on paper plates, while my ma scrambles around with Quentin's mom to set up the baby shower games. Ali sits beside Ms. Barrera, showing her pictures of his dorm for summer school, excited by the fact that he has to buy shower shoes for the communal bathrooms. On the surface, the small, intimate nature of the party feels mismatched. Leti's parents aren't here, and we're playing baby shower games at a baptism party. But even in everything feeling backward, I feel the promise of forward.

Quentin is holding Alma, bouncing her on his knees. I look around to find Leti, but don't see her anywhere. I peer outside, where I see her sitting on the front steps, looking across at the skyline. Ali's ma brings out coffee for everyone, and in the moment of distraction, I slip outside and sit beside Leti on the steps.

"Are you okay?" I ask.

She presses her knees together, worrying, even now, about her modesty. "Yeah, I just needed a second."

"What's wrong?"

She purses her lips, returning her gaze across the way, at the skyline darkening around us. "It's stupid. But I just wish my parents were here."

"That's not stupid."

She lets out a sigh. "Yes, it is. Everybody in there cares more about me and Alma than my parents ever would. And I'm so grateful, and so sad."

We're quiet for a while, sitting in soft silence until we hear pops up ahead. Somewhere in the distance the Oakland A's have miraculously won a game—green and yellow fireworks break against the dark of the sky, light illuminating around us.

I look at Leti, who is staring at the earthquake cracks on the concrete. I remember when we argued here, when she said my pa had just left. Even then, in my fit of anger, I didn't wish for her to know this type of pain.

"It's okay," I assure her. "It'll take some time to adjust."

She looks over at me, her brown eyes sloping in worry. "Does it get easier?"

"Yeah," I tell her. "I spent a whole year trying to understand my pa's absence. I don't think I'll ever fully get it, but it just helps to make the presence of others feel more important."

She looks away, her braid falling over her face. "That's what I worry about."

I lean back. "About what?"

"That I won't have people around me like that. I'm moving so far—"

"Leti, come on," I tell her, turning her toward me to look her in the face.

It's strange seeing her worry about something that I'm attempting to reconcile. But I am grateful that loss has brought company, that we can hold hands through it.

"You're my family," I say. "I know that doesn't always mean a lot when you come from families like ours, but I want you to know it means something coming from me."

"I know it'll never be the same after I go," she says, "but, I just—"

I shake my head, my curls falling down my back. "You're right, it won't be the same. My life wasn't the same after my pa left. Your life won't be the same since you left your parents. But things shouldn't be the same. Things should be better."

In the grass, I see Quentin's shadow. He hoists Alma over his shoulder, gently patting her back. Leti glimpses the scene, her shoulders falling in some type of relief. Then she smiles at me. It's meek, but it stays on her face long enough to tell me that it's hopeful.

We sit on the steps, just the two of us, the way things used to be before Alma and Quentin and my pa. The one person who has been with me through it all, in absence and in presence.

We look ahead at the skyline. The fireworks sizzle in the atmosphere, then fade, clouding the horizon in darkness. In the dark, I imagine the Barragóns watching WWE, I imagine Alexis climbing up the hill to his house, I imagine our frutero picking mangoes from milk crates.

And in the dark, I can even imagine my pa. I wonder if he has this same view from his new home, if we are both gazing at the night with the distant promise of each other.

Leti leans her head against my shoulder, her braid cascading down the length of her back. I wrap my arm around her, my cheek resting on the crown of her head. And we sit like this for a moment, in the summer that grows shorter as we get older. Cradling each other, the way our parents did and did not cradle us.

ACKNOWLEDGMENTS

As a child, I loved acknowledgments sections. To me, they were the lagniappe of literature. The rolling of credits. The breaking of the fourth wall. The humanity in authorhood. I would read *every* section, studying them in an attempt to discover how I could publish my own book. Instead, I'd often be left squinting at long lists of names, wondering how *that* many people could even possibly be involved in creating a book. This is funny to me now, when there are probably names I've unintentionally forgotten in the printing of these pages, because there is no way a book is birthed without a profound team. And I am deeply grateful for the team I've been blessed with.

Publishing a book was never a goal of mine. Since I was eight, it was the dream of my entire life. You holding this book in your hands, to me, is a testament to God's work. I have never, never—I wish I was exaggerating—*never* wanted anything the way I wanted to be an author. The creation of this book has been the most emotionally expensive thing I have done to this point of my life—because if you know, you *know*. So many tears. So many. In my classroom, in my car, in crowds.

Because trust me when I say I often thought this would not happen. I vividly remember being twelve years old and sitting in the public library, shedding different tears. I was so angry, so caught in the thought, *How could everyone have written a book but me?* It really makes me laugh now—to have been that impatient.

But if you, like me, are a young writer who takes the time to read the acknowledgments section because you just want to write *that* badly, cherish that commitment. You will need to sustain it. Talent pales in comparison to training and tenacity. So train and be tenacious. But let me be proof that it can happen for you. In due time, it will happen.

Writing this section came with its own very ugly (but fortunately very private) cry. Sobs. Tear-stained T-shirts. Calls to my friends. Lots of prayer. If you got one of those calls, here is what I wrote. I know this is not a typical acknowledgments section—but I needed to make it work. Because the least I can say is thank you. Thank you, thank you, thank you.

Thank you to Elizabeth, my agent. You were the first person to give Belén an overwhelming yes. Thank you for that validation, for your invaluable guidance in this process, and for advocating for me and for these characters so fiercely.

Thank you to Jen, my editor. Your early enthusiasm for this book still brings me to tears. I'm still in awe of how you read and emailed Elizabeth with interest in six hours. I reread that email embarrassingly often, and it always brings me warmth on the coldest days. Thank you for crying alongside Belén when she and I both needed that compassion. And thank you for understanding why this acknowledgments section needed to be this long.

Thank you to the entire team at Quill Tree Books and Harper-Collins. The dedication you've all had to this book blows me away. In the midst of selecting a publishing house, I knew Quill Tree would be the best fit for Belén because books published by Quill Tree inspired me to write a character like her. To be published by an imprint that has produced so many of my favorite titles, some of which I read to my students on a yearly basis, is an honor. Thank you.

Thank you to Rosemary Brosnan, my publisher and a legend! Working alongside someone who is responsible for publishing some of my favorite books is truly, truly an honor. To add Belén to that list makes me painfully sentimental. Thank you.

Thank you to Shona McCarthy, our production editor, for her help in this process.

Thank you to Joel Tippie, whose invaluable design direction helped design the book you are holding. And isn't it beautiful? Thank you.

Thank you to R. Kikuo Johnson. It is an *honor* to have you as our cover artist. When I got emails about cover artists, I vividly remember thinking this collaboration would never happen because I am a *fan*. I am privileged to have this book curated by your careful eye. Thank you for capturing Oakland in such a poignant and profound way.

Thank you to Raquel. It is so easy to block blessings in a world as competitive as publishing. Thank you for every alley-oop and for your true sincerity as you held the door open for me. To be in conversation with you is a privilege, and I am so grateful you were my mentor in this process. To the Latina writers: look up Las Musas.

Thank you to Mahasin J. A. Aleem, our sensitivity reader, for your feedback and guidance.

If you are a young writer who is looking to become a better writer, you must be a student. And to be a student, you need to read. Widely. Thank you to the authors who nurtured me on the path here: Elizabeth Acevedo, Jason Reynolds, James Baldwin, Erika L. Sánchez, César Vallejo, Tomás Rivera, Claudia Rankine, Adrian Tomine, John Green, Daniel Alarcón, Kiese Laymon, Ashley C. Ford, Angie Thomas,

Raymond Carver, Danez Smith, Raina Telgemeier, Jhumpa Lahiri, Kali Fajardo-Anstine, Ann Brashares, Hanif Abdurraqib, Dan Charnas, Sarah Dessen, Crystal Maldonado, Morgan Parker, Ned Vizzini, Nate Marshall, Stephen Chbosky, Rubén Darío, Sor Juana Inés de la Cruz, Toni Morrison, Pam Muñoz Ryan, Jerry Craft, J. D. Salinger, Rita Dove, Rainer Maria Rilke, Aria Aber, and Terrance Hayes.

Thank you to 102.9 KBLX for raising me. A specific thank-you to Kevin Brown, wherever he is. The Bay misses you.

Thank you to *Reading Rainbow* and to LeVar Burton.

Thank you to Baron Davis and the Golden State Warriors.

Thank you to the Scholastic Art & Writing Awards for their continual support and belief in my work. To all the young writers: submit!

Thank you to *Split Lip Magazine*, *PANK* magazine, and *580 Split*.

Thank you to every magazine that ever took the time to read my work and sent me a rejection letter.

Thank you to Ocean Vuong for writing "Someday I'll Love Ocean Vuong," a poem I memorized and recited through my own heaviness.

Thank you to Frank Ocean, for so many things. But, today, for writing "Skyline To."

Thank you to D'Angelo for writing "One Mo'Gin."

Thank you to Damian Lillard.

Thank you to the good teachers. Yes, only the good ones, because it is so easy to be a bad one. Thank you.

Thank you to my teachers: Ms. Katz, Ms. Paul Castro, Mr. González, Ms. Fajardo, Ms. A, Ms. B, and Mr. Doan; professors Cathy Thomas, Micah Perks, and Melissa Sanders-Self; profes Fernández, Poblete, y Pérez.

Thank you to Yahdon Israel. The Language Barrier Lectures have been invaluable to my development as a reader, writer, and scholar. I think about them daily. Thank you for that guidance.

Thank you to all the good syllabi.

Thank you to all the libraries and librarians.

Thank you to all the bookstores and booksellers.

Thank you to the Libby app and thank you to audiobooks.

Thank you to all the public-school students—you can do anything in this world.

Thank you to all the students who have a top choice for university. Thank you, especially, to all the students who have no idea what they want to do after high school. Don't let the height of a precipice scare you—there is so much you can see from an edge.

Thank you to BE3 (RIP). A large, profound thank-you to Sonal and Nives for always pushing our cohort to dive deeper. I could not have written this book without the knowledge you all offered me while at Berkeley. Piggybacking-kickflipping-skateboarding off of that, thank you to what has to be the best and hottest cohort that ever graced that building. A warm thank-you to Karen, Cristina, Barbara, and Raha for their continuous friendship.

Thank you to my SLUSD community. A sincere thank-you to every family who has ever brought me lunch or coffee or flowers or made my copies or cleaned my classroom or decorated my door. It means more than I can put into words. Thank you to Ari for always listening when I needed to talk. Thank you to Dina for always keeping an eye on my kids. Another warm thank-you to Sonal for keeping me beneath your wing. Gracias, Clara, por todo el chisme y café.

Thank you to the creative writing program at UC Santa Cruz. A special thank-you to the creative writing interns, who I still cherish fondly. And a specific thank-you to our poetic genius, Sarah. I am so fortunate to be debuting alongside you.

Thank you to Marlene and Kayla. You both literally saved my life my freshman year of college. Thank you for being the best roommates—and friends—Santa Cruz could have ever brought me. 521 triple forever.

Thank you to coffee for its dichotomous promise of megalomania and anxiety.

Thank you to Luna.

Thank you to geometry.

Thank you to poetry.

Thank you, in order, to circles, squares, perpendicular lines, parallel lines, and triangles. Thank you to Stevie Wonder for audaciously titling an album *In Square Circle*.

Thank you to the swelling sound of synthesizers and string sections.

Thank you to staccatos and ostinatos.

Thank you to the past participle tense.

Thank you to every BART train I've cried inside of.

Thank you to Sufjan Stevens for a *Pitchfork* interview that changed my life.

Thank you for the cyclical promise of seasons. Thank you to petrichor and the smell of sunshine. A sincere thank-you to the summertime.

Thank you to the citrus and drupe trees outside of my bedroom window. Thank you to hummingbirds. Thank you to spiders.

Thank you to the month of March.

Thank you to gold hoop earrings and nameplate jewelry.

Thank you to em dashes. Fuck you to semicolons.

Thank you to all the Mexican immigrants.

Thank you to all the single mothers.

Thank you to all the street vendors.

Music was a foundational part of writing this book. There are too many artists to name—but I'll list some of the most important here. A deep thank-you to D'Angelo, Frank Ocean, Sade, SZA, Saba, Prince, Solange, Beyoncé, Slum Village, Little Brother, the Internet, Rosalía, and Kendrick Lamar for scoring my book playlist as I wrote. If you are interested, you can find that playlist on my website.

Thank you to Julie. As a proud Leo, I have to thank my hairdresser. Thank you for pulling up for a house call before my headshots with no hesitation. I am so grateful for you.

Thank you to Sneha for always keeping my nails beautiful and somehow still the perfect typing length.

Thank you to Talia for seeing me through many versions.

Thank you to Leila. You are a genius! I am so grateful to have found your friendship and your sincerity in this community.

Thank you to Kaitie. So much of our friendship in high school was woven into this book in the most unexpected ways.

Thank you to Reena, my work soulmate. Thank you for embracing me with such open arms and for putting up my bulletin boards when you were nine months pregnant. You hugged me when I cried and always reminded me how amazing this feat is. Your mentorship and friendship in my life is something I cherish so deeply, especially in a school that often did not offer that for me. We did not meet by chance, and I will always thank Sanjana for bringing us together in this lifetime.

Thank you to Kiana, one of my favorite Virgos. Your ability to love your friends made me deeply consider how love would be shown in the friendships of this book. You have shown up for me in ways that are so soft and sincere. You are a beacon of light in every single life you touch. I am so grateful you touched mine.

Thank you to Nene. Do you remember that time you woke me up during orientation training? And talked to me about books while we disassembled flagpoles? That summer and that job was a fever dream. I am forever grateful it brought me to you. Thank you for your giving nature, for always listening when I needed an ear, and for your insightful wisdom about bread.

Thank you to Juno, who sat next to me every day of senior-year English (the times I would show up) and printed all my essays for me. Who read a blurb I'd written and said, "Dude, you need to rename this character." And who renamed that character to Ms. Foley. Please: start journaling.

Thank you to Nick for always dreaming with me! Now we get to discuss new dreams together, and it makes me so emotional. So many years of those pendulous conversations, oscillating between "our lives are amounting to nothing" all the way to "no, just wait . . . one day we're gonna do it." And we did it. Together! I am so proud of you and so proud of us. Maybe that yearbook committee was really onto something. Now we're laughing all the way to the next Beyoncé show.

Thank you to Alberto. Here we are, from that Night Owl bus to intermediate fiction to Berkeley to a summer residency to this page. Thank you for all of those winks around campus that turned into winks around life. Thank you for listening to every phone call and voice note where I was blubbering in tears over this book. Thank you for your careful eye and your critical honesty. And thank you for telling me, "You're supposed to be having fun. Calm down. Have fun."

Thank you to Sharon, my future dentist. Thank you for your consistent and nurturing friendship and for somehow always making me laugh. You know so many sides of my brain—from makeup to tears to Jesse McCartney lyrics. I'll always be grateful that we met at that Applebee's.

Thank you to Xiadani and Alyssa. I LOVE you. Thank you for helping with this therapy scene, for diving into Ali's Medi-Cal coverage, and for introducing me to LeQuy. Thank you for telling me, "No, you're wrong, you can't do that" when I needed to hear it. Xiadani, I will always laugh a little at how God brought us together and at the Venn diagrams of our lives. Thank you for picking up when I needed to talk about the Bible. Be honest, be brave, go write something!

Thank you to Rosa. I was so nervous asking you to read this book because you are one of the smartest people I have ever met. I knew no one would read this book with the critical lens you offered me. And I needed it! Your friendship and your feedback has been such a backbone to this book. I am forever indebted to your honesty and thoughtfulness. You were one of the largest pillars in this process, and I will always cherish both Frank Ocean and Berkeley (and Frank Ocean's love for Berkeley?) for bringing us together.